while *you* were sleeping

Also by Kathryn Croft

The Girl With No Past
The Stranger Within
Behind Closed Doors
The Girl You Lost

KATHRYN CROFT

while *you* were sleeping

bookouture

Published by Bookouture, an imprint of StoryFire Ltd.

23 Sussex Road, Ickenham, UB10 8PN,
United Kingdom

www.bookouture.com

PAPERBACK ISBN 978-1-78681-095-3
eBook ISBN 978-1-78681-094-6

For Dad, never forgotten.

PROLOGUE

I open my eyes and know immediately something is wrong. Nothing is familiar. The dark blinds, shutting out all but a tiny sliver of sunlight, are not mine, and neither is the black silk sheet covering my body, nor the too-soft pillow beneath my head.

This is not my bedroom.

With eyes still groggy from sleep, I rely on all my other senses to comprehend where I am, but I have no idea.

Something else is wrong.

I should be warmer than this – it was over eighty degrees yesterday evening, yet now I feel cold. And as I become more alert, it only takes a few seconds to work out why this is.

I am naked.

Forcing my eyes to focus, I squint into the darkness, and try to take in the rest of the bedroom. Everything is white and neat, deliberately minimal. Furniture I would not have chosen. Furniture that is both strange and familiar.

Someone is next to me.

'Noah?' I whisper. But I already know it's not him. The shape under the sheet is not my husband's.

Now I begin to panic because none of this makes sense. Slowly I lift the sheet, and take in the familiar dark hair and suntanned skin of his back.

I know this man.

Gently I nudge him, wait for the awkward response, as I start to remember brief flashes of his face last night. The smile as he invited me inside.

'Lee?' Another gentle nudge, but harder this time.

Nothing.

On rare occasions I have seen Noah like this. Too intoxicated from celebrating something or other to wake up, unless I shout directly in his ear.

Flinging my legs over the side of the bed, I search for my clothes. My black skirt hangs over the radiator, my underwear scattered on the floor. I can't remember what else I was wearing. I can't remember anything other than turning up here.

I retrieve what I can and hastily dress. I don't want him to see me undressed. But he already has. He must have. And when I walk to his side of the bed I know immediately something is wrong. Something else. Something worse than waking up naked in my neighbour's bed.

He is dead. I know this already. No one with life in them can lie so motionless.

With heavy robotic movements, I pull back the sheet, preparing myself to call an ambulance. He is young, but he could still have had a heart attack or something similar. I have heard of this happening when people exert themselves. But no, I cannot allow myself to believe I slept with him. I wouldn't do that to Noah. To Rosie and Spencer.

This I am prepared for. It is the large pool of blood which is the shock. The gash in his chest. The way his mouth forms an 'o' shape. The accusation in his wide-open eyes.

I scream into the silence.

PART ONE

CHAPTER ONE

24 Hours Earlier

I lie in bed and watch Noah pack. He is methodical and precise, ticking off items on the 'To Pack' list he created days ago on his phone. Everything is placed neatly inside his immaculate suitcase, every inch of space utilised to its full potential. I smile to myself. This is Noah all over. The complete contrast to me.

'Are you looking forward to having the house to yourself?' he asks. 'A bit of peace for a change.'

Yes, I am. I love the kids, and I love Noah, but I need to get back to me, if only for the weekend. The chance is a rarity I must make the most of. 'I'm just worried about Rosie,' I tell him. 'She's. . . well. . .'

'Has something else happened?' He stops folding a T-shirt and searches my face. He always thinks I'm not telling him everything as far as our seventeen-year-old daughter is concerned. But if I've kept anything from him, it's to preserve her trust in me. Not that it makes any difference to Rosie. We are both against her.

I sit up and draw my knees to my chin. 'Nothing new. But she's still talking about Anthony.' I wait for the fallout.

'Oh, for Christ's sake! Does she want the police here again? Why doesn't she just leave the poor guy alone? He's not interested. End of story.'

But in Rosie's world it isn't. Anthony chased her for weeks, an affirmation of the beauty we can all clearly see, but then after only a kiss he lost interest. It happens. Most of us can move on from this rejection, but not Rosie. It wasn't the first of her meltdowns and it won't be the last. It's just the one we're currently dealing with.

'It will be fine,' I say. 'She just mentioned him, that's all. I think she'd seen him at school and it. . . well, it must have triggered something.' Because there is always a trigger with Rosie. It doesn't even have to relate to her current trauma.

With a heavy sigh, Noah resumes folding. 'We need to get her to Dr Marshall again. He helped last time, didn't he?'

Not really. But, at a loss as to what else to do, I've attempted to take her back to him, only to be met with huge resistance. Screaming. Shouting. Smashing of fragile objects. Silence as she withdraws into herself and won't speak to anyone. And then, finally, the other Rosie. The Rosie who convinces us she's fine, makes us believe it, so that we cancel the appointment for fear of wasting the doctor's time.

He couldn't give us an answer either. His voice said depression, but his eyes told a different story. She'll grow out of it. She just wants attention. Now get on and deal with it.

'I've got it under control,' I say, 'you just focus on New York. Get that account.' And my silent thoughts say: *don't come back and tell me it's happened again, that after everything you're in the wrong place here with us.*

Noah zips up his case and pulls it down from the bed, placing it in the corner of the room, out of the way. He crosses to me and plants a soft kiss on my forehead.

'Make sure you get your painting finished. I know you artistic types need to get in the zone, or whatever you call it, but we'll all be back on Sunday night.'

I have already counted how many hours I will have: fifty-six. Fifty-six hours to finish my submission for the London Art Gallery competition. The chances of winning are slim, but the prize is representation in the gallery so I will give it my best shot. And having the house to myself will aid me tremendously. It will also give me a break from thinking about school, disciplining students and, most of all, my colleague, Mikey.

Noah interrupts my thoughts. 'So Spencer's staying with your parents, and Rosie's going to Libby's? I'd feel better if they were both staying with your mum and dad.'

He's already gone through this with me three times since yesterday. And each time I've told him that, yes, I've double-checked with Libby's parents that they're having Rosie for the whole weekend. It's all covered. And Bernadette is aware of Rosie's troubles. She will keep an eye on our daughter.

'Remember what happened last time?' I tell him. 'I don't want to put my parents under any more stress.'

He curls his mouth and I know he's recalling the events of two months ago. Remembering the pain it caused my parents to have to report to the police that their granddaughter had gone missing. 'Hmmm. True,' he says. Then he delivers that sigh again: the one that only Rosie can inspire.

From out in the hallway I hear a door opening, and floorboards creaking. It is only ten minutes to seven so I know it will be Spencer, creeping along the corridor so he doesn't wake his sister. I've told him many times that Rosie could sleep through a hurricane, but he tells me it's best to be careful. Spencer wakes early so that he can enjoy the calm before the storm. I forgot to tell him yesterday that Rosie has no classes today, so the likelihood of her emerging from her room before one p.m. is zero.

'Oh, good, Spencer's up,' Noah says. 'I'll get to see him before I leave. Cab's coming in half an hour, so I need to jump in the shower.'

I wonder if Noah said goodbye to Rosie yesterday, but don't ask him. It will spark another long conversation, and I need this time to be for Spencer.

Downstairs I watch our son pour cornflakes into a bowl, and marvel at how different he is to Rosie. How easy. I don't play favourites, and even in the private recesses of my heart and mind, I love them both equally. But Spencer makes it so much easier.

'Mum, will Grandma and Grandad let me watch a DVD this evening?'

His face flushes with excitement. It is very rare not to see him happy, and even when Rosie is kicking off about something, he puts on a brave face, tries to see the best in the situation, and his sister.

'That depends what DVD it is,' I say, taking a sip of my coffee to wake myself up.

'Well, um, it's actually a 15, but everyone at school's seen it.'

'Spencer, you're eleven. So pick another one.'

He doesn't protest at this, just resigns himself to it, and it's not long before he's content again, filling me in on the new English teacher who's just started at his school. I can't help but smile when he tells me nobody's giving her a chance, but he was nice to her because she's done nothing wrong.

It is confirmation that I must be doing something right.

'Dad!' Spencer calls, when Noah walks in, his hair still damp from his shower.

Noah hurtles over to him and ruffles his hair, pulling him into a bear hug. And behind my cup of coffee I smile at this scene. But we are missing Rosie. The Rosie I know is there somewhere.

Later, once I'm showered and dressed, I get ready to paint in the sunroom. The whole day stretches before me, and I'm excited to see what I can produce. I have decided on a lake – the branches of a large tree reaching out to it, trying to touch the scattered floating leaves – which exists only in my imagination.

I don't hear Rosie appear until she's standing right behind me. It is only ten a.m. but she's already dressed in skinny jeans and a loose V-neck T-shirt. Her shoes are the same coral colour as her top, and her glossy dark hair fans around her shoulders. She always looks lovely.

'Hi, Mum,' she says, peering at the easel. 'What are you going to paint?'

When I tell her what I've decided she nods, a thin smile forming on her face.

'A landscape. That's a good idea.'

'Are you ready to go to Libby's? Shall I give you a lift?'

'It's okay, we're meeting in Putney. I'll get the bus.'

Even though Putney is not far from Richmond, I can't help feeling anxious. But today Rosie seems in a good mood, calm, and I know she's been looking forward to this weekend.

'Okay, if you're sure.'

'Stop worrying about me, Mum. I'm fine. Okay?'

So I relax a little, because this is the Rosie who inspires confidence. The girl I wish she always could be. I squeeze her hand and dare to believe that she's through the worst of it. That she's forgotten all about Anthony.

'Bye then,' she says, floating through the door like a butterfly.

She will be okay today. I know she will.

I'm so engrossed in my painting that it's past two p.m. when I finally remember to eat. I am making progress, so taking a break won't do any harm.

When my mobile rings while I'm eating my sandwich, I'm pleased to see Lisa's name on the screen. My sister is always travelling, or doing something adventurous I can only dream of, so it's rare that we get a moment to speak.

'Everything okay?' she asks, once she's told me about her latest trip to Thailand.

I fill her in on Rosie's latest escapades, and she whistles into the phone.

'That girl needs to come away with me somewhere,' she says. 'That will sort her out. But at least she'll be having fun with her friend this weekend.'

Rosie travelling with Lisa is an interesting idea, and one I will consider when she's finished her A-levels. Perhaps she needs to be aware that there is a whole world out there – not just the tiny one which revolves solely around Rosie.

'How's Harvey?' I ask.

Lisa hesitates. 'He's great. Planning our next trip as we speak. He's thinking of Australia.' She lowers her voice to a soft whisper. 'To tell you the truth, Tara, I'm getting a bit tired of it. It would be nice to be in the country for longer than a few weeks.'

I have often wondered how Lisa has the energy for all this jet-setting, but then, at thirty-six, she is three years younger than me, and not yet having children probably helps. Is that enough to make a difference? I'm exhausted just contemplating a trip to the West End. But I love that she lives her life to the full. She always has.

'Is everything okay between you two?' I sense something is not quite right, but Lisa doesn't like to share details of her relationships. And, after only six months, theirs is a fairly new one.

'It's going fine, actually. We've got a lot in common.'

But does he excite you? I want to say. Does he make you feel as though you can do anything, be anyone? Because that's the way it should be. I think of Noah. He still makes me feel like that, but somehow I doubt I do the same for him.

'I miss you,' Lisa says, forcing me to focus. 'Hey, if you're going to be alone, shall I come over this evening? I'll bring a bottle of wine and you can tell me everything that's been going on.'

Her offer tempts me – it would be nice to catch up with her – but the competition deadline looms before me and I need to use every moment I can.

The calm before the storm.

She falls silent when I tell her this, but tells me she understands. 'It's been so long,' she says. 'When was the last time? It was months ago when we went out for drinks at that piano bar.'

Yes, she is right. But I don't remind her how drunk she got, or how Noah had to drive her home early.

We say goodbye as we usually do: with hope-filled promises to meet up soon.

Despite my good intentions to paint all day, somehow I fall asleep while I'm taking a break on the sofa. I am roused by the ping of my phone: a text from Noah, and am shocked to notice it's nearly seven p.m. He writes that he's just landed at JFK, and is on his way to the hotel to meet his client.

Nearly twenty years with Noah has taught me a little about the advertising industry, and the main thing I've learned is that it's a dog-eat-dog world, one in which Noah has to battle hard for every account he gets.

I reply to his text, wishing him luck. The two kisses I add I wish I could give him in person. I will never be possessive or stop him doing anything he wants to do. I only need to know that he wants to come home.

His reply is immediate. '*I love you.*'

Closing his text, I see that I have another, unanswered, one, this time from our neighbour, Serena. I flit between labelling her and her husband friends and neighbours, because really they are both. But at different times they seem to mould into each individual label, so perhaps they are truly neither. But, whatever they are to us, and we are to them, they are a decent couple and we're lucky to live across the road.

'*Can you come over ASAP?*' Serena asks. '*Need a shoulder to cry on!*'

Her exclamation mark tells me this is tongue-in-cheek, but you never know with Serena. She's a strong woman, but I know she's going through a lot at the moment.

I'm about to type back that I'm on my way, but am distracted when Rosie texts to ask if Libby's mum can take them to the West End for dinner. This is fine as long as they are being accompanied, and by the time I've confirmed this with Bernadette, I don't bother replying to Serena. I will just get over there, but I need to change first. I may only be heading across the road, but I can't leave the house in paint-splattered joggers.

Lee answers the door, dressed only in shorts. But being a landscape gardener, I am used to seeing him like this.

'Oh, hey, Tara, how are you? Come in, come in.' He holds open the door, standing aside to let me in. 'Excuse my state of undress; I'll just throw a T-shirt on. It's so bloody hot, though, isn't it?'

'Don't worry about that, I'm, um, sorry. I just got Serena's text. Is she okay? Are you okay?'

His forehead creases. 'We're fine. But Serena's not here. She just left actually. Her friend's hen weekend.'

This is a puzzle to me. 'But she just texted to ask if I could come over. At least I'm sure she did.' I have never misread a text before, but start to doubt myself.

To prove to Lee I'm not losing the plot, I pull out my phone and scroll to Serena's message. It is there, the words exactly as I remember them.

'Oh,' Lee says, when I show it to him, the frown back on his forehead. 'Hang on a minute.' He swipes the screen and then smiles. 'I see what's happened. She sent this text in the morning.'

He shows me the screen, and there it is: ten fifteen a.m. Hours ago.

Feeling foolish, I apologise profusely for my mistake, and turn to go back home.

'Don't be silly,' Lee says, 'you're here now. Why don't you stay and have a drink? I've literally just opened a bottle of red.'

I hesitate, pulled in two directions. Across the road my unfinished painting waits, but it would be nice to have company. And Lee is a good laugh.

As soon as I sit down on their cream leather sofa this feels like a mistake. There is something wrong about being here without Serena; as much as I like Lee, she is the one I have bonded with. But I am here now.

Lee pulls on a T-shirt then hands me a glass of wine, and I sip it slowly, wondering how wise it is when I've barely eaten today.

'So, Tara, how are things? We haven't seen you for a while.'

My mind searches for a memory but I only draw a blank. Surely it hasn't been that long? It's funny how you can live so close to someone yet not bump into them on a regular basis. Our cul-de-sac has only ten detached houses, surrounding a large green, which only makes it stranger.

I tell him about my painting, pleased to notice he is listening intently.

'So, you've given up teaching?' he asks. 'Don't blame you. Must be the hardest job in the world.'

I don't bother correcting him. I haven't taught art for over a year now. 'Well, I'm still the Year 9 head of pastoral care, but, yes, I'm hoping that, eventually, I'll be able to make a living from my painting.' This is usually when people's eyes glaze over, when their silent thoughts scream at me. Most artists are penniless. There is too much competition. Perhaps you should just stick to your real job. But their doubt only fuels my determination.

But not Lee. He asks me what genre I paint, and explains how much he admires creativity of any kind. 'I love your passion,' he says, and I flush at his compliment.

'What about you and Serena?' I ask, hoping I'm not crossing a line. I have only ever spoken to Serena about their problems, and can't be sure Lee knows his wife has shared so much with me.

He does seem taken aback for a moment, and perhaps he is trying to determine how open he can be with me, but it doesn't take him long to speak freely. 'We've been trying for years, and I have to be honest – it's exhausting. Sometimes I just want. . .'

'A break?'

'Yes, that's exactly right. A break. I want to forget we're having trouble, and just focus on living.' He smiles, and takes a long sip of wine. 'I just want Serena and me to be. . . us again.'

As always happens when I speak to Serena, I am shrouded in a veil of guilt. Getting pregnant with Rosie happened without us even trying, and Spencer only took a few months to conceive. But everything comes at a cost.

There is no advice I can offer Lee, so instead I tell him what I firmly believe. 'You'll both be okay.' Because we have no choice. Whatever afflictions we are dealt, unless it's a terminal illness, we find a way to survive.

'To be honest, Tara, I'm not even sure I want a baby any more. At least not yet. We're still pretty young: I don't think life should be this. . . heavy.'

I know Serena is thirty-three, so Lee must be close to that. He is right: they have time on their side. But, of course, that is not how Serena feels.

'Another one?' Lee asks, gesturing to my now-empty glass.

'No. . . thanks, but I should get back.' To my painting, and the empty house I've been looking forward to for weeks.

But Lee starts filling my glass. 'It's still early. You can have one more while you tell me more about this art competition.'

But I don't just have one more, and after another two glasses, I'm enjoying myself too much to go home. It is too late to paint now, the sun withdrew long ago, so there is no harm staying here chatting to Lee.

And this thought is the last thing I remember.

CHAPTER TWO

Now

I don't know how I make it home, but somehow I am here, sinking to the floor the second I close the door. My heavy breaths echo through the house, and surely any moment now I will take my last one.

I left him there. Dead. And now there is no going back, no calling the police, because I have left a crime scene. Nausea overcomes me and I rush upstairs to the bathroom, only just making it in time. But the panic does not abate.

Instinctively I pull off my clothes and examine each item, but I can find no traces of blood or anything else. Even my body – shades paler now – is untarnished. At least visibly.

But I turn on the shower, the temperature almost too hot to bear, and scrub every inch of my skin until I am red raw. My tears merge with the water, and the noise I make doesn't sound human.

I have no idea how much time passes before I feel ready to emerge, to take the first step towards dealing with this mess I am in, but it is still only six a.m. Time is at a standstill. Wrapping myself in a towel – Noah's because it's the first one I grab – I sit on the edge of the bed, trying to control my breathing.

Panicking will do me no good. I need to calm down if I'm to make sense of any of this. But the image of Lee's vacant face, his lifeless body, refuses to leave me. Fifty years will pass and it will still be there, as vivid as if I am still standing next to him.

I steady my breathing. Focus on the facts. One: I didn't kill Lee. There was no blood on me, his or my own, so I couldn't have done it. Two: whoever did that to him saw me there in his bed. His killer knows my face. What if they come back for me?

I rush around the house, checking every window and door, and when I've done that I recheck them all, driven by fear and paranoia I have no control over. And then I curl up on the sofa, and try to assess my situation.

It's not too late; I will go to the police. After all, I have the truth on my side. And once they have investigated they will see that I am innocent.

My phone rings, making me jump. It has to be the police. Somebody saw me leaving Lee and Serena's house, and now they will never believe I was about to tell them everything.

But it is Spencer, and seeing his name forces me back to normality. I take a deep breath and answer.

'Hi, love, is everything okay? You're up early.' It takes all my effort to keep my voice upbeat.

'Yeah, I got up early with Grandad to take Jackson for a walk. But Mum? Grandma and Grandad wouldn't let me watch a DVD. Even a 12. And I'm nearly twelve, aren't I? It's only a few weeks away, so why won't they let me?'

My head pounds. How can I have a conversation about something so trivial when Lee is dead? 'Spencer, they're just doing what they think is best. But don't worry, you'll be home tomorrow. And I'll check the film and see if you can watch it next weekend.'

But my son is full of quiet determination – a trait I usually admire in him. 'You could speak to them this morning and they might let me watch it tonight?'

'I'll see,' I say, too weary for this conversation.

The excitement in his voice makes my heart ache. 'Great! I'll just put Grandma on now, she's—'

'Not now!' My request is more a command, and I deliver it too harshly.

Spencer falls silent. Seconds tick by. 'Okay,' he says eventually.

'I'll call you later, Spence. I just have some things to do.'

'Bye, Mum,' he says. He can tell there is something wrong. For an eleven-year-old, Spencer is highly intuitive.

For half an hour after I've hung up, I sit clutching my phone, wanting to call the police and do the right thing, but unable to move. If there was any way I could help them find Lee's murderer then I wouldn't hesitate, but with no memory of that night other than turning up at his house, there is nothing I can tell them, so I can't risk hurting my family for nothing.

I cross to the living room window. The sun is already bright in the cloudless sky, in complete contrast to the blackness inside the house it shines down on. There is no sign of life, and I can only assume Serena is not yet back.

At this moment she could be waking up in a hotel, soothing her hangover with a black coffee – despite trying to get pregnant, I know she still occasionally has alcohol – and she will have no idea her husband lies dead in their bed. His life extinguished by. . . who?

It wasn't me. I know it wasn't me. But the front door was shut before I left, and there were no signs of a break in. Don't think too deeply about that, it will be your undoing.

But I am already undone, because I was there and somehow I am embroiled in this, an unwitting participant in my neighbour's murder.

The curtains are still drawn from the night before, but I don't recall Lee closing them. I have no memory of anything but sitting on the sofa, drinking wine.

I consider texting Serena, explaining that I only just got her message from yesterday morning, because she will wonder why I haven't replied. Panic surges through me as I realise just how lucky I was that I got distracted from texting her. I would have told her I was on my way. Then she, and eventually everyone, would know that I'd gone there. That I was the last person to see Lee, so surely I must have killed him.

But it's okay. I am safe for now.

As I stare at the house across the road, I once again waver in my decision not to go to the police. I am making a difficult choice, but I have to choose my family. Rosie and Spencer both need me, so I can't be the woman who has woken up next to her dead neighbour. I'm also doing it for Noah, although he needs me less. It is not about me, and fear of consequences, because I know I did not harm Lee.

All of this, more than anything else, I know to be true.

Without further thought I lift my mobile and begin typing a message to my friend. A lie. A betrayal.

And when her reply comes, a kind '*no problem, we'll chat when I get home on Sunday xx*', I stifle the tears, swallow the lump in my throat and tell myself I'd better get used to this. For my family.

The rest of the morning passes agonisingly slowly, a blur of staring through the window and strong coffee. I cannot stomach anything else.

The postman delivers a pile of letters through their door, oblivious to the fact that the property he stands on is a murder scene. Life goes on for everyone else, while it has halted for me, and for Serena.

I want my family back here. I need the noise and the life, and even Rosie's tantrums. Anything to pierce this awful silence.

While I'm contemplating this, Noah texts, telling me it all went well with his client, and I calculate the time difference – New York is five hours behind – and wonder why he is up so early. Don't think about that. It's jet lag. There is no other reason he is awake at this time.

Painting is impossible now; all I can do is sit and stare at what I've already started – the greeny-blue of the lake – unable to lift my brush and make even the tiniest of strokes on the paper. Yesterday, I had the finished piece pictured in my head; today, it is dead.

And when I can no longer bear being alone with my thoughts, I call Lisa. I have to tell someone, and if anyone will understand it's my sister. With liberal views, even if she suspects I've slept with Lee, she will not judge me.

'Hey, Tara,' she says, her voice thick with sleep. She must have had a heavy night. 'I'm a bit hung-over,' she says, confirming my suspicion. 'Went bar-hopping last night. Great fun, but I'm paying for it now.'

'I was going to ask if you wanted to come over.' My choice of phrasing hopefully masks my desperation. 'But I understand if you can't.'

'Are you okay?' she asks.

Of course, she will detect something different in my voice. She knows me better than almost anyone.

Now is the time to tell her. Then she will come straight over and offer me the support we always give each other. I open my mouth to speak, but the words die before I can set them free.

'I'm. . . just really struggling with this painting. I've got a lot riding on this competition.'

'I know you do, sis. And you'll get it done. Isn't it all part of the creative process? Look, I would pop round if I could, but Harvey's planned something for us today. Not sure what it is, but he's not too thrilled that I'm still in bed.'

I tell her it's no problem, that I should try to crack on with my painting, and I hope she enjoys her day.

'You'll be fine, Tara. I'm sure you're just finding it hard to paint because you're missing Noah and the kids,' she says. 'Being on your own isn't all it's cracked up to be, is it?'

In the evening I'm sitting in the kitchen, a brief respite from my reconnaissance at the living room window, when I hear something. I freeze, my mind playing only one scenario: whoever killed Lee has come for me.

But when I turn, it is Rosie standing in the doorway, her head tilted as she watches me.

'Rosie, is everything okay? You're home early.' Please don't let her be here because of another incident. For the moment, I have to push thoughts of Lee aside.

She takes a step into the kitchen, walking carefully as if this is a stranger's house and not the home she's lived in for most of her life.

'Why do you always assume I'm in trouble?'

Of course, I don't tell her it's because she usually is. This is not the time for an argument. 'I'm just surprised you're back.'

She walks closer towards me and peers at my face. 'You don't look well, Mum. Are you ill?'

Her words are those of a concerned daughter, but the tone she delivers them in is anything but warm. I try to work out what she might be angry with me about. Have we argued lately? Have I punished her for something she believes is unjust? But everything before Lee has been overshadowed, temporarily erased from my memory.

Like last night.

What happened, Lee? What did we do?

I tell her I'm fine, but she raises her eyebrows. If I can't even fool Rosie, who half the time doesn't notice anybody except herself, then what chance do I have?

She pulls out a chair and sits next to me. 'It's just that I need to talk to you. It's important.'

Whatever Rosie needs to tell me is a welcome distraction.

'Go on, you know you can tell me anything.' This is what I've tried to get across to her since she was a toddler. There is nothing she can't tell me.

Her face lights up then as her mouth spreads into a smile. 'Mum, I've been seeing someone.'

My heart sinks. 'Oh, Rosie, is this about Anthony? Because—'

'No, it's not Anthony!' She shrieks her words.

'Calm down, Rosie. Just tell me all about him, then.'

Normally instructing my daughter to calm down results in the exact opposite, but this time she doesn't protest.

'His name's Damien. But just promise you won't be angry.'

I am used to Rosie deliberately taking an eternity to get to her point – it's just her way – but today I struggle to humour her. 'I won't be angry because, whatever it is, at least you're telling me.' And I am the biggest hypocrite.

She sucks in her breath. 'Well. . . he's a bit older.'

Once again that sinking feeling, this time in my whole body. 'What do you mean by a bit?'

She shrugs and narrows her eyes. 'I dunno! Maybe twenties. Who cares?'

'You mean you're seeing this man and you don't even know how old he is?' I realise too late that I'm handling this all wrong. That it could be an example in a textbook of how not to connect with your daughter.

Standing up, she flings her chair aside. 'Why can't you and Dad just be happy for me? You weren't happy with Anthony and now you're not happy with. . . I can't win, can I?'

And then she is gone. Thundering up the stairs and slamming her bedroom door. And I have no clue why she came back early or who she is supposedly seeing.

But at least I am no longer alone. I have to focus on my daughter now. She will come back downstairs once she's calmed down, and I will give her all my attention because she needs me. And whoever this man is or isn't, I will be understanding.

But while I'm waiting, I cannot escape the prison of my mind, and I head back to the living room to resume my post at the window. Nothing has changed in the last hour, everything outside still has the façade of normality. Our peaceful cul-de-sac. And tomorrow Serena will arrive home, expecting her husband to greet her, but instead. . . How can I let that happen?

I could drive somewhere far from here and make an anonymous call to the police from a payphone. But anonymity doesn't exist any more. They would trace the call and track me down.

My mobile rings, startling me because I'm so on edge.

'Tara, how's everything at home?' Noah's voice is a comfort.

I fill him in on Rosie, and he sighs into the phone.

'We're going to have to have that chat with her again, aren't we?'

This conversation is good, an anchor to normality.

'I don't know what's more worrying – whether she actually is seeing an older guy, or the fact she might be stalking someone again.'

'I'll talk to her. But, anyway, you should go, this call will be costing a fortune.'

'Yeah, you're right,' Noah says, 'I'll text from now on until I'm back.'

We say goodbye, and I make a quick call to my parents to check on Spencer. He is happy to hear from me, and still begs to watch the DVD he's so desperate to see, so I give in and tell him it's fine. Right now there are worse things to worry about.

As soon as I end the call, I plummet back to my new reality. But all I can do is carry on, and focus on my family.

I knock on Rosie's door and wait for her to invite me in. But seconds pass with no reply, and behind her door is only silence.

Deciding she must be asleep, I creep across the landing to our bedroom, knowing there will be no rest for me tonight.

But before I open my door, Rosie calls out: 'Let's just talk tomorrow, Mum. I don't think either of us is in the right state to have a proper discussion.'

Enveloped in guilt, it is easy to misconstrue her words. She cannot know about last night; it is just my mind playing a cruel trick.

Once I'm in bed, I switch off the lamp, pull the sheet tighter across me, despite the heat, and close my eyes. But the image of Lee won't disappear, and it's intermittently broken up with snatches of past conversations I've had with him. Tears fall from my eyes as I remember him helping out in the garden when I was too busy with work, and his refusal to accept any money. He didn't deserve this; he only ever showed us kindness, and even Serena, who knew him better than anyone, never complained about him. Not once. So why would anyone want him dead?

It is just a waiting game now. Someone knows I was there, and sooner or later everything will come crashing down around me.

CHAPTER THREE

A loud pounding wakes me, but I don't move. Perhaps I imagined it? But there it is again. Thud thud thud. There's no mistaking it this time, or the fact that it's our front door.

'Mum? There's someone trying to break the door down.' Rosie stands in my bedroom doorway, still wearing her pyjamas, her hair tousled from sleep.

I pull myself up. 'It's just someone knocking,' I say. But then I remember what's happened, and the few moments of oblivion I've had are lost.

Rosie tuts. 'I know, Mum, I was being sarcastic.'

I glance at the clock on my bedside table. Eight a.m. Too early for anyone to be knocking on my door on a Sunday morning. This can only be about Lee.

'I'm going to get it,' Rosie says, already making her way to the stairs.

'No! I'll go. It could be anyone.'

Jumping up, I grab my dressing gown from the back of the door and race past Rosie, who is ignoring my suggestion and heading downstairs.

Thud thud thud.

I can't let her get there before me, but I also can't make too much of it. 'I'm expecting a delivery,' I call. 'It might be heavy. Let me go.'

'Oh,' she says, slowing down as she loses interest. But then she turns to me, and I am convinced she sees through my lie. 'What have you ordered?'

There is no time to make something up on the spot, something that could later come back to haunt me, no matter how trivial it seems.

Thud thud thud.

'Just let me get the door, Rosie.'

'Sorry,' she says, but I feel her eyes on me as I walk through the hall, my stomach flipping inside me.

I shouldn't be shocked to find myself face-to-face with a uniformed police officer. They have come for me, and my daughter will see me dragged away in handcuffs. The sight will stay with her for the rest of her life, and my innocence won't matter.

The officer glances at my dressing gown. 'Sorry to wake you, Madam, but there's been an incident across the road, at number five, and we're just questioning all the neighbours to see if anyone saw anything.'

A surge of relief. They have not come for me. Not this time.

I stare past him to Lee and Serena's house, which is now a hive of activity. Police officers, and other officials I can't name, rush around purposefully, leaving and entering through the open front door. Someone has erected a barrier; scene of crime tape I've only ever seen on television, and I am momentarily mesmerised.

'Madam?'

'I, um, yes, sorry, I'm. . . what. . . happened?' The officer will think my hesitation is due to the shock of what I'm witnessing.

He doesn't answer my question. 'Can you tell me if you saw anything at all at number five on Friday night or early Saturday morning?'

It scares me that they already know the exact time frame, but I assume they've pieced it together from what Serena must have told them.

Perhaps he is not allowed to inform me that someone has been murdered. Is that the protocol?

'I. . . well, I was at home but I didn't see anything. What exactly has happened? Are Serena and Lee okay?'

Again he ignores my question. 'How well do you know your neighbours across the road?'

'We're friends,' I say. This might encourage him to provide more information. Perhaps they already know who did it. For the first time since waking up on Saturday morning, my spirits lift with hope.

'What's going on, Mum?' Rosie appears beside me, staring at the police officer. And then she, like I have just done, registers the scene across the road. 'Oh my God. Mum? What's going on?' Her voice is higher, bordering on hysteria.

I need to protect her from this, but it is too late.

'Miss?' The officer attempts to get her attention. 'If you could just stay calm, I'm just trying to determine if anyone saw anything.'

'But what's happened?'

She turns to me as she asks this, and I shudder. Why does she think I have any answers? All I can do is reach for her hand.

'Miss, could you tell me if you saw anything at number five – anything at all – on Friday evening or early Saturday morning?'

Rosie is suddenly calm, a different girl to the one she was only moments ago. 'I wasn't home. I only came back yesterday evening.'

The officer asks for our names and scribbles details on a form; once he's finished, thanking us and requesting that we contact the police if we think of anything later.

He leaves then, and I am just about to close the door when Rosie stops me and pulls it open wider.

'Look, Mum!'

Against my better judgement I look out to see what's got her attention. They are bringing him out on a stretcher, a black cover pulled over his face. An unmistakable dead body.

Rosie screams and grabs hold of me, her nails digging into my flesh. 'Mum! Who is that?'

I'm about to tell her I don't know, that we need to close the door and stop rubber-necking, but then Serena appears. A woman I've never seen before has her arms around her, holding her up because, even from this distance, it looks as if she's about to collapse.

'Oh, God – that's Serena! So it must be Lee under that. . . something's happened to Lee, Mum!'

It takes me half an hour to calm Rosie down. We sit in the kitchen – my ploy to make sure she can't see out of the living room window – and stare at our untouched glasses of water.

'Maybe he died of natural causes,' she says. 'I mean, he was quite old, wasn't he?'

She is straight-faced as she says this – as if she is stating an indisputable fact. Under any other circumstances I would point out that thirty-five is absolutely not old – but it must be to a seventeen-year-old. And now is not the time for trivialities.

I want to tell her, yes, that must be what's happened, but any second now she will realise why this can't be true.

'Oh, wait,' she says. 'The police wouldn't have come here then, would they?' She contemplates this for a moment, and as I watch her facial expressions while she assesses it all, I feel a pang of envy.

My daughter can talk about this easily because it is nothing to do with her. Any time now she will call Libby and report what's happened, the two of them pondering it in hushed, excited voices. While I cannot speak of it, or think of it, without a suffocating dread encroaching me.

'Someone's actually been murdered on our road,' she continues. 'Maybe it's a serial killer and he'll come back for one of us.'

'Don't be ridiculous. Don't say things like that, it's not a joke. A man is dead, Rosie. Our friend.' But I know Rosie is deliberately playing games now. This is what she does.

'Your friend. I hardly even knew him.'

But this is not true. Both Serena and Lee have always had a lot of time for her, and Spencer, so her callousness is inexplicable.

I take a deep breath, try to stay calm. 'I'm going to let this go because you're in shock. But I don't want to hear you speaking like that again.'

She ignores my admonishment. 'I can't believe this. I have to call Libby.'

And then she is gone, her footsteps pounding on the stairs as she rushes to share the gossip with her friend.

I stand on the doorstep and brace myself for the task ahead. I can do this. I can be there for my friend and offer her support, because only one thing matters: I did not kill Lee.

But I am a liar by omission. And I'm about to expand my lies by looking Serena in the face and telling her I'm sorry this has happened when I should be telling her what I know about his death, filling in the details she will be desperate to know.

The same woman I saw her with earlier answers the door, standing aside to let me in once I've explained who I am. She tells me her name is Gwynn, and that she's a police liaison officer. She is a tall woman, with a stocky build, but she's not threatening at all; her face is too kind.

I knew coming here would be hard, but I'm unprepared for the feeling I get stepping through the door. Flashes of that evening bombard me, but none of them show me what I need to know. I recall nothing other than Lee letting me in, giving me drinks, opening up to me.

It is only now, as Gwynn leads me through the hallway, saying something about Serena wanting to see me, that I realise I've made a horrendous mistake.

Lee and I were drinking wine that night – perhaps bottles of it – but it didn't occur to me to wash up my glass, or dispose of it, as I fled the house. My only thought was to get out of there as quickly as possible to escape the nightmare. But now I realise my fingerprints will be plastered all over the glass, traces of my DNA in the wine residue left behind.

I feel as if I'm standing in fire, my body slowly burning. I should have called the police. Serena would detest me, would never believe I didn't sleep with her husband, but at least I would have morality on my side. But now it is too late for that.

'Tara.'

I barely recognise her voice, and even her appearance doesn't belong to the woman I know. Serena is always neat, never a blonde hair out of place, even all the times she has cried on my shoulder, shedding tears for the baby she is desperate for. Now she is a shadow of that immaculate woman: her long blonde hair seems greasy and smudges of make-up are dotted around her face. The Serena of before would be horrified for anyone to see her in this state. But, of course, none of that matters now.

'Tara,' she says again, as if she needs to confirm it's actually me standing here.

My body stiffens as I wait for her to assail me with accusations. But they do not come. Instead, she rushes over to me and flings her arms around my neck, almost dragging me to the ground as her body collapses. I pull her up and grip her tightly, trying not to let her fall.

'Lee's. . . dead! I. . .' Her wail is animalistic, a testament to the pain she's in. The pain I have a hand in.

'I'm sorry,' I whisper into her hair. 'I'm so sorry.'

She pulls away then, and stares at me. 'It doesn't make any sense. He. . . they found him in bed. . . stabbed. They said they won't know for sure yet but it looks like a knife went straight through to his heart so that's why there wasn't lots of blood, and that if so at least it would have been...quick. But nobody broke into the house! So how could it happen? He couldn't have done it to himself – they told me that would have been impossible. So. . . so how? Who?'

I squeeze her arm. I need to find some comforting words to offer her, but I'm struggling.

'Let's go and sit down,' I say eventually, hoping a move to the living room will buy me some time to get myself together.

She nods and lets me lead her there. My eyes immediately scan the room, ignoring the bodies milling around as I look for the wine glasses Lee and I drank from. But there is no sign of them, or any bottles. Perhaps Lee cleared everything away before we went upstairs. I shudder to think of us heading upstairs together. Surely that's not what happened? More than likely the police have already taken them as evidence. I can find out from Serena if I question her carefully. But I will have to wait for the right moment.

I focus again on the distraught woman before me. 'Serena, I'm here for you, if you need anything at all, day or night. I'm just across the road, okay?'

She nods gratefully, and I can barely look at her. My stomach heaves, and I am a second away from bolting through the door. Just hold it together. You know you didn't do this, so just hang in there.

'I found him, Tara, it was terrible. If only I hadn't gone on that stupid hen weekend, then he'd still be alive, wouldn't he?'

I fight the urge to scream, yes, he would still be alive. Why did you have to go away and set in motion this horrific chain of events? But, of course, it is not her fault.

'You couldn't have known this would happen. None of this is your fault, Serena.'

She erupts into fits of tears again, and all I can do is hold her hand. 'But it is my fault! I texted him on Friday night, and all day Saturday, and he didn't reply to a single one. If I'd known something was wrong I would have come straight back home, and maybe. . . maybe I would have found him still alive and. . . and called for help.'

I can't let her believe this. 'Serena, it's not your—'

'We'd had a huge row before I left. He said he wasn't sure about having another go at IVF, and I just lost it. So I just thought he was ignoring me because he was so angry. He did that sometimes, and I usually just let him get over it in his own time. But. . . but I had no idea. . .' Tears drown out her words.

There is little I can say to comfort her; nothing will bring Lee back. But I try my best to help her see she is wrong about it being her fault. 'You didn't do this to him,' I say. 'There is only one person responsible and that's the one who. . .' I can't say the words, even though my mind will not let me forget the vision of Lee's slaughtered body.

Through her tears, she offers a slight nod. 'But who would want him dead? He's never done anything to anyone. He didn't deserve to die like that.'

I want to tell her that life is not always fair. There are no hard and fast rules; anything can happen to any one of us, no matter how good or bad we supposedly are. But she doesn't need to hear this. She will need me to agree with her, so this is what I do.

We sit like this for a few moments: together, but alone with our thoughts, while the crime scene officers buzz around us. For them it is just another day at work. For us, it is the beginning of the end.

* * *

When I get home, Rosie is sitting on the stairs, facing the door as if she's been waiting for me. 'Have you been over there?' she says. 'To see Serena?'

'Yes, I did shout up to tell you I was going, but you mustn't have heard me.' Although I'm certain she did, am sure I heard her shouting a response over the pounding bass pumping from her speakers. But perhaps my mind is playing tricks on me.

'She must be in a real state,' Rosie says. 'Poor woman. But she's quite pretty. I'm sure she'll find someone else eventually.'

I open my mouth to yell at her, but think better of it. Rosie always wants us to rise to her bait, but today I will not. So instead, in the calmest voice I can muster, I tell her to think about what she's just said. 'Put yourself in her shoes, Rosie, before you say anything else about Serena or Lee, or anyone else for that matter.'

She seems surprised that I haven't admonished her more harshly, but nods her agreement.

I need a distraction from everything so I ask her what she'd like for lunch. It is Sunday so we always have a roast at lunchtime, and I won't break that tradition now. It will just be the two of us – my parents are feeding Spencer before I pick him up later, and Noah isn't due home until after eleven p.m.

'Can't we have those beef parcel things you make instead?' Rosie asks. 'If it's just us two. I love them so much.'

This is good; the recipe is simpler than a roast but complex enough for me to shut out all other thoughts – to try, at least.

It is a surprise when Rosie follows me to the kitchen and offers to help. But I set her to work, and for the next hour everything is calm, and it is easy to pretend nothing exists outside of this house and my family.

'It's so sad, isn't it, Mum?' Rosie says, as she peels potatoes. 'I mean, how is Serena going to have a baby now?'

My hands freeze halfway through slicing an onion, and I turn to my daughter. 'How do you know about that?' Serena is fiercely protective of her privacy, and the only reason I know about their troubles is because I happened to be with her when she had her first miscarriage. It had been hard for her to tell me, but eventually I had earned her trust. But Rosie? I cannot believe she would talk to my seventeen-year-old daughter about her infertility.

And there is no way Lee would have told her. He has barely even spoken to Noah about it. And our conversation on Friday night was the most I'd ever heard him speak on the subject.

'I can't remember how I know,' Rosie says. 'I thought everyone did. I must have heard it somewhere.'

But there is nowhere she could have heard it. The only other neighbours we know well enough to say more than a hello to are Guy and Layla Watts next door, and there is no way Serena would have shared personal information with them.

I am about to question Rosie further when my phone beeps in my pocket. I pull it out to check who has texted, and am surprised to see it's from Libby's mum. Before I read any further I already know this means trouble. Rosie has done something over the weekend that Bernadette wants me to know about. I take a deep breath and open the message.

And once I've read it I turn to my daughter, rage boiling inside me that I can't let out. Calmly, I ask her where she was all weekend.

'You know where I was, Mum. At Libby's and then here.'

I shake my head. 'No, you weren't. Because that was Libby's mum, telling me what a shame it was that you couldn't stay with them this weekend, and that she hopes you feel better soon. Now what the hell is going on?'

CHAPTER FOUR

When Noah arrives home he has already heard about Lee's murder. It is plastered all over the local news now, but at least this saves me having to tell him about it myself. Of course he is desperate to talk about it, shocked that it's so close to home, and that he only spoke to Lee on Thursday night, but when I tell him about Rosie, this trumps any other topic of conversation.

'What do you mean she didn't stay at Libby's? Then where the hell was she?'

I tell him to brace himself for this next part, because it doesn't make for easy listening. 'She's been seeing someone. An older man. And she finally admitted that she'd been with him on Friday night.'

We're sitting at the kitchen table, a glass of wine each in front of us, and Noah takes a long swig of his.

'So our teenage daughter has spent the night with – and probably slept with – a stranger?'

I have to defend Rosie here. 'He's only a stranger to us, Noah. That doesn't mean I'm condoning it, but we have to stay calm about this.'

But he isn't able to. 'She's seventeen,' he says.

'And how old was I when we met? When I fell pregnant with Rosie? How old were you?'

'There's a world of difference between seventeen and twenty-one. And I'm only three years older than you. How old is this guy she's seeing?'

'She claims she doesn't know, that it doesn't matter.'

Noah finishes the rest of his glass, while I cannot touch mine.

'I think we're forgetting something here,' I say, raising my eyebrows to show him that it's obvious, that he should know.

And then he understands.

'She's making it up,' he says, with a sigh of relief.

But how is this any better? I tell Noah I'm afraid Rosie might have fixated on someone again, and it can only end badly. But there can be nothing worse than waking up next to your dead neighbour.

Noah pours himself another glass of wine.

'If that's true, though, then where did she sleep on Friday night?'

This is what I intend to find out. Because this doesn't feel right, and Rosie is slipping away.

Not long after our conversation in the kitchen, when I am exhausted but know sleep won't come easily, I stand by our bedroom window, listening to the sound of Noah brushing his teeth in the en-suite.

I cannot stop myself peeking through the curtains and am surprised to find that, other than the crime scene tape surrounding Serena and Lee's house, everything is quiet, and there is no sign of anyone.

Serena has gone to stay with her parents in north London, declining my offer of our spare room because it was too close. Too painful to be here. Secretly I was relieved when she said this, but it has only added to my guilt.

'It's hard to believe, isn't it?' Noah says, startling me.

I didn't hear him come out of the bathroom, but now he is standing next to me, and we both stare through the window.

I manage a nod.

'It's funny, but suddenly it feels different being here, doesn't it? I don't know, like it's not quite home any more. My whole perspective of our road has changed in an instant.'

'But whatever we're feeling, it's worse for Serena,' I say.

'Oh, I know, of course it is. Poor woman.' He grabs my hand and pulls me towards him. 'If it was you. . . instead of Lee. . . I don't know what I'd do.'

Ordinarily I might use an opportunity like this – where his words are flowing without inhibition – to ask him if he's certain this time. If he's sure this is where he wants to be, but now is not the time. I have my secret to keep hidden, my daughter to protect, and a son whom I need to make sure feels cherished rather than neglected because his sister needs so much of our attention. There is no room for anything else.

'You haven't told me about your trip,' I say, turning from the window and closing the curtains to shut out that house.

'Oh, it was fine. Everything went well. But you look so tired, Tara, let's go to bed and I'll tell you all about it in the morning when we've sorted Rosie out.'

But Noah knows Rosie cannot be sorted out with one conversation.

He climbs into bed, only pulling the cover up to his waist because, despite all the windows being open, the heat is stifling.

'Aren't you getting in?'

But I cannot seem to move. The thought of getting into bed next to someone suddenly frightens me, but I am not surprised as to why. I am about to tell Noah I think I will sleep downstairs on the sofa, where it is several degrees cooler, but I won't let fear beat me.

So I cross to the bed, and turn back the sheet, sliding in next to him. I turn to face away from him and he cuddles into my back, wrapping his arm around my waist. Inside, I am frozen, praying his hands stay still, that any second now I will hear the heavy breaths that signify he is asleep.

I squeeze my eyes shut and count to ten, and when I reach the end neither of us has moved. So for tonight, at least, I don't have to pretend, or fake enjoyment in a mockery of our marriage.

I end up downstairs, after all: sneaking out of our bedroom and curling up on the sofa once Noah is asleep. The television is on, and I hold a book in my hand, but neither can distract me. I don't know how the hours pass, but perhaps I do fall asleep because, one second I am alone, and the next Spencer is jumping on the sofa.

'Why are you down here, Mum?' he asks.

'It was too hot upstairs. I couldn't sleep. Are you okay, Spence?'

'Yup. Can I watch TV?'

I haven't yet told him about Lee. Spencer liked him a lot, and yesterday evening I couldn't bring myself to break it to him. For more than one reason. And Noah got home too late to even say good night to him, so now he sits beside me, oblivious, and I can't let him find out from the news.

'Not right now. Let's have some breakfast first.' It's the last thing I want, but it will give me a chance to talk to him.

'Okay,' he says, because he doesn't argue or cause a fuss when he can't get his own way. My two children are opposites in every way.

I let him eat before I break the news, and at first he grins, clearly in disbelief. But when my face remains sombre, it quickly fades and his mouth hangs open.

And then he is crying, so I grab him and pull him into the tightest hug I can manage, telling him not to be worried. Not to be scared.

Despite his gentle nature, Spencer is tough, and he soon recovers. 'I really liked him, he was cool. He was always so nice to me.'

'I know, Spence. It's very sad, but we all have to be strong so we can support Serena.'

He nods. 'She's nice too.' He pauses. 'Shall we go and see her?'

It both stuns and saddens me how different his reaction is to Rosie's, until I remind myself not to compare my children. Rosie isn't a bad person. She's just Rosie.

'Does Rosie know?' Spencer asks. 'She must be gutted too.'

I recall her reaction yesterday: hysterical at first but quickly calm, and even detached in the end. Gutted is far from how she appeared.

'Why do you say that, Spencer? She didn't really talk to Lee or Serena, did she? I know you did, but Rosie never bothered with them, did she?'

'No, but. . . Mum, can I watch TV now, please?'

'What were you about to say?'

He shakes his head and gets up from the table. 'Nothing, Mum. Can I watch TV now?'

I try one more time to get him to finish his statement, but he insists he can't remember what he was about to say. I let it drop for now. But clearly there is something going on with Rosie that only Spencer knows about.

More secrets to rip my family apart.

It is past midday when Noah emerges from the bedroom. He is off work today, because of the travelling yesterday, but I know he planned to do some work at home. He is freshly showered and has clearly slept off his jet lag, but his expression is serious. He is desperate for us to talk things through with Rosie. For him, this has overshadowed what's happened to Lee, but then it is even closer to home. Our daughter has to come first. But for me everything mingles together, unrelated incidents, but fully entwined in my mind, because everything has happened at once, over the same period of time.

Noah and I go outside in the back garden to talk, and to get some air.

'I can't believe this heat,' he says, pulling at his T-shirt. 'I'm not used to it.'

'But it's hotter than this in New York, isn't it?' It seems ludicrous that I'm standing here discussing the weather in the midst of all that's happened.

Noah nods. 'Yeah, it was. But I was inside, in meetings, most of the time, so I barely noticed it. Anyway, have you had a chance to talk to Rosie yet?'

'There was no time before she left for school, so we'll have to do it later. But I told Spencer about Lee.'

'Poor kid,' Noah says, shaking his head. 'It just makes you realise you can't shelter them for ever. Anyway, we'll talk to Rosie this evening. When Spencer's gone to bed, of course.'

It is true that we can't always shelter them, but we can do our best to protect them from whatever might happen. And that is what I intend to do.

I agree with Noah's plan, and tell him I'm going upstairs to have a bath. I have a pile of paperwork to see to before I am back at work on Thursday, but it will have to wait.

'You didn't tell me how your painting's going,' he says, as I head back into the house.

I don't mention that I haven't been able to look at it, let alone do anything with it, since I woke up on Saturday morning. 'Not too bad.' My lie is a safe one: I never show anyone my paintings, and always keep them turned to the wall until they are completed, and he would never try to look without my knowledge.

'Great,' he says. 'I'm really proud of you, Tara.'

I offer him a faint smile then walk inside. There is nothing to be proud of right now.

On my way past the front door, I notice a tall, thin silhouette through the glass. And even though someone is clearly out there, I still jump when whoever it is thumps on the door. I curse our broken doorbell for the hundredth time, and cautiously open the door, preparing myself for anything.

It is a shock to see Layla Watts standing there when I've been expecting it to be the police.

'Hi, Tara,' she says, her voice quiet. 'I guess you've heard?'

She turns around and we both stare at Serena and Lee's house. Once again, now daylight is here, various people bustle around, although far fewer than yesterday.

'It's awful,' I say.

She nods. 'Poor Serena. I can't even imagine how she's feeling. But anyway, I just wanted to say Guy's calling a meeting tonight at eight, just so we can all discuss what to do as a neighbourhood. You know, as far as security goes. And what we can do for Serena. I hope you and Noah can make it?'

I want to say no. Noah and I have been notoriously bad at attending the monthly Neighbourhood Watch meetings that Guy and Layla take such pride in hosting. But how would it look if we weren't at this one?

'Of course, we'll be there. Can I help with anything?' I pray she will say no.

'No, it's all under control. It's a bit last minute so there won't be the refreshments I usually put out, but I'm sure I can manage some nibbles.'

I picture the scene: people munching crisps and cakes while we all discuss the death of our neighbour.

'Well, let me know if I can bring anything.'

'Just yourselves,' she says, not even attempting to hide the judgement in her tone.

'No way,' Noah says, when I tell him about the meeting. He is sitting in the garden on a sun lounger, under the shade of our huge oak tree, his laptop balanced on his knees. 'Why would we go when we never bother with those things? I can't think of anything worse.'

I sit on the grass beside him. 'We have to go, Noah. It's the right thing to do. For Lee.'

He sighs. 'But it's not going to be about Lee, is it? It will just be all our neighbours, most of whom we've never even spoken to, gossiping about his murder as if it's an episode of a soap opera. Lee would hate it. He never went to those things either.'

This is true, but Serena did, and has tried to get me to go on many occasions. Although, like me, she wasn't keen on Guy and Layla, she liked the idea of community, of getting to know the people around us. I wonder if she feels the same way now.

I'm about to tell him I agree when a thought makes me reconsider. As the person in charge of the Neighbourhood Watch programme, Guy might have information from the police to share with us. As well as being sad that this happened to Lee, he will be horrified it took place on his doorstep, right under his nose, where, clearly, nobody was watching.

And I need information.

'I'm definitely going,' I say. 'I understand if you don't want to, but one of us should at least show our face.'

Noah sighs again. 'I'm not letting you go alone. I still don't agree with it, but of course I'll come.'

I leave him to work and head back inside the house, telling him I'm going to try to paint. The deadline for the competition is in three days' time, and he will ask questions if he thinks I'm not working on it. And Noah will not let me give up on my dream, so the only thing I can do is try to finish it. It won't need to be perfect; I no longer care about winning, all that matters is that I have something to send to the gallery.

But once I'm in the sunroom, sitting in front of my easel, all I can think of is that I'm making a huge mistake going next door for the meeting tonight.

What if someone saw me going to Lee's house that evening? Or worse, what if they saw me fleeing the next morning?

CHAPTER FIVE

Rosie is late home from school. It's almost five p.m. when she strolls in, slinging her bag over the bannister. 'Hi,' she says, when she sees me standing at the bottom of the stairs. She doesn't follow this up with an explanation of where she's been, but she is eighteen in a few months – an adult – so what can I say except to let her know the right thing is to notify your family when you'll be late home.

'I'm sorry, Mum,' she says, when I explain this to her. 'It won't happen again. I don't want you to think I'm dead, like Lee.'

'Rosie, cut it out.'

'Sorry.'

This time she actually does appear remorseful so I let it go. I have more important issues to talk to her about. 'Let's talk in the kitchen,' I say.

'But I've got homework and—'

'That can wait. We need to discuss some things first.'

'I know,' she says. 'Come on, then, let's get this over with and I can start my homework.'

Despite her difficult behaviour at times, I know Rosie studies hard, and is desperate to do well in her A-levels. She does care about her future – despite her actions sometimes suggesting otherwise.

Noah is already waiting in the kitchen, his arms folded as he leans against the worktop.

'This is an ambush,' Rosie says, although she doesn't appear distressed. 'Hi, Dad.'

'Sit down, please, Rosie.'

'This is all very formal,' she says, pulling out a chair.

I sit opposite her, but let Noah have his say. I've already lectured Rosie about this topic so she knows my feelings.

Walking around to where I sit, Noah leans on the table, his arms ramrod straight.

'First of all, we love you, Rosie. You know that.'

She shrugs. 'Yeah.'

'So if it seems like we're going on at you it's just because we want you to be safe. Happy, of course, but safe.'

'Okay. . .'

'So you must understand that we want to know who you're seeing.'

She rolls her eyes. 'You mean so you can vet him? Make sure he meets your approval?'

I can't help but chime in. 'That's not what your dad means, Rosie.' But it is exactly what he means, and I feel the same way. We both want to make sure our daughter is with someone who will treat her right.

Noah chooses to ignore her comment. 'We know you're nearly eighteen, and you can make choices for yourself, but all we ask is that we meet him.'

As he says this, I wonder if Rosie realises we have doubts about her story, that we can't be sure this man she's talking about is actually in a relationship with her. Anthony certainly wasn't.

But then I remember what Noah pointed out last night: if she's making up that she has a boyfriend, and is stalking someone, then where did she spend the night? Rosie might be obsessive, but she would never camp out on the streets. She loves her creature comforts far too much.

As prepared as I am for a battle, I am shocked when Rosie agrees.

'Okay, fine. You can meet him. Now can I go and do my homework, please?'

* * *

Later, I sit once again in front of my easel, waiting for inspiration. I stare at the river, the tree branches, the heron searching for its lunch, which I added as an afterthought. It is no good. Even though I no longer care about winning, what sits in front of me just cannot work. Then, almost unconsciously, I reach for a fresh canvas and begin again, my fingers furiously sketching what is only, for now, a seed of an idea.

An hour later, I have a charcoal outline of a scene on the canvas. A man and a woman in bed, the sheet pulled up to their waists, their bodies turned away from each other. And then I begin to paint.

Lisa calls before I'm finished, but it is time I had a break. Spencer will be home soon, and I need to get dinner ready for us. Life has to go on.

'Hey, Tara,' she says. 'How's your painting going?'

Studying what I have created, I tell her it's going well, that I've almost finished.

'That's great. I hope you win,' she says.

I shake my head, even though she can't see me. 'No, it won't win, but as long as I'm happy with it, then that's all that matters.' This was not how I felt before Saturday morning, but now everything has changed.

'I suppose,' she says. 'Anyway, I miss you – how about I pop over tomorrow? We can go for lunch at that pub near you. It's only a five-minute walk, and you'll need to eat, even if you're painting.'

There are many reasons why I should say no, and top of the list is because she's my sister, my closest friend; so how can I trust myself not to tell her what happened? While only I know, I can try to carry on as normal because, to everyone else, I'm the same person I was before. But once someone knows – even my sister – I will be that same person, but with a huge question mark hanging over me. The one who can't be trusted.

My pause lasts too long.

'Oh, go on,' she says. 'I could do with a chat.'

That decides it for me. 'Yes, let's do it.' I debate whether to tell her that a neighbour of ours has been murdered but I can't manage to say it. I will have to tell her tomorrow, though, as not mentioning something so important would cause her to question me. 'Are you okay, Lisa?' I say, because I don't want to focus on Lee.

'Oh, yeah, I'm fine. I just miss our chats. Anyway, I better go – Harvey's calling me for something. But I'll see you tomorrow.'

And when I put down the phone, I feel a surge of strength. I will not burden my sister with this just so I can ease the weight I'm carrying. No, tomorrow will be just another lunch date with my sister. We'll talk about her and Harvey, Rosie and Spencer. Even Noah. Anything but Lee Jacobs. He is for my thoughts only. I am not callous or heartless; I only know that I did nothing wrong.

But tonight still won't be easy.

'Do you have to go out?' Spencer says, when over dinner I tell him Noah and I are popping next door. 'You never go to those Neighbourhood Watch meetings.'

'Yes, but this time it's different,' Rosie chirps in. 'Someone's been murdered on our street, Spencer. It's serious. Mum and Dad have to go, otherwise people will think they don't care. Isn't that right, Mum?'

Ignoring her, Spencer turns to me to refute this, but in a way Rosie is right.

'We do have to go, Spencer. Lee is. . . was a friend of ours, and we need to support Serena as best we can.'

He considers this for a moment then nods. 'But won't it be strange for her? Everyone talking about it like that in front of her?'

I tell him she's not going to be there, that she's still staying with her parents, but don't add that I'm not sure how she'd feel about this meeting. If it descends into panic or gossip, then she would be appalled.

'We won't be long,' Noah says, glancing at me as if to say please let this be true.

I give a slight nod, because I, too, don't want to be there any longer than we have to.

'We'll just be next door if you need us. And Rosie will be here with you,' Noah continues.

'Um, yeah,' Spencer says, and I'm sure we both know what he's thinking.

But Rosie will most likely ignore him, and shut herself in her room. He will not have to deal with anything.

We still haven't pinned her down to a day we can meet her so-called boyfriend, Damien, but she insists he's busy at the moment, and that even she hasn't been able to see him. This appears to be true: because since she came home on Saturday she's been at home every evening.

'Just don't bug me,' Rosie says to Spencer.

The moment arrives too soon, and I begin to lose my nerve. I still have no idea what I'm walking into – will I be confronted with my lie? – so I need to be on my guard. Ready with an excuse.

But there isn't one. I could have said I was looking for Serena, after her text message, but I've already told her I didn't get it until it was too late. Plus, I would have mentioned to the police that I'd seen Lee that evening. No, there is only one thing I can do and that's lie. If anybody did see me, it would be their word against mine; there won't be any proof.

And running from their house in the early hours of Saturday morning would be even harder to explain, so, again, I will have to lie. It wasn't me. It was too dark for anyone to make a positive identification. It's a weak defence, but there is no other option.

'Let's get this over with,' Noah says, grabbing my hand tightly as we leave the house. There is no way he can know anything, but it is almost as if he senses how nervous I am.

Guy opens the door, wearing smart black trousers and a white shirt and tie. He takes this so seriously, and I wonder if secretly he is relishing the fact that this tragedy happened. He certainly appears to be in his element as he ushers us in and directs us where to sit.

Although their living room is large, like ours, it is crammed with extra chairs, beanbags and even kitchen stools, so we struggle to squeeze past everyone to the seats Guy has pointed us to. It is only just eight p.m., yet it appears at least one person from every house is already here.

I turn to Noah and he raises his eyebrows, clearly already fed up.

'Look at him,' he whispers to me, flicking his head towards Guy. 'He's so smug.'

Noah is right. Since the moment we moved in, Guy acted as if he was in charge of everything. But he didn't reckon on a family like ours moving in. People who won't just sit around and take orders. People who will speak their minds.

'I know,' I say to Noah. 'He lives for this kind of thing.'

Guy is at the front of the room now, rubbing his hands together and smiling as he takes in the people before him. Layla sits by him, in an armchair, and I try to catch her eye, so that she knows I kept my word, but she is too busy watching her husband.

'Ahem.' Guy claps, and the room quickly falls silent. 'Thank you. Now, as you know, this is an impromptu meeting, brought about by the tragic untimely death of Lee Jacobs, my friend and neighbour.'

I glance at Noah. 'My friend.' Lee despised Guy, and I am appalled that he has found a way to make it about himself.

'It's a terrible tragedy, and we will be offering Serena Jacobs our full support when she returns home but, in her absence, I want to speak about what this means for us as a neighbourhood.'

Low murmurs spread around the room, but Guy continues. 'Some of you may be feeling afraid – I know I am – but it's important we don't panic. I've spoken at length to the police, and they've assured me the chances of this happening to anyone else here are as good as zero.'

Not if they come back for me.

Noah leans in towards me and whispers in my ear: 'Who does he think he is? The Prime Minister delivering a speech or something? I actually think he's written it down and rehearsed it all day.'

The couple who live next door to the Jacobs – is it the Kerrs? I always forget, and have only ever smiled at them since they moved in – turn around to glare at Noah, so although he is right in what he says, I don't respond. The less attention we get, the better.

Guy continues his sermon. 'But, having said that, we need to be vigilant, and I cannot stress enough the importance of our Neighbourhood Watch scheme. We live in a lovely area, and houses like ours can be a huge attraction for burglars. Our alarms are just not enough, I'm afraid. But, on the positive side, I'm thrilled that since I've lived here we've not had a single break in.'

Again there are murmurs, and then someone shouts from the back of the room: 'But it didn't help Lee, did it?'

It seems as if everyone turns simultaneously to see who has spoken out like this. I am surprised to find it is the middle-aged woman from number one. I've never spoken to her, but have seen her coming and going from her property, and she's always appeared shy, refusing to fully meet my eye whenever our paths have crossed.

Guy tries not to appear ruffled by her question. 'That's actually partly why we're here,' he says, pausing to give everyone a chance to focus on him once more. 'I know from the police that nobody has come forward to say they've seen anything, and I'm not expecting a miracle, but I'm hoping that, since everyone was interviewed, something – anything – might now seem relevant that wasn't before.'

Somehow I am both relieved and fearful at the same time. Nobody has seen me. I silently pray that nothing comes up now. The hushed murmurs begin again, and each second ticking by feels like an hour.

'If you prefer,' Guy says, when nobody raises their voice to speak to him, 'you can come and see me after the meeting and talk to me in private.'

Beside me, Noah tuts, making no attempt to do it quietly. 'He is unbelievable.'

Again, I don't respond, but grab his hand, hoping he will understand my silent plea to be quiet.

I tune out after this, only hearing snippets of Guy's monologue on the importance of being vigilant and reporting anything that seems unusual. But he is wasting his time. People will listen for a while, but eventually time will erase the fear and they – we – will carry on as normal: Lee's death confined to the distant past.

Finally, he draws his speech to an end and invites questions from us. As I have expected, anyone putting their hand up only wants to know details, and the more gruesome the better, it seems. I learn nothing I didn't already know, except that the police are certain it was someone Lee knew.

'There was no sign of forced entry, you see,' Guy takes pleasure in informing us. 'So, they're deducing that it was someone who either had a key, or he let in.'

Once again the no-longer shy woman calls out: 'So it could be his wife?'

Someone gasps, and people begin talking amongst themselves.

'No,' Guy says, raising his voice to be heard over the increasing volume. 'It was most definitely not Serena – Mrs Jacobs – because she was away and has several people to prove it. But, as I said, they do think it was someone he knew. That's all I can tell you, I'm afraid.'

'It could just as easily have been a stranger who knocked on the door and forced their way in.'

It takes me a moment to realise the person who's just spoken is Noah. I have no idea what he's doing, but assume he's just trying to put Guy in his place.

For once, Guy seems to falter. 'I. . . well, I suppose. I don't know. The police haven't mentioned that possibility, but I am certain they'll be looking into every angle.'

Layla stands up to rescue her husband, joining him in his preacher's position.

'Well, I think that's about it, but I'll be bringing out refreshments now so please stay and talk to each other. There are some of you here who won't have even spoken to half the people in this room, so it's a good opportunity to get to know everyone. And the better we know each other, the more tight-knit we are as a community, the better prepared we'll be to prevent this happening again.'

Noah and I glance at each other, and I am certain we're thinking the same thing: does Layla actually believe the garbage she is spouting? Especially when her husband has just told us the police think Lee was murdered by someone he knew.

But everyone obliges and people are quickly out of their chairs, swarming towards others they already know rather than taking Layla up on her advice.

I stay seated and turn to Noah, about to discuss with him how we can make an early exit, but I don't get a chance because someone is tapping my shoulder. Layla.

'Hi, Tara. Noah. Glad you actually made it.'

Noah and I both stand up, but he excuses himself to use the bathroom, which I know is just a way for him to escape from Layla.

'You really should try to come to our meetings more often,' Layla says, as soon as Noah's out of earshot. 'It's just so important. Especially now.' She shakes her head. 'I still can't believe it. I just hope they quickly find out who did it. I'm sure they will, though. People don't get away with things like that, do they?'

Now is not the time to tell her that plenty of murders go unsolved, so I nod and let her carry on.

'Anyway, it's hard to believe nobody saw anything.' She waves her hand around. 'I mean, there may be only ten houses on our road, but look how many people are here now, and this isn't even everyone. I just can't understand how nobody saw a thing. Especially as the road curves round in a horseshoe, so we're all pretty much opposite someone else.'

I shrug. 'But just think about how little any of us actually bump into each other, Layla. I can count on one hand the amount of times I've seen. . .' I scan the room for someone to pick. 'Him. That man in the striped T-shirt.'

Her eyes follow to where I'm pointing. 'You mean Robert from number three? Oh, I see him all the time. Lovely man. Bit reclusive since he retired and his wife passed away, but I make it my business to pop in and check on him at least once a fortnight.'

This doesn't surprise me, but only because Layla makes everyone's business her own. I'm sure she can't bear to think there might be things going on behind the walls of our homes that she knows nothing about.

'Well, I don't, so you can see what I mean.'

'Hmmm. Anyway, I better go and mingle. Thanks again for coming. Oh, I meant to ask – did Noah enjoy his meal on Saturday night?'

My mind ticks away, trying to make sense of her question. Why is she asking about what Noah ate while he was away?

'His meal?'

'Yes, at that new restaurant in Piccadilly. I forget the name, now. Rechelle's, is it?'

'Oh, no, Noah was in New York this weekend.' I take pleasure in pointing out her mistake.

Layla frowns. 'Impossible – I saw him there as I walked past. Having dinner with a client I assumed. Some Mediterranean-looking woman. Very pretty. I tried to wave at Noah, but he didn't see me.'

This description is all too familiar, but still I try to convince Layla, and myself, that she's got it wrong. 'Perhaps it was someone who looked like him?' But somehow I know this isn't true.

Layla frowns. 'I don't mistake people, Tara. It was Noah, and he was wearing a blue polo shirt with a yellow logo. I can't tell you what make it was. And it was definitely this weekend because I was in town shopping, and I rarely go to the West End.' And then realisation dawns on her. 'Wait, are you saying you thought Noah was in New York this weekend?'

Although I feel as though my legs will give way any second, I somehow come up with a way to salvage this.

'Oh, no, sorry, I thought you said last weekend. Confusion over. And yes, he did love the food at Rechelle's.'

CHAPTER SIX

The house is quiet when I get home, only minutes after Layla's revelation. Spencer will be in bed, but I can't let Rosie know I'm home yet; I need a few moments. Any second now Noah will realise I've gone, and I need to compose myself, calm down, so I can speak rationally without losing it.

So I creep upstairs to our bedroom, relieved that the soft music emanating from Rosie's room drowns out the creak of the floorboards.

I sit on the bed, surprised by how detached I feel. Perhaps this is because nothing is as bad as what happened on Saturday morning. Not my husband lying to me, or the inevitable fallout from this.

He was with her. What is she doing here when she's supposed to be in New York? If Noah has changed his mind, then he only has to tell me. Yes, I want my family to be together, and I love Noah, but I will not keep him in chains. I want him to be free to do what is in his heart.

What hurts the most are the lies; he will have had to tell me so many of them to keep his presence in this country a secret. And the reassurances he's constantly given me since he came back six months ago, they now mean nothing.

Five minutes later, I hear the front door open, followed by silence, probably as Noah checks all the rooms downstairs. Then, when he bounds up the stairs, I sit up straighter, and wipe away my tears. I am ready.

He walks in and squints into the darkness.

'Tara? What's going on? Why did you leave without telling me? And why are you sitting here in the dark?'

I don't answer any of his questions. 'Come and sit with me,' I say. I will not shout or accuse. I will listen and then we will work out how to go our separate ways. 'Tell me about New York,' I say. I want him to be honest, to prove we all mean something to him, because when he lies to me, he lies to our children. But isn't this exactly what I'm doing? For a different reason, I tell myself.

He sighs and sits beside me on the bed.

'There's nothing much to tell – I. . .' He trails off and turns to me. 'Tara, I need to tell you something. I. . . this is really. . . difficult.'

'Go on,' I say; even though I could make this easier for him, I want to be sure he will tell me the whole truth. With everything else that's going on, I at least want this to be set straight.

He takes a deep breath and grabs my hand.

'I didn't actually go to New York.'

I don't pull my hand away, but I don't say anything either. I just wait.

'I love you, Tara, and this is where I want to be, this is the life I want. You three are my life. But. . . I needed to sort some things out in my head. And she's over here on a business trip for the week, so I went to see her.'

'You spent the whole weekend with her?' I say, surprised by how calm I'm managing to be.

'No. Not the whole weekend. We just had dinner on Saturday night. Oh, and she stopped by my hotel room on Friday night to try to get me to talk earlier, but I sent her away. I promise. I told her I wasn't ready to see her until the next day. Tara, I didn't want to hurt you so I made up the New York trip.'

This has stopped making sense. If Noah just wanted to see her briefly then why did he need a whole weekend away? I ask him this, and he shakes his head.

'I don't know, I just wanted some time by myself.'

'To work out your feelings?'

'No! I know how I feel. I love you. I never loved her; it was the idea of New York and a new life I loved, in my head she just got tangled up in that, somehow. But seeing her at the weekend made me realise I have no feelings for her whatsoever. You have to believe me.'

I stand up and cross to the window, but I don't look out this time. I think about Noah's words for a moment. He did not cheat on me with her, or lie to me about anything he'd done. If anything, I was the one who left him, because when he wanted us all to start a new life in America I refused. I knew how stressed he was here, how much he needed a complete change of life, but I would not give in. My career at the school was too important, and I was too fearful of teaching in America, with a whole new system and different breed of students. But even more than that, the kids didn't want to go, and I could not bear to uproot them and disrupt their lives.

So I had let Noah go, and I had no idea he'd come back a year later, begging to be part of the family again. But it came with a price, because a lot can happen in a year. On his part, he knew I could live without him, while I had to live with the fact he'd met someone else in that time. Amelie. A pretty name to go with a beautiful woman. That was my price to pay for letting him go.

I think about all this, as I resist the urge to pull apart the curtains and once more stare at the house across the road. Noah and I have gone through the toughest test already, so we can deal with this.

'It's the lying that's the problem,' I say, swaddled with guilt that I'm doing exactly the same. Worse.

'I know. I just couldn't risk you leaving. I can't go through a year like that again. Being away from you all. Please understand that, Tara. Look, we both know if this wasn't what I wanted, I wouldn't be here. You know me.' He stands up and joins me at the window. 'I will fight for us.'

'So how is Amelie?' I ask. I am not speaking sarcastically; I genuinely do want to know how she's dealt with all this. After all, she was the one who was hurt when Noah came back to his family. And she only got involved with him in the first place because she thought our marriage was over.

'She's still hurt,' he says. 'But she understands I love you, and that she could never come close.' It would be just like Noah to express it to her in these words, sparing no thought for the added pain they would cause.

I've heard enough now. The boundary between truth and lies has been blurred and I no longer know what to think, or what to believe. He could still be lying. But it is what it is. Perhaps now we both have our secrets. But just as mine is bound to surface, so will his too, in time. Noah has at least admitted this much, but I won't let him think it's okay. I am a hypocrite.

'I'm going to bed,' I say.

'Not downstairs again?'

Without another word, I head to the bathroom to get ready for bed. When I come out, Noah is already in bed, and I leave him there and go downstairs.

I no longer know whose lies I am running from.

Rosie wakes me in the morning, pulling open the curtains and letting in harsh bright sunlight. I cover my eyes, but greet her with a good morning.

'Oh! Mum, I didn't see you there. What are you doing on the sofa? Is everything okay?' Despite the heat, she is wearing a dressing gown, and her loose pyjamas are visible underneath.

'Our room's like a sauna,' I say, reverting to the previous excuse I used with Spencer. 'It's much cooler down here.'

Her eyes narrow and she twists her mouth. She is old enough to understand too much. She doesn't believe me. 'Are you and Dad okay?'

This is the funny thing about Rosie: just when you wonder how a person can be so wrapped up in herself, she will surprise you by showing you she does notice things, does care if things aren't right with the family.

And then something occurs to me: we are all contradictions, each of us double-sided. Except Spencer. What you see is exactly what you get with him. And before Friday night, I was a straightforward person. Now I have changed beyond recognition. The only difference is I can't show the other side of me to my family.

'Dad and I are fine, Rosie. You don't need to worry about us.'

But my words have no effect.

'He's not leaving again, is he?'

'No, of course not.' I can say this with confidence now, after our conversation last night. If Noah wanted to leave, then he would have done so already.

I try to steer Rosie off the subject and once more question her about Damien.

'Oh, Mum, don't you ever give up?' She pulls out her mobile and begins tapping the screen. I wonder if I have pushed my luck, if the Rosie of a few seconds ago has now vanished because I've said something she doesn't want to hear.

'Not until we meet him,' I say. 'Then maybe I'll think about it.' I keep it light-hearted – this is the best way with Rosie.

'I'll call him tonight,' she says, her eyes fixed on her phone.

I pull myself up so that I'm sitting, and Rosie joins me on the sofa. I see from the cable box that it's only six fifteen.

'Why are you up so early?'

'I was finishing some homework. I was up late last night but couldn't get it all done.' She puts her phone in her dressing gown pocket and turns to me. 'Mum, are you sure you and Dad are okay?'

I give her a hug, but half-expect her to pull away. When she doesn't, I pray that this Rosie sticks around for a while. I also pray that she's telling the truth about this Damien. His age is not my main concern right now; I will deal with that later. As long as their relationship isn't a figment of her imagination.

By mid-morning I have added the finishing touches to my painting, and I sit in front of it, pleased with what I've managed to achieve, despite how inspiration struck. I have done this for Lee, and it is Serena lying next to him, as it should be. It is my way to say sorry to them both, although they will never know it.

As I stare at Lee's supine body, I am forced to confront what's been gnawing away at me since Saturday. Something I've not allowed myself to think of, but can now no longer escape. If my memory loss is simply down to alcohol consumption then surely I would remember snippets of things, snatches of the conversation Lee and I had, how we got from the living room to his bedroom. But there is nothing but a gaping black chasm, a void, which terrifies me when I allow myself to think of it.

I package my canvas, the acrylic paint already bone dry, and am grateful for the brief respite doing something so functional gives me, and then on my laptop I book a courier to deliver it to the gallery.

Once my task is completed, I stay online and Google memory loss after drinking alcohol, hoping to find that it is common. That even though it's never happened to me before when I have previously drunk more than I did that night, it can still happen at random.

But everything I find tells me blackouts after drinking are rare.

Which leaves me with two options: either Lee gave me something more than alcohol that night, or someone else did. Both these scenarios make me shudder. If Lee drugged me then his marriage, and his life, were a sham. But he had no way to know I would knock on his door that evening. And if he and Serena had been arguing then she probably wouldn't have told him she'd asked me to come over. He didn't appear to know about her message when I knocked on the door.

And if his killer was responsible, then why did they leave me alive? I try to remember if there was any blood anywhere other than on his body, but I didn't notice any, so he must have been killed in the bed. So maybe I walked in after, and the killer didn't see me at all? But this is unlikely, and I cannot shake the feeling I now have that Lee is dead because I was with him that night.

I sit across from Lisa, at an outside table overlooking the river, and smile when she tells me in more detail about Thailand. I don't mind when she repeats herself – forgetting she's already filled me in on the phone – because I can only half-listen. But I try my best to smile in the right places, even though I am burning up from the heat outside and the dread that's been growing inside me.

'I'm sorry I'm going on,' Lisa says, snapping me back to the present. 'Let's talk about you.'

It is now or never. I have to tell her about Lee, leaving out the most important part.

Her mouth hangs open when I tell her what happened.

'I can't believe it. You never think that kind of thing will happen to someone you know, do you? Poor guy. His poor wife!'

'It's just terrible. He was a good person.' I know he was. Despite everything.

'Well, if there's anything I can do to help... Poor woman.'

I need to change the subject, otherwise we will end up talking about this all afternoon. 'Let's talk about something nicer. Tell me more about Thailand. Did Harvey enjoy it?'

'He did, but. . . He loved it.'

Once again it is clear that something isn't right with the two of them.

'Lisa, what is it?' She wouldn't admit anything was wrong on the phone the other day, but perhaps face-to-face she will be more forthcoming. I only hope that *I* am not.

'Oh, Tara, I don't know. He's just getting really heavy, but I don't think I feel the same. It's only been six months. I just want to keep it casual to see where it goes. Does that make sense?'

I tell her it does, and that she shouldn't feel bad about feeling that way. But I know my sister, and when I search her face I see sadness in her eyes.

'But he's a great guy, Tara, he really is. He'd do anything for me. . . I just. . .'

'Don't have those feelings.' I finish her sentence for her, something we both used to do when we were kids. Before our lives took us in different directions.

She nods and is about to say something when the waitress appears with our food.

I have very little appetite, so have only ordered a prawn starter, using the unbearable heat as an excuse, but even this feels like too much.

'You're right,' she says, picking up her burger, which is bursting from its bun. 'That's exactly it. You always did understand me, Tara. Even if you didn't agree with me about something, you always got it.'

'Same with you,' I say, digging my fork into a prawn I know I can't eat. This is the perfect moment to tell her, because I know without a doubt she would stand by me. But it is a line I cannot cross. If I tell Lisa then she will have to carry the guilt as I do, and I can't put that burden on her shoulders.

'So tell me about my lovely niece,' Lisa says, oblivious to the turmoil I'm feeling. 'What's the latest? I hope she's okay after. . . you know. . . your neighbour?'

I avoid mentioning Lee and fill Lisa in on Rosie and the boyfriend we're yet to meet.

'Sounds like trouble,' Lisa says, and she is right, even though she barely knows half of it. 'Do you want me to talk to her? I'm no expert on kids, but I think sometimes they find it hard to talk to parents. You know, you're the ones with all the rules and sanctions.'

I am tempted by her offer. Lisa has been away travelling so much over the last couple of years that she has barely spent much time with the kids. It might do Rosie some good to speak to someone like Lisa. Someone carefree, whose life is far removed from my own.

'If you can spare the time,' I say, 'I think that would be good for Rosie.'

Lisa nods and puts down her burger. 'It will be good for me too. I miss the kids. I saw so much of them when they were younger and I miss them.'

My sister has always been great with Rosie and Spencer: attentive to them without spoiling them, so it's always been a surprise to me that she's never wanted any of her own. I'm too busy living my life, she would say, whenever our parents mentioned it. I wonder if that's still true now.

'Not enough to want my own, though,' she says, as if reading my thoughts. 'So don't get any ideas. Anyway, what about Noah? How is everything going?'

Once again, it would be easy to tell her about Noah's fake trip to New York. But that would mean talking about Amelie, and I can't bear to mention her name. Even though I trust Noah's feelings about her, she is still a woman who has slept with my husband.

'It's good,' I say, plastering a smile on my face. 'He's happy to be back home, and the kids are more settled now.' I leave it at that, not wanting to discuss how Rosie's troubles began once he left. She was never an easy baby or child, but things fell apart for her when she realised nothing was secure.

She must sense I don't want to discuss Noah any longer, because she soon changes the subject, telling me about her freelance photography work instead. And just for a few moments, I soak up her words and allow myself to believe that everything is normal.

'Are we okay?'

I turn to Noah, who sits on the sofa, clutching his iPad. We've both been here since the kids retreated upstairs after dinner, and have barely said a word to each other. I don't think it's a deliberate act on either side, we're just both too engrossed in what we're doing.

I am pretending to work. The school timetable for the next academic year, which I've ended up being in charge of, needs to be tweaked, but no matter how much I rearrange the classes, it's still not right. So I have given up and am now staring at Lee's website, his smiling face silently mocking me.

I look up at Noah. 'We'll be okay,' I say. 'It may just take time.' Although he is asking about our marriage, all I can relate his question to is Lee's murder.

Murder. It's a horrible word, a thousand times worse than just saying death. But it is what it is.

'Good.' Noah smiles, and his body visibly relaxes: his shoulders less hunched, and his leg no longer twitching. Somehow I have managed to notice these things, even though my eyes have been glued to Lee's website.

I don't know what I'm expecting to find here, but I need to get a sense of him. I still think it may be possible he drugged me to get me to sleep with him. It doesn't feel like the Lee I knew, but then how well do we ever know anyone? Including our own husbands or wives.

Nothing jumps out from the screen other than what a talented landscaper Lee was, and how satisfied all his customers have been with the work he has done for them. And in the whole time I've known him and Serena, she's never said a bad word about him. Lee's comments on Friday night about finding their journey to parenthood stressful, and Serena's revelation about their argument, are the first whiff I've ever caught of any disharmony between them.

But nobody is that perfect are they? And it's clear that Lee had an enemy.

I glance up at Noah, who has gone back to tapping on his iPad, and then I Google date-rape drugs. It is a shock to me to find there is more than one available, as I have only ever heard of Rohypnol, but there they are, and all of them cause memory loss and blackouts.

But surely I would know if I'd had sex, willingly or otherwise? I look up at Noah, and am racked with guilt. What if I drank so much that I slept with Lee? I haven't even entertained this idea before, because it's not who I am, but nothing else makes sense. Nothing else explains why I was naked in his bed. But there was no blood on me, and surely there would have been if I'd been in any proximity to him when it happened.

So I couldn't have been in the room, and somehow I ended up there after. In my drunken state? Yes, that has to be it. Relief floods through me as this explanation expands in my mind to become the only one that fits.

Someone bangs on the door, startling me. Quickly, I snap my laptop shut.

Noah says he will answer it, and I watch him leave, expecting it to be Layla or Guy doing their rounds, inviting us to another meeting.

When Noah returns a few minutes later, his skin is pale, and there is fear in his eyes.

'That was the police,' he says, searching my face. 'They're waiting in the hall.'

My heart almost stops. It has caught up with me, just as I knew it would.

But what Noah says next is something I have not seen coming: 'They want me to go down to the station. They said I lied about where I was that night and now they want to question me about Lee's murder.'

CHAPTER SEVEN

I am no fool, and nor am I a pushover. Although I cannot imagine that Noah is a murderer, I will not be blind. He has lied to me before, kept things hidden, shown me that there is another side to him. So, I have to consider that there is a chance he did it – especially when finding me with Lee would be his motive – even though my heart screams it's impossible.

Time ticks slowly, and I count the minutes since he left. Forty-four now. Forty-four bleak minutes when I've had to consider the most horrendous possibility in all this. But there is nothing to do but await the outcome.

When someone knocks on the door, I almost don't answer, frozen as I am to my usual spot, staring out of the living room window at the murder house. That's what I call it now; I cannot think of it as anything else.

But if I don't answer it then whoever it is might keep knocking. The lights are on and I don't want Rosie or Spencer rushing down and having to deal with whoever is there.

I am expecting more trouble, but not to find Layla standing on the doorstep, her arms folded, and an ugly frown on her face.

'Tara. Can I come in?'

There is no warmth in her voice, and I wonder if it's because I left the meeting early yesterday. But of course it's not that. She is here because she already knows about Noah.

'It's not a good time,' I say. 'The kids are in bed.'

She steps forward anyway, and lowers her voice. 'I don't think you'll want me saying what I've got to say out here on the doorstep.'

Despite my temptation not to give in to her, I hold open the door, because I already know what she's about to say, and she is right. I don't want my family's private business being overheard by any of our neighbours, or the media vultures who have set up a vigil across the road.

I lead her through to the kitchen and close the door, but don't offer her anything to drink or eat.

'What is it, Layla?'

'Did you know?'

I will not make this easy for her. 'Did I know what?'

'That Noah was lying about being in New York? Because if you did then you're just as guilty as he is.'

'Woah, slow down, Layla. Just what exactly are you saying?'

Despite her forceful words, for the first time since I've known her she seems flustered, her confident façade all but gone. She is scared to be standing here in my house.

'I didn't know it was anything really,' she says. 'But when you told me Noah was in New York, something didn't feel right. And then you tried to say you'd got the wrong weekend, well, I wasn't buying that. But I might have let it go if you hadn't disappeared so fast.'

It's not hard to work out what she means.

'So you told the police Noah lied about where he was at the weekend.'

She shakes her head. 'I didn't know what he'd told them, but I thought I should report it. Just in case.'

Just in case my husband is a murderer.

'And then when the police knocked on your door,' she continues, 'I just knew I'd done the right thing.'

I cannot contain my fury, and all the years of frustration with her and Guy erupt from my mouth. 'You stupid woman. You just can't help yourself, can you? Noah saying he was in New York has nothing to do with. . . Lee's. . . what happened.'

'The police will judge that,' she says.

Yet this is exactly what she's doing. But I don't have the energy to point out her hypocrisy.

'Get out of my house,' I say, edging towards the kitchen door.

I expect her to ignore me, that she will stand here all night and argue with me, but she wastes no time scurrying to the front door.

'I'll be calling Serena too,' she says, once she's outside.

I slam the door in her face.

Even though I'm fuming inside, I don't have a chance to calm down because the second I turn around and flop back against the door, Rosie is standing there. Appearing silently from nowhere seems to be a regular occurrence for her now. She doesn't speak for a moment but stares at me, her expression unreadable.

'What's going on, Mum?' she says, after what seems like hours.

'Oh, nothing, love. That was just Layla trying to get us to go to another meeting. I told—'

'Isn't it time you stopped lying?' Her words echo through the house. 'Why are you always lying? Both of you. It's just lies, lies, lies all the time, isn't it?'

I step towards her and hold out my arms. 'Rosie, nobody is—'

'And you were about to do it again! I heard everything, Mum.'

I need to check what she knows before I involve her in this. 'What did you hear, Rosie?'

'That Dad lied about going to New York. And that witch Layla's told the police about it.'

I grab her hand and lead her to the stairs, checking first to make sure Spencer isn't hovering around up there. When I'm sure he's still in his room, I sit down and tell Rosie to do the same.

'I'm going to be honest.' The word sits uncomfortably in my mouth. 'Your dad didn't go to New York this weekend.'

'Because he was with someone else. He's having an affair, isn't he? And he's going to leave you again.'

It takes me a second to register that Rosie is focusing on the wrong thing. She should be asking me why the police want to talk to Noah, but this doesn't even seem to register with her.

'No, he's not having an affair, Rosie.'

She shakes her head. 'Then why else would he lie about the weekend?'

'Shhhh! Keep your voice down. I don't want Spencer waking up.'

'Of course you don't. We must protect Spencer at all costs. Heaven forbid Spencer hears about anything upsetting. But it's all right for me to know about it.'

I calmly explain to her that I didn't want either of them to know what Layla was saying, and that I had no idea she could hear us, but of course she ignores me.

'This family is a mess,' she says, flinging herself up so that she's towering above me. 'I can't wait to move in with Damien and start my life. I'm sick of this.'

I am used to Rosie overdramatising things, but right now it is all out of place. She still hasn't mentioned her father being arrested, and I wonder if she really did hear everything.

'Rosie, don't you want to know what's happened to Dad?'

'So he's talking to the police. Who cares? They'll soon realise he had nothing to do with it.'

And then she is gone, thundering up the stairs, and slamming her bedroom door. Seconds later her music starts up on full blast.

And I am left wondering how she can be so sure, and have so much faith in her father, when I am plagued with doubts.

It is past eleven p.m. when Noah returns home. I am sitting on the living room floor with the fan in front of me, because tonight even downstairs is stifling. Once again, I have barely looked at the book I hold in my hand, but it comforts me to think that any minute now I can pick it up and resume where I left off five days ago.

'Tara,' Noah says, joining me on the floor. 'I can't believe they wanted to talk to me. I mean, how could they possibly think I could have—'

'Because you lied. And because Layla made it look that way.' But they haven't arrested him. He is here so they must believe him, or at least not have enough evidence against him. 'I'm sure they're just tying up loose ends,' I say.

He nods, clearly comforted by my suggestion.

'And I don't have a motive, do I? There's no reason on this earth I'd have to. . . do that to Lee. We were friends.'

But I am the reason. A motive no judge or jury would have trouble believing.

Noah grabs my arm, urging me to look at him. 'But what do you think? Please tell me you don't believe I could do that.'

I've had several hours to consider this exact question, and have determined the following: if Noah killed Lee it would be because he found me in bed with him. That would be the only reason he'd have to do it. But if that is what happened, would Noah be able to carry on as normal with me? Wouldn't he, deep down, harbour resentment and jealousy? But I've seen no sign of this in his words or actions, and I don't think he's that good an actor. But he fooled me about New York. He talked about the trip before the weekend, and even stood packing his case in front of me.

I am torn, and I no longer know what to believe. I search Noah's eyes, and find only desperation there. But again, he has fooled me before.

'Just tell me what happened tonight,' I say, because I don't know how to answer his question.

'It was awful, Tara. They wanted to know why I lied about New York. I had to sit there and bare the details of our marriage to strangers, just so they would believe I didn't kill Lee. And I could tell they still didn't believe me; they treated me like a criminal.'

It seems strange hearing Noah say that. 'I didn't kill Lee.' Those words don't belong in our house, in our world.

'Telling them about Amelie was the hardest part, though, because even as I was speaking it sounded so. . . wrong. So implausible. And I have to admit my lie does seem so elaborate. But that's only because I don't want to lose you.'

I am not interested in this; I only want to know what the police said. 'But they believed you?' I ask.

'No, I don't think so. They didn't exactly say it but I could tell from their tone. And that was even before they spoke to Amelie—'

'The police spoke to her? She was there?'

Noah shakes his head. 'No, but they contacted her while I was still in there, that's why it all took so long. I had to wait for ages for someone to come back to me.'

I hate the thought of Amelie being involved in this, but at least now Noah will be in the clear.

'So now they know you were with her and you couldn't have. . . been anywhere else.'

But his silence tells me how wrong I am, before he even speaks.

'That's just the problem, Tara. She told them I was with her on Saturday night for dinner, but that she never saw me on Friday night.'

This can't be right. 'But you told me she went to your room to try to talk.'

'Yes, that's the truth.' He stares at me, his eyes begging to be believed. 'So why has Amelie decided to lie to the police?'

And once I've had a chance to digest Noah's words – this is exactly what I want to know too.

CHAPTER EIGHT

Everybody lies. I read that once. That no matter how moral and good we think we are, we all tell lies. It is only the scale of them that varies. I'm not sure I took much notice of it at the time, but now I know it to be true. But there is always a motivation behind every lie, and that's what I've come to find out from Amelie.

Perhaps a small part of me is also curious. I want to meet the woman Noah fell for because, no matter how things ended up, at one time he had feelings for her.

Noah doesn't know I'm here, hanging around a hotel lobby at seven a.m. so that I won't miss her when she leaves for whatever meeting she's got today. I don't know what room number she's in, but am sure they will not tell me at reception. Unless I can fool them, and her.

I head to the desk and ask to be put through to Amelie Forrester's room. It is a long shot, but worth trying. I will get more out of her if she's not rushing to get somewhere.

I hold my breath and wait for the receptionist to ask me which room. But she doesn't, and I feel both sick and excited that so far my idea has worked. She hands me the phone, stepping away to assist someone checking out, and I wait to hear a voice I've never heard before.

'Hello?'

I turn away from the receptionist, even though she is now preoccupied.

'Hi, I've got a package for room 103, is it okay if I bring it up now?'

There is a brief pause. 'Oh, no, you've got the wrong room, sorry.'

She is not going to make this easy for me. 'That's not room 103?'

'No, it's 207, not even close.'

'Oh, sorry, I'll try again.' I hang up, and head to the lift, trying to ignore my forebodings.

I've seen photos of Amelie, but she is far more beautiful in person. She answers the door in a fitted dark trouser suit, and her dark curly hair bounces around her shoulders. How has she had time to look this good so early in the morning?

I remind myself that it doesn't matter how good she looks, or what kind of person she is. Noah came back to me. But still, it is hard to erase the thought that this woman has slept with him, and knows his body as I do.

She knows immediately who I am. I can tell from the way her eyes suddenly widen, and how she looks me up and down, assessing me as I have already done to her. She doesn't say anything but steps sideways so that more of the door is hiding her.

'I think you know who I am,' I say.

'Noah's wife.'

She must know my name, but my title will be all I'll ever been to her.

'Can we talk?' Although I phrase it as a question, I won't give her a choice, not now I am here.

'I'm. . . on my way out. I've got a meeting to get to, and I can't be late.'

She looks ready to leave so I'm sure she is telling the truth, but I am already taking a step closer to her. I don't want to intimidate her, but she needs to know I'm not leaving until I've found out why she lied about Noah. If she lied. Either way, I'm determined to know by the time I leave this hotel.

'Please,' I say, to assure her I won't be causing any trouble. 'Just give me five minutes.'

She sighs, but opens the door further, and I barge past her into a room I have no right to be in.

The first thing that hits me is the overpowering smell of perfume, and I almost gag. Amelie must have thrown the whole bottle over herself for it to be this strong. And the next thing I notice is how neat the room is. The bed is already perfectly made, even though it is far too early for room service, and there is nothing out of place. If it wasn't for the suitcase in the corner of the room, it would be easy to think nobody was staying here. Noah must have loved this about her.

'You may as well sit down,' she says, gesturing to the small sofa opposite the bed.

I'm about to tell her I'd rather stand, but I need to get her onside so I do as she suggests.

Amelie removes her suit jacket before sitting on the edge of the bed, and carefully places it next to her.

'You're here because I spoke to the police, aren't you?' she says, smiling, because she thinks she's got it all worked out. 'Noah's in some serious trouble, and you thought you'd come here and. . . what? Why exactly are you here?'

'I'm just here for the truth, Amelie. I don't want anything more than that. I'm not angry that you met up with Noah at the weekend, and I'm not here to gloat.'

She snorts. 'Really?'

'I promise you. I'm sorry you got hurt, but you have to understand he's my husband. We've been together a long time. We have two kids and—'

'I could never compete with that, could I? I never stood a chance. It was always you. The funny thing is, I knew that the whole time. He never stopped talking about you and the kids. And when he wasn't talking about you I knew he was thinking of you.'

It is hard not to feel buoyed by her words, an affirmation that Noah does want to be at home with us, but I will not let her see my pleasure.

'Like I said, I'm sorry about it all. But I just need to know why you told the police you didn't see Noah on Friday night. Why lie when you've got nothing to gain? You've already lost him, Amelie.'

She stares at me for too long without speaking, and I only hope she's realising there is no point lying. But then she shakes her head.

'I had no idea why the police were asking me about Noah to start with. It was only later I realised the man who'd been killed was your neighbour, and that somehow Noah was tied up in it.'

But he's not, I silently scream. He can't be.

'So what I told them was the truth. I asked Noah to meet me on Friday night, but he said he couldn't because he was busy. And if you're here to try to get me to lie to the police then forget it.' She reaches for her jacket and stands up. 'Now, I have to go to a meeting, so please. . .'

I slowly rise and head to the door because there is nothing else I can do here. And I don't want to hear any more. But before I step into the hallway, Amelie calls to me.

'I guess I've had a lucky escape, haven't I?'

I stand outside the hotel, in the bustle of Tottenham Court Road, and let the noise drown out my thoughts. But eventually I have to move, and with each step I take nearer home, my mind forces me to make sense of everything. If Amelie is telling the truth, then Noah has lied again, but that doesn't make him a murderer. So where was he if he didn't come home that evening and see me going to Lee's house? What other reason is there for him to lie? And why would he only tell me half the story?

But the police haven't arrested him, so, for now, at least, he is innocent. That's what I have to focus on.

It's almost ten a.m. when I approach the house, and I am exhausted, even though the day has barely begun. As always, I can't help but stare at the number '5', but it gives me no answers. Someone came there that night and saw Lee and me together. Is that why he ended up dead? There are other possibilities, though: he could have been involved in anything.

I am so consumed with this thought that I don't notice someone is on my doorstep, banging on the door, until I am inches away.

Serena.

She must have heard that the police spoke to Noah, and she wants answers. I can't blame her.

'Hi,' I say, before she has a chance to verbally attack me. 'How are you doing?' A stupid question, but I hope she will see I mean well.

'Tara, thank God you're here. When nobody answered I didn't know what I'd do. . .' She looks beyond me to her house, then quickly turns away. 'Can we. . . go inside?'

She doesn't appear angry so I wonder if she does know about Noah being questioned.

'Of course,' I say, reminding myself I must still be prepared for whatever it is she has to say.

But as soon as we step inside, Serena shrinks against the door, hugging herself as if she might fall if she unwraps her arms.

'Are you okay?' I ask. 'Do you need some water or something?'

'No. It's just. . . weird being here now, that's all.' She stares around her at the hallway she's seen many times before. A hallway that is identical to hers in all but décor. 'The last time I was over here, Lee was still here and everything was normal. And now. . .'

I wish I could tell her that I understand. That, although it is much worse for her, I know her desperation for the life we knew.

'Perhaps fresh air would help? Shall we go and sit in the back garden?'

She offers a faint nod, and we head outside in silence.

Once we're sitting at the garden table, shielded from the fierce sun by the huge parasol I normally don't bother using, I decide to confront this head on.

'I know you must be here because the police questioned Noah,' I say. 'But, please let me assure you, he would never have—'

'Oh, I know. That's not why I'm here. Sorry if you thought that. I don't want you to feel uncomfortable. The police told me they were just double-checking his alibi. And that he was meeting up with some woman.'

She stares at the floor as she says this, as if she's worried she will upset me. I have never told her about Amelie, although she knows Noah and I were separated. I see now how unfair that was, given that she shared so much with me about her infertility.

'Yes. It's complicated, Serena. But when. . . soon I'll tell you all about it. When you're ready.'

'Are you splitting up?' she asks.

'I hope not.' I am touched by her concern, her ability to think of me when she has just lost her husband. Her life.

I assure her that Noah and I are fine and tell her not to give it another thought. She looks so small sitting across the table, as if she's shrunk to half her size, and I fight the urge to reach out for her and tell her I'm sorry.

'We're friends, aren't we, Tara?' she says. 'I mean, I can trust you, can't I?' Thankfully, she doesn't wait for an answer. 'The police think it was someone he knows. They say in these types of situations it usually is, and being stabbed straight through his heart like that shows that person wanted him dead.'

I lean across the table and grab her hand. 'You don't have to tell me all this,' I say.

'It's fine,' she says. 'I want to. Not talking about it doesn't mean I can escape it. It's always there. Will always be there.'

Again, I could have spoken these words myself. There is only brief respite, short distractions, but never escape.

Serena stares up at the bright cloudless sky, but clearly takes no pleasure from it.

'If I didn't have an alibi the police would think it was me.'

I shake my head. 'Of course they wouldn't. Why would they?'

'I found something, Tara.'

Bile rises to my throat. She knows I was there that night. She has found something I left behind, or strands of hair that are unmistakably mine.

Reaching into her pocket, she pulls out a watch. A man's watch. Nothing to do with me.

'This is Lee's,' she says, sliding it across the table towards me. 'He bought it for himself last summer to celebrate finishing a huge job he was doing in Surrey. It's expensive. A Tag Heuer. But he loved it.'

My mind struggles to compute where she is going with this, and how it links to me.

'Look at the back of it,' she says.

I pick up the watch and turn it over. There is a message engraved on it, but I have to twist it to see the words.

'*For ever My Love*'

'You didn't get Lee this watch?' I already know the answer but have to check that I understand this correctly.

She shakes her head. 'No. And he never took it off so I had no idea about the engraving.'

'Then—'

'He was seeing someone, Tara. Lee was having an affair. And this is the proof.'

CHAPTER NINE

For the rest of the afternoon I puzzle over Serena's revelation. If Lee was having an affair, how do I fit into it? But no matter how much I ponder this, my head aching from the effort it takes, I am left with no answers.

It is a relief when Spencer gets home, bounding into the kitchen, where I am nursing my fourth black coffee since Serena left.

'Mum? You look sad, what's wrong? Are you worried about your painting? Did you miss the deadline?'

He heads to the fridge and pulls out a carton of orange juice.

I try my best to smile. 'I sent it off, but let's just see what happens.' It is neither an admission nor denial of what's troubling me, because I am sick of the lies.

Spencer's smile fades. 'But you didn't show it to us!'

I tell him I'm sorry, that I had to get it sent to the gallery and nobody was at home to show it to.

'Oh.' He cannot hide his disappointment.

'But you can see it when I go and collect it.'

He shrugs. 'Okay. But that's if you don't win. Otherwise it will be for sale in the gallery, won't it?'

I can't help but smile. Spencer is eternally optimistic, and we could all learn a lesson from him. Thinking of this makes me sad for Rosie. Life is not the same for her; she always sees the worst in every situation, as if negativity courses through her veins. Despite everything that's going on, she still hasn't told us when Damien can meet us.

'Did you see Rosie at school today?' I ask Spencer, as I make him a sandwich. He is always hungry after school and usually makes it himself, but I need my hands to be busy to still my mind.

He shrugs. 'I don't think so, why?'

'Just wondering if she's okay.'

'Ha, Rosie okay?' He doesn't need to elaborate.

I know it's a long shot, but I need to find out if he knows anything about Damien.

'Spence, have you seen Rosie with any boy lately?' The word 'boy' sticks in my throat because, apparently, Damien isn't one. It makes me uncomfortable that I know nothing about him.

Spencer scratches his head. 'No. Why? Is she in trouble?'

'No,' I say, hoping this is true.

'Do you mean Anthony? Because he's seeing someone else now so I think Rosie leaves him alone.'

After months of her obsession, I am pleased to hear this. But I cannot help thinking Rosie has replaced him with someone else.

'Are you talking about me?' Rosie asks, slipping in through the patio doors.

'No,' Spencer says, but he avoids looking at her, instead focusing on the peanut butter sandwich I place in front of him.

'Liar, I heard you.'

'Rosie, cut it out.'

Every day I wait for her to grow out of this childish behaviour, but it only seems to get worse, right after I think she's turned a corner.

She dumps her bag on the table and pulls out a chair to sit on. 'I just don't want people talking about me behind my back. Is that so wrong?'

'One, we're not just people, we're your family, and two, there's no need to be aggressive. Okay?'

She shakes her head. 'Whatever. I'm going out. I said I'd meet everyone at the park. And before you start checking up on me again – Libby's not going. She's got a study club thing.'

I want to ask her about Damien, but Spencer is still here, busy tucking into his sandwich, and I don't want him involved in this. But when Rosie comes back down after changing, I follow her out to the garden.

'Have you had a chance to talk to Damien?' I ask. 'We're really looking forward to meeting him.' This is the truth, because it will mean their relationship is real.

She turns and studies my face before answering. 'Mum, he's still really busy.'

Now I know for sure she is lying. Even Noah and I are not that busy.

'To be honest,' she continues, 'I don't actually think he wants to meet you. That's a bit too heavy for him when we've only just got together. Sorry.'

But she is anything but sorry and is gone before I have a chance to respond.

I make sure Spencer is busy doing his homework downstairs before I slip into Rosie's room. I have never done this before, and feel sick to my stomach that I've resorted to snooping through my daughter's things, but then this is a week of firsts. A week when everything has been turned upside down.

Reminding myself to put everything back exactly as I've found it – Rosie notices if anything is a millimetre out of place – I begin opening her chest of drawers.

I have no idea what I'm looking for; all I know is that something is not right with Rosie, and the sooner I find out what, the sooner I can help her. And it is a relief to throw myself into doing this, to be distracted from thinking of Lee and what Serena told me.

But after searching every drawer, the whole wardrobe and under her bed, I have found nothing.

I'm about to leave when I notice Rosie's school bag hanging on the back of her door. I take it down and rifle through her books, every inch of me feeling like I am betraying my daughter.

I flick through her notebook, pleased that she is so thorough with her lesson notes. And then I flip it over and stare at the back cover. It is covered in neat doodles and biro sketches. I smile to myself because it is clear Rosie has an artistic streak, just as I do. Moments like these, when I focus on how clever and talented she is, overshadow the other times when I wonder what will become of her.

I'm about to slip the notebook back in her bag when something catches my eye. Rosie has written two initials in the middle of the cover, but they are faint compared to the bold shading of all the other doodles.

' LJ'

I freeze. Perhaps it is just coincidence, or my mind jumping to conclusions because of the heavy weight I bear, but those initials can mean only one thing to me.

Lee Jacobs.

My head pounds as I put the notebook back in her bag, and leave Rosie's room to check on Spencer.

He's still at the kitchen table, engrossed in a poster he's producing for his homework. I tell him I need to make a quick phone call, and head out to the back garden, walking all the way to the fence at the end before I pull out my mobile.

Now I've had a few moments to get over the shock, I am sure there is an innocent explanation – there has to be. Anyone in Rosie's school could have those initials. It is my dark secret that won't allow me to see anything other than Lee.

'Hi Bernadette, how are you?' I say, forcing joviality into my voice.

'Tara! How lovely to hear from you.' And then she must remember I only call when Rosie is in trouble. 'Is everything okay?'

'Fine, thanks. Nothing to worry about, but I was just wondering if Libby was home?'

'Actually, she's just come in from study club. Shall I get her?' Bernadette doesn't wait for an answer – perhaps she is tired of getting involved in our problems with Rosie – but calls out to her daughter, and after a brief shuffling, Libby comes on the line.

'Hi, Mrs Logan. Is everything okay?'

'Yes, Libby, nothing to worry about, but I was just wondering if we could have a quick chat about Rosie.'

'Oh. . . Oh no, is she okay?'

'Yes, she's fine, but, well, I am a little worried about something.'

'Oh, Mrs Logan, I have helped her stay away from Anthony, and she doesn't seem to be—'

'No, it's not that. Actually, do you think we could meet quickly? Now? I'll buy you a coffee. But please don't mention it to Rosie.'

There is a pause, and in the silence I can almost hear her say *no*, that she can't meet me behind Rosie's back.

'Okay, sure. Meet me at the Coffee Bar in half an hour.'

I feel nervous waiting for Libby. It's not only that I'm betraying my daughter, it's also fear of what I'm about to learn. She is over fifteen minutes late. Perhaps she has changed her mind, and decided it's weird to meet her best friend's mum for a coffee and chat about what Rosie has been up to.

I haven't yet ordered anything and consider leaving, but then Libby walks over, hurrying past tables to get to me.

'I'm so sorry I'm late,' she says.

Her jeans cling to her skinny legs like tights, and I wonder why she's not sweating. I'm dressed in shorts and can feel perspiration drip from the crease under my knees. I tell her it's no problem, and ask what she wants to drink.

'I'll have a cappuccino,' she says, without any hesitation.

I have known Libby since the girls started secondary school and it feels strange that she is drinking coffee. They are now on the cusp of adulthood, and with Rosie, at least, that's only bringing more trouble.

I get up to buy our drinks, and when I come back Libby is doing something on her phone.

'Thanks,' she says, when I place her drink on the table.

She slips her phone in her bag and I am relieved I won't have to compete for her attention. She's not like Rosie, I remind myself. And as I have done many times over the years, I find myself wondering just how two girls as different as Rosie and Libby ended up being so close.

'Has something happened, Mrs Logan? Rosie is okay, isn't she?'

I'm glad Libby has asked this; it saves me wasting time with small talk. I like her a lot, and she is good for Rosie, but I need to know what's going on with my daughter before more time ticks by.

'She's fine,' I say. 'But I am worried about something, and I was hoping you could help. Rosie doesn't know I'm talking to you, and I don't want to upset her so it's probably best she doesn't know.'

Libby nods and tells me she'll help in any way she can. She is a credit to Bernadette.

'I'll just get straight to the point, then. Do you remember all that business with Rosie and Anthony?'

'Yes, it's a bit hard to forget. Poor Rosie. She kind of lost it a bit, didn't she?'

I nod, remembering the police cautions, the constant worrying over where she was or what she would do next, and worst of all, the pain it caused Rosie.

'It's just that, lately, I've been worried she's doing it again.'

Taking a sip of her coffee, she shakes her head. 'Oh, no, like I said on the phone, she really isn't interested in Anthony any more. And he's got a girlfriend now so—'

'I don't mean Anthony. I think it might be someone else. Has she mentioned someone called Damien to you?'

Libby thinks this over. 'No. I've never heard that name before. I don't think there's anyone in school called Damien either. Who is he?'

This is worse than I thought, and I haven't even asked her about those initials yet. Lee's initials.

'Rosie told us he was her new boyfriend.'

Her eyes narrow. 'But. . . he can't be. Rosie would have told me.'

I know this must be true. There is no way she would keep something so huge from her best friend. Unless she had to.

'And there's nobody else she might be seeing?'

Libby shakes her head. 'No. We always tell each other about boys. And there's nobody she likes at the moment.' Her eyes drop to the table. 'Unless. . .'

'Unless what?' My heart races.

'No, I'm sure it was nothing.'

'Libby, just tell me whatever it is. Even if you think it's not important. I'm just trying to help Rosie here.'

'Well, a few weeks ago I walked in on her talking to someone on the phone. She was in our textiles classroom during lunch, and she didn't hear me at first.'

'What was she saying?'

'That's just it. I couldn't hear her properly because she was whispering, but as soon as she realised I was there she quickly said she had to go and hung up. I asked her who it was, and she said it was a mobile phone company trying to get her to upgrade.'

'But you don't believe that?'

'Well, I let it go at the time because people were starting to come in for the lesson, and I forgot about it after. But now I remember, it did seem strange. And she was definitely trying to keep her voice down, as if she didn't want anyone hearing her.'

I try to make sense of this. 'So, are you saying you think it might have been a guy she was talking to?'

Libby nods. 'I think so. I mean, you can tell when someone's talking to someone they like, can't you?'

This is true. Especially in the early days of a relationship. Especially if you are young like Rosie and Libby.

She stares at her cup. 'Look, I'm not being unfair to Rosie, I'm only telling you all this because I'm worried about her.'

'I know. I really do appreciate your help. So you're sure you've never heard her mention Damien?'

'No. Never.'

I have been putting off asking my next question, because I was hoping Libby would tell me that, yes, of course Damien exists and that she's met him many times.

'Libby, is there anyone you can think of with the initials "LJ"? Maybe someone in school or someone Rosie might know from somewhere else?'

She considers this for a moment. 'I don't think so. "LJ"? Um, actually there's Laura Jenkins. She's in Year 13. We don't really know her that well, though.'

I tell her I was thinking more of a male.

'I don't think so. Why?'

'Rosie wrote those initials on the back of her notebook, and I wondered who they referred to.'

Again she shakes her head. 'Nope, I can't. . . wait. "LJ"? Could it be Lee Jacobs? Your neighbour who was killed? Rosie is always talking about him.'

CHAPTER TEN

'No way. I think you're reading too much into this.'

Despite knowing everything that happened today, Noah remains calm. It is not the reaction I have expected when, to me, it all makes perfect sense. But I need his input – I cannot trust that I'm not overreacting, making everything about Lee because of my guilt.

'But there's nobody else with those initials,' I insist. 'And why is she talking about him all the time? She told me that she barely knew him.'

Noah shuts the en-suite door and climbs into bed beside me. He bought a small fan after work so now there is no reason for me to sleep downstairs. But this is a good thing – we need to be united. Even though I am lying to him. And maybe he is to me.

'Lee's death has shaken us all, Tara. It's not surprising that she's focusing on it. Nothing like this has ever happened to her, so it must all be confusing. It's bad enough for us, isn't it? And she's a teenager – everything gets magnified a hundred times by them, doesn't it?'

I cannot understand why he is so calm with the lie he told the police hanging over him. I haven't told him I went to see Amelie, or that she is sticking by her story that she didn't see him on Friday night. But I will not blindly take the word of my husband's jilted lover. Not without evidence.

'But it does sound like she's lying about this Damien guy,' Noah continues.

And now, in the midst of everything else that's happened, this seems like the least of our troubles.

'We'll have to talk to her tomorrow,' I say.

There was no opportunity to catch her alone this evening, and she didn't answer when I stood outside her bedroom door, once Spencer was asleep, and called her name. I assumed she was asleep, and didn't want to risk waking her.

'Let's just try not to jump to conclusions,' he says. 'Anyway, just what are you thinking it means?'

This is the problem, because I can't be sure.

'I just want to know what those initials mean, that's all.' To know if my daughter is somehow connected to Lee.

On the bedside table, my phone beeps. 'It's Lisa,' I tell Noah, because I can tell from his stare that he's wondering who is texting me so late at night. I read the message. 'She's invited us to have dinner with her and Harvey tomorrow, at her place. Says she won't take no for an answer. But I'll tell her we can't.'

Noah turns to face me. 'Actually, it might be good to get out for a couple of hours. I'm telling you, Tara, that interview with the police really shook me up.' He shakes his head. 'Let's go, I'm sure your parents won't mind coming over to keep an eye on Spencer.'

Perhaps he is right. And maybe I can talk to Lisa about Rosie, and see what she thinks. But I will never admit the whole truth.

'Okay,' I say, texting her back to let her know we'll be there.

'You'll see, it will do us some good,' Noah says. 'We might need some respite after talking to Rosie tomorrow.' He pauses. 'But remember, we shouldn't jump to any conclusions.' He grabs my hand and turns over.

Staring at his back, I wonder if he is also talking about his situation.

'It's nice to have you in bed again,' he says.

And as I lie there, my eyes wide open, while Noah drifts off, I wonder if it will ever be nice to be next to him in bed again.

* * *

Today is the first day I have ever dreaded going in to work. I might have lost my passion for being in a school since I decided to make a go of my painting, but this is not why my legs feel as if they're restrained by lead weights as I make my way through the corridor to my office. How can I focus on work, on being there for the students, when my family and life are dangling by a thread? And it's all about to come crashing down, it has to.

And then I see Mikey Bradford standing at my door, and I know this day is about to get a lot harder.

'Hey, Tara,' he says, stepping back to let me into my own office. 'I knew you'd be here any second. Are you ever late for anything?'

Today I can't manage a fake smile, as I normally would, and I can't care if it offends him. He is one of the reasons I cut down my hours, but I will never admit that to anyone else, not even Noah. I can handle him. He is harmless. After all, he's not doing anything worse than my own daughter has done to Anthony.

'Can I help you with something, Mikey?' I say, not bothering to invite him in because I know he will be right behind me.

'Nope. Just wondered if you fancied a quick coffee.' He glances at the kettle sitting on my windowsill. I should never have given in that first time he asked.

'Can't really today,' I say, 'I've got a load to catch up on before the bell goes. Don't you have to set up for your first lesson?'

'Already done,' he says. 'I've been in for over an hour already.'

Engaging him in small talk is another thing I should never have let happen. Noah tells me I should make it clear I don't want him around me, but it's not that simple. Mikey has never been inappropriate or suggestive, has never overstepped any boundaries. He's just always there, wherever I am in school, he finds me.

'Well, I'd better get on,' I say, and wait for him to move.

'Okay, Tara, but I'll catch up with you later.'

I watch as he walks away, and exhale a deep breath. This morning I have been lucky. Normally it takes several more direct statements for him to get the message.

By lunchtime I have barely accomplished anything. My mind won't let me think of anything but Lee and Rosie, and what it means that she scribbled his initials on her notebook. Noah might be able to dismiss it easily, but I cannot. But I stop myself before I let my mind think the worst scenario. I will heed Noah's advice not to jump to conclusions and speak to Rosie first. When I look her in the eyes, I will know whether or not she's lying.

I'm outside doing lunch duty in the playground when Mikey tracks me down again. It won't have been difficult for him; I'm sure by now he knows my whole timetable.

'Hey, Tara,' he says. Under one arm he carries a pile of yellow exercise books, and in his other hand a shop-bought sandwich.

I will him to move along, to be in a hurry to get somewhere, but, of course, he is only here in this playground for one reason. Mumbling a greeting, I turn and scan the playground. A group of Year 9 girls walk past us, giggling as they whisper to each other. But I'm used to this. The kids rarely see me without my shadow.

'Just ignore them,' Mikey says, but I'm sure he is secretly pleased by the gossip. 'Hey, listen, I meant to ask you earlier. Was Lee Jacobs your neighbour? It's been all over the news, and I'm sure you live in King George Square.'

Hearing Mikey say Lee's name renders me speechless. There is something wrong about it, as if the two of them should have nothing to do with each other. I force myself to stay calm. Mikey is only talking about what everyone else will be too: a murder on their doorstep.

'Yes, he was my neighbour. But I—'

'Did you know him well?'

'Well enough. But I'm not going to stand here and gossip with you about him, okay? I'll see you later.'

I have no choice but to walk off, because if I don't I will say something I regret, and Mikey doesn't mean any harm, not really.

'But you're still on duty,' he calls after me, his words mingling with the chatter of students buzzing around the playground.

I don't turn around.

'I can't believe Rosie's not back yet.' Noah is already dressed for dinner at Lisa's so now he has nothing to distract him from worrying where our daughter is. He even came home early from work today, hoping to talk to her before we left, but it's as if she has sensed we want to talk to her so is avoiding us.

I am getting changed in our bedroom, but have no clue what to wear, so am standing in my underwear, unable to make the simplest decision.

'Tell me exactly what she said when you saw her after school.'

I quickly throw on the first smart thing I can find: a royal blue fit and flare dress I can't remember ever wearing.

'Not much. She flounced in here and bleated something about going to Libby's. I tried to get her to stay, but other than locking her in the house, what could I do? You look lovely in that, by the way.'

It occurs to me that Noah didn't try very hard. He's normally a great advocate of laying down the law, so why has he taken the easy option this time? But I'm too exhausted to question him right now.

'Are you okay?' he says, when I don't answer his question or respond to his compliment. 'You look tired. How was your day?'

As I reapply more make-up I tell him about Mikey, and he rolls his eyes.

'Why doesn't he just leave you alone?'

'He wasn't really bothering me. I just didn't want to talk about Lee.' I struggle to say his name, and wonder if Noah notices.

Spencer walks into the room before Noah has a chance to respond. 'Grandma and Grandad are here,' he says. 'They're in the kitchen, and I told them you'd be right down.'

Ordinarily I would be pleased to see my parents, but my mum will immediately know things aren't right, and I'm no good at lying to her.

'You go first,' I say to Noah, who is already dressed for dinner. 'I just need to finish getting ready.'

I feel a wave of sadness when I see Mum and Dad standing in the kitchen. They are laughing at something Spencer has just said, oblivious to how I've changed all our lives.

All eyes turn to me when I walk in, and Mum is the first to speak.

'Don't you look lovely, Tara! And it's so nice that you're getting together with your sister. The two of you don't do it enough.'

I give them both a hug and thank them for coming over to babysit.

'It's not babysitting,' Spencer tells me. 'I'm eleven years old, so not a baby.'

Both my parents laugh once more, in unison, because having been together so long they seem to have morphed into one person, and Dad ruffles Spencer's hair.

'You're certainly not, young man.'

'We'd better get going,' Noah says. He turns to my parents. 'Rosie's at her friend's house but she should be back any time.'

'Go and have fun,' Mum says. 'And give Lisa a huge hug from us.'

I can't remember the last time I was in Lisa's flat in north London but there is something different about it. It's usually minimalist, the home of someone who's yet to put down roots, but now she has decorated it with ornaments and photos so that it feels homely.

'I love what you've done,' I say to her, as she leads us through to her kitchen. Beside me, Noah frowns. He won't have noticed that anything's changed.

'You remember Harvey,' Lisa says, gesturing to where he sits at the table.

I have only met him once before, but he also seems different. Perhaps it is because he seems more secure now, more comfortable in Lisa's flat. He immediately stands and holds out his hand.

'It's great to see you both again. Please, sit down. Can I get you both some wine?'

I ask for water, and turn to Lisa, whose mouth is spread into a tight smile.

'Everything okay?' I ask her, when I'm sure Harvey is too busy with Noah to hear.

'Oh, yeah, we're fine. I'm really working through things. But what about you? How is Rosie doing?'

'Let's talk about that later,' I say.

Lisa has gone to a huge effort tonight, and the steak we tuck into is perfect. It is the first food I've been able to make a dent in since Friday night, but I still can't finish my meal.

'I'm sorry,' I say to her, when she frowns at my half-full plate. 'I stupidly ate too much at lunchtime.'

Her eyes narrow – she doesn't believe me. But then, she has always been able to see through to the core of me.

I told Noah I would drive tonight, so when Harvey offers him another glass of wine he doesn't hesitate. He has a long day at work tomorrow but I can't blame him for needing to escape, even if only for a few hours.

'How's work going?' Noah asks Harvey, and I struggle to remember what exactly he does. I think Lisa mentioned computer programming, but I can't be sure.

'It's good, actually,' Harvey says, his hand making circles with his glass of wine. 'Gives me time to travel. I mean, you've got to have a life, haven't you?'

I sense Noah tense because, other than his work trips, neither of us has had time to go anywhere. 'It's difficult when you have kids,' Noah says, taking a sip of wine. 'Everything changes.'

Harvey nods, even though he can have no idea how it feels. 'Yes, it's all worth it, though, I'm sure.' He glances at Lisa, but she looks away, choosing to stare into her glass rather than contribute to this discussion.

Oblivious to the tension between them, Noah continues. 'But don't rush into it,' he says, and I know he is thinking of Rosie. How we've had some tough times with her. 'Just cherish the time you have alone together.' He looks at Lisa, but she refuses to meet his eye. Changing the subject is the only way out of this.

'Noah's thinking of getting a new computer,' I say. 'What would you recommend?'

Harvey's face lightens and I sense he is pleased that we're no longer talking about children.

'Oh, definitely a Mac. In fact, come and have a look at Lisa's – I just bought it for her – and I'll show you a couple of things.' He stands up, still holding his glass.

When I turn to Lisa, she is staring at him, and I can only imagine what she's thinking. This is her flat, they've only been together a few months, and yet he has made himself fully at home. That might be okay if she felt the same way about him, but I am convinced now, more than ever, that she doesn't.

Lisa and I can finally talk once they've disappeared. But we will have to keep our voices down; her computer is in her bedroom – right next to the kitchen where we sit – as it's the only place it will fit in her flat.

'Is everything okay?' I ask.

She doesn't answer straightaway, and I know it's because she is worried about something. 'It's. . . fine. He's just been a bit weird today. I just feel as if he knows I'm not happy and is trying everything to. . . I don't know, stamp his mark on me, if that makes sense?'

I reach for her arm. 'Lisa, if you're not happy then you need to leave him. It's not as if you live together – although he's certainly acting like it.'

She nods. 'I know, but I'm not sure. I do like him. And it's about time I settled down a bit, isn't it?' She chuckles at this. 'Ha, can you imagine? Me, settled down?'

She is talking at a hundred miles an hour, a habit of hers she's had for as long as I can remember. There is no slowing down for Lisa. It's as if she's afraid to stand still and take anything in. Which is strange, considering she has to do just this to take the amazing pictures she always captures.

'I can actually,' I tell her. 'You would be great at it. You're so good with the kids.'

Lisa snorts. 'You sound like Mum. Anyway, while Noah's keeping Harvey busy you can tell me about Rosie.'

It is a relief to unburden some of the weight I bear, and by the time I've finished, Lisa knows everything other than the part about me seeing Lee that night, and waking up next to him.

'Oh, Tara, I can't believe all this. But what exactly are you thinking here?'

And for the first time I allow myself to speak the thoughts I've been trying to suppress. 'At first I was just wondering if Rosie was obsessed with Lee. She's done it before, hasn't she? So it's not unrealistic. He was much older than her, but still good-looking.' Inside I cringe as I say this. 'But now I think something even worse.' Until I say these words I have been too afraid to admit even to myself that this is what I'm thinking.

Lisa frowns. 'What?'

'Well, Serena said he was having an affair. And somebody bought him that watch. What if. . . what if it was Rosie he was seeing?'

Lisa shakes her head. 'I understand why you might think that, after seeing his initials on her book, but she's seventeen, Tara. She's just a kid. And from everything you've told me, this Lee was a decent kind of man.'

But he was having an affair, so how decent could he have been? I tell this to Lisa, but can't emphasise my point with the evidence of me ending up in his bed.

'But still. An affair is one thing. But an affair with your neighbour's teenage daughter is something else.'

'She's almost eighteen,' I say. 'She's practically an adult.'

'Yes, but Rosie doesn't behave like one, does she? No offence. But I still don't think you're right about this. You're just being protective of your daughter and assuming the worst. I think you should talk to her about it. Treat her like an adult and see what she says.'

I tell her that's my plan, but the opportunity has yet to arise.

'Remember we talked about me having a word with Rosie? Well, why don't I come over tomorrow and talk to her. You could take Spencer out somewhere so we have the house to ourselves, or if she prefers I could take her shopping or something.'

'I don't know, Lisa. It just feels a bit like you'd be doing my job for me. I mean, things are much worse now than last time we spoke.'

Noah and Harvey's voices grow louder.

'Don't think of it like that,' Lisa whispers, before they appear in the kitchen. 'Think of it as doing whatever you can to help Rosie.'

She is right. And Lisa will be more likely to stay calm. I thank her, and help clear away the dinner plates.

And all the time I try to suppress the feeling that there is far worse to come. For now, at least, I keep hidden the fear that somehow Rosie is involved in Lee's death.

CHAPTER ELEVEN

'What do you make of Harvey?' Noah asks.

He has been silent on the drive home until now, and I wonder what he's been thinking of. His thoughts can't mirror my own; he doesn't believe Rosie is somehow mixed up with Lee. Whether her obsession stems from her imagination or not, she is still linked to him somehow. And where do I fit into that?

'He's okay. I hardly spoke to him, though, so I wouldn't say I really know him enough to make any judgements.'

'I don't think he's right for Lisa,' Noah says.

There is no need for me to ask how he's drawn this conclusion, because fuelled by alcohol he doesn't hold back.

'He just seems a bit. . . I don't know. . . controlling? But in a passive way. He's not a bully or anything, but I think he knows how to get exactly what he wants.'

I tell him that Lisa is the last person who anyone would ever be able to control, and he laughs.

'Yes, that's true.'

We are still ten minutes away from home. That's ten minutes for us to talk without fear of the kids hearing us. And it angers me that Noah doesn't seem to think there's anything other than Lisa's relationship to talk about.

'I still think those were Lee's initials on her notebook. I know you don't, but it's too much of a coincidence to be anything else.'

'To be honest, Tara, I'm trying not to think about it all. Somehow, because of Amelie's lie, I'm embroiled in Lee's death, and I just wanted a few hours when I didn't have to think about him. I know it sounds awful but it's still hanging over me, and the police aren't going to let it go, unless she retracts her lie.'

The chances of her doing this are zero, but I keep that to myself.

'So, it's messing my head up to think Rosie might have been. . . I don't know, what? Obsessed with him? Let's just talk to her tomorrow and take it from there.'

I understand Noah's need to escape, so I let it go for now. Tomorrow we will hear Rosie's side of the story.

And surely I will know if my daughter is lying?

I wake to the sound of muffled voices. And an empty space beside me in the bed. Rushing downstairs, because I already know what Noah is doing, I find them in the kitchen, sitting at the table with untouched cereal in front of them.

Rosie stands up. 'Mum! Can you please tell Dad to leave me alone? Why is he harassing me about Lee?'

I tell her to calm down. 'Let's talk about this as adults, okay?' It is worth a try.

Rosie eyes me suspiciously. 'Okay,' she says eventually. 'But you can't go crazy or anything. If you do I'm out of here.'

My heart thuds in my chest. Moments from now I will wish I was oblivious. I know this with certainty. I assure her I won't, and tell her to sit back down.

Doing as I ask, she stares at the ceiling, her arms folded. Seconds tick by, and it is disconcerting as I have never known Rosie struggle to say something.

When she speaks, her voice and manner is more mature than I've ever known.

'A few months ago Lee tried it on with me.'

'What do you mean "tried it on with you"?' Noah jumps straight in before I've had a chance to make sense of her words.

'Oh, Dad, what do you think I mean? He. . . he tried to get me to sleep with him.'

And now I really do feel as if my heart will stop. But I have to be strong for my daughter. I force myself to breathe normally. 'Go on. Tell us exactly what happened.'

'Do you remember the barbeque you had last summer? I—'

'You were sixteen.' I cannot keep my voice from shouting.

'No, I wasn't, Mum, I was just seventeen.'

'What's the difference?'

Noah grabs my arm. 'Keep your voices down, otherwise Spencer will wake up. And let Rosie continue.'

Our roles have reversed: now Noah is the voice of reason, while I am almost hysterical. But she is my daughter. My baby.

'Nothing happened at the barbeque, Mum. I'm just trying to explain everything.'

Despite my blood boiling, I urge her to go on.

'He didn't do anything, but I could tell he liked me. He was, you know, kind of flirting.'

'But Serena was there,' I say. 'She would have noticed.' I try to think back to last summer, but it was too long ago for me to remember any details, and we'd all had too much to drink.

Noah shakes his head. 'Remember she couldn't make it. She'd had a hospital procedure or something and was resting in bed.'

Now I remember. It was the time of their first round of IVF. She was too scared to be up and about, fearing that the embryo wouldn't implant unless she stayed as motionless as possible. Lee had commented that she was overreacting – how did I not spot the signs of discord between them?

I turn to Rosie. 'So nothing happened? He was just being over-friendly?' My hands clench into fists, even though the man I want to pummel is no longer here.

'No, it was much later on. Like I said, a few months ago.' She picks up her spoon and starts mixing around her cornflakes, even though she's yet to add milk or sugar. 'He was out in his front garden when I came home from school one day, and we just got talking. I didn't like him or anything, I mean, he looked good and everything, but he was far too old for me.'

I remind her of Damien, although we are yet to know if he is real.

'Damien's not that old. He's twenty-four.' So now she suddenly knows his age, and is sticking by her story that he is her boyfriend.

'Just tell us what he did,' Noah says, losing his patience, as I am.

'I can't remember the exact conversation but he said I looked really pretty and then asked if I wanted to go inside with him. Upstairs.'

Hearing this feels even worse than waking up next to Lee's dead body.

Noah slams his fist on the table. 'Damn that arsehole.'

I, though, am now strangely calm, because it has just occurred to me that this could be another one of Rosie's stories. But why would she lie? She has nothing to gain from making this up. It's not as if she's telling us they were in a relationship.

'He's dead,' I say, to no one in particular. 'That's enough punishment, isn't it?'

Rosie stares at me for a second, as if she can't quite believe I'm not flipping out, threatening immediate punishment. 'Yeah, well. We all know what he was like now, don't we? And, if you've finished with your interrogation, I need to get ready for school.'

She stands up and leaves, her untouched breakfast still on the table.

'Do you believe Lee did that?' I ask Noah a few minutes later, while he's getting dressed for work. I keep my voice low because Spencer is up now, rushing around because I woke him up a bit later than usual.

'Yeah, what a piece of scum. If he was here I'd. . .'

'But how do we know she's telling the truth?'

Noah stops buttoning his shirt. 'Because this is a bit different from Anthony. Why would she make this up? The man's dead.'

'Anthony and Damien. We still don't know he exists.'

'Maybe we should just give her a break,' Noah says. 'She said we can meet Damien, so let's give her a chance to introduce us.'

His tone is not harsh, but I can tell he no longer wants to talk about this. It is a puzzle to me why he would let this go so suddenly, but confronting him when he is about to leave for work is not an option.

'She's got until Sunday,' I tell him. 'And if we still haven't met him I'm calling Dr Marshall.'

As soon as the house is empty I call the school and tell them I can't make it in due to a family emergency. Although I feel guilty that I'm letting my students down, my family comes first. And I need to find out what's going on with Rosie.

Once I've cleared my day, I text Serena to ask if I can come and see her. I would just turn up but I don't have her parents' address; I only know they live in Palmers Green, close to Lisa's flat in Winchmore Hill.

Serena's reply comes by the time I've had a shower, and I'm relieved to find she can see me today.

I am there in just over an hour, and it's still early morning so I have plenty of time before I need to be home. Spencer is having dinner at a friend's house, so that buys me even more time.

Serena's parents live in a well-maintained Victorian terrace house, and even before I step inside I imagine the tiled floor in the hallway and original fireplaces downstairs and up.

A man who is far too young to be Serena's father answers the door, staring me up and down before he speaks.

'Tara?' he asks.

He is dressed in a suit, but his ruffled hair and stubble are a contrast to his smart clothes.

I nod, but before I have time to speak, Serena appears behind him.

'This is DCI Hunt,' she says. 'Sorry, I was just in the bathroom.'

It is my paranoia that convinces me I've walked straight into a trap. But I must be getting used to this because, for the first time, I don't feel as if I'm about to crumple. I take a deep breath and step inside, ready for whatever awaits me. I just have to cling on to one thought: I didn't kill Lee.

But maybe I know the person who did.

'DCI Hunt's in charge of the investigation,' Serena says, and I'm sure she is almost smiling.

'How's it going?' I ask, because surely this is what anyone else would want to know?

The detective nods slowly. 'We're going to find who did this,' he says.

And beside him Serena lets out a sigh. She believes in this man.

Someone's phone rings and all of us reach for our phones before we realise it is Serena's. She stares at the screen for a moment before telling us she needs to take the call and heading towards the kitchen.

'Maybe we should wait in there?' DCI Hunt says, gesturing to the living room.

Although I readily agree, I silently pray for him to leave. Surely he won't stay here the whole time? If he does, there is no chance of talking to Serena about Rosie.

'She's mentioned you often,' he says, as we sit on her parents' sofa. 'It's good that she has close friends around her.'

This is a trick. It has to be. He's trying to make me comfortable so he can trip me up. But I try to be rational; if he knew anything about me he would be arresting me at this moment, not making small talk.

'And it's good that she has you looking out for her too.'

DCI Hunt smiles. He knows I am referring to what he is still doing here. 'Well, her parents are out so I just wanted to make sure she wasn't on her own,' he says.

Normally I wouldn't buy this for a second, but there is something in his tone, and the way he sighs, that tells me it's true.

For a few minutes we sit in silence, both of us staring around the room, the muffled sound of Serena's voice the only audible noise, but then he breaks the silence.

'So you're a teacher?'

'Head of pastoral care, so I don't actually teach lessons any more.'

He nods. 'Ha, when people ask me how I do such a hard job, risking my life every day, I just tell them it's not as hard as teaching. And I know that because my mother was a teacher.' He smiles, and I wonder if his referral to her in the past tense means she is no longer alive. But of course I don't ask. 'Anyway, good on you,' he says. 'It's an admirable job. Any role in a school, helping kids.'

Before I have a chance to respond, Serena comes back in, and the detective rises to his feet.

'I'll get going now, but I'll be in touch,' he tells her.

Turning back to me, he shakes my hand, and I hope he doesn't take my clammy palms as a sign of guilt.

'I'm glad he was here,' Serena says, once she's seen him out. 'He's such a nice man. It's being alone that's the worst thing. It gives me too much time to think.'

'I can imagine. It must be awful.'

She looks well, though, almost like the old Serena, neat and groomed in her skinny jeans and floaty vest top. She sits on the sofa, and invites me to do the same.

'Do you know what's strange, though? It actually helps knowing Lee was having an affair.'

She waits for me to digest her statement, waits for the inevitable question I must have.

'Why is that?'

'Because I now hate him more than I ever loved him.'

I know she doesn't mean this. It is the grief speaking in her place.

'You think I'm awful saying that, don't you? But what I mean is, it taints everything we shared together, every special moment. All those times he held me while I cried after a failed treatment cycle. None of it was real. And that's why I feel better now.'

I tell her I can understand this, but don't add that maybe she's just passing through a grieving stage.

'How is the investigation going?' I ask.

'DCI Hunt is really nice. He just seems to have taken me under his wing a bit. I think he feels sorry for me that Lee was cheating. I mean, it's bad enough that he's dead. . . Anyway, they have no leads, but they're looking into his clients. Maybe he was seeing one of them. I just can't see where he would have met anyone else. He rarely went out without me so how would he have had a chance?'

I remember all the times Serena was off with friends or family, trying to escape her infertility at every chance she could. How does she know what Lee was doing then?

But there is no time for that. I need her to focus on what I have to say. I take a deep breath and begin. 'Serena, this is really difficult to say, but it's something you need to know. I just hope you know I don't want to hurt you in any way, but. . . well, it's too important not to mention.'

She lifts her head, suddenly more alert than I've seen her since Lee's death. 'Go on. You know you can tell me anything, Tara.' But her tone is wary; she is bracing herself for my news.

'Rosie told us this morning that. . . Lee tried to. . . get her to sleep with him. A few months ago.' I have said it now and there is no going back. My heart thumps because I have no idea what I've set in motion with this revelation. But I'm doing it to get to the truth.

An uncomfortable silence hangs in the air, and I begin to wonder if Serena heard me, or if she's choosing not to acknowledge what I've said. She doesn't look at me, but stares at her feet, cushioned in slippers that seem too old-fashioned for her.

'Tell me what happened,' she says, eventually, still not looking up.

I repeat what Rosie told us, cringing inside that I have to give details to Lee's wife, but I am hoping she will tell me it's ridiculous, that Lee would never have done that. That even though he wasn't perfect, he had some boundaries.

She shakes her head, and relief surges through me. 'No,' she says. 'I can't believe that. Rosie is practically a child. No, it can't be true.' She finally looks up. 'Believe me, I'm no fool. I realise there was a huge part of Lee I didn't know, but there's one thing having an affair where the woman mentions love, but it's another to try to sleep with a teenager. No, I'm sorry, Tara, I don't believe it. And I have to be honest, Rosie does have a history of. . . this kind of thing.'

I cannot deny this, but still I must defend Rosie. 'Well, to be fair to her that was a bit different. An imagined relationship is not the same as what she claims Lee did. But that's why I wanted to talk to you, Serena, because I needed to hear it from you. You know Lee better than anyone, and if you think he wouldn't—'

'That's just it – I didn't know him at all did I?' She is almost shouting now, but I know it's not me she's angry with.

She stands up and paces the room, her arms folded defensively, and for minutes I wait for her to say something.

When she finally speaks, I am surprised by her words. 'Oh, Tara, what if. . . Do you think he could have? I just don't know anything any more. And now that I think about it, he was fond of Rosie. And even when she was having her meltdown over that boy, he never said a word against her.'

'Wait, what are you saying, Serena?'

She looks me in the eye. 'I don't know, Tara! When you told me just now, I didn't want to believe it, but. . . but what if it's true? Because none of us really knew Lee, did we?'

CHAPTER TWELVE

I walk into the doctor's surgery, grateful they could fit me in at such short notice. But this emergency appointment won't be with my usual GP, something I'm pleased about because I don't want Dr Pathak remembering what I have to say today whenever I have a future appointment.

For once the waiting room is almost empty, only three other patients sit here, and I slip into a seat, my leg shaking as I wait for my name to flash up on the screen.

It is half an hour before I'm eventually called, and I almost change my mind and head for the way out, but the receptionist is watching me, so I make my way to room six instead.

The doctor is a small man in his early fifties, and he smiles when I walk in, putting me at ease.

'How can I help today?'

I summon my courage, and remind myself this is my chance to get some answers. But still it is hard to find the words.

'I . . . um.'

He swivels his chair to face me and leans forward. 'Take your time. I can tell this is difficult for you.'

'It's just. . . I think I may have been drugged. I had a blackout, and I can't remember anything that happened.' I have said it now, and it will be on my medical record, evidence if anyone thought to look for it.

'Okay, why don't you tell me exactly what happened?'

I have concocted a story on the way over here. That I was out drinking with work colleagues and can't remember anything after a certain time, until I woke up the next morning. This is all he will need to know; it won't make any difference to the information I need.

'Right, and you don't think it was the alcohol that caused it?'

I tell him I can't be sure, but that it's never happened to me before, even on the odd occasion I've had even more to drink.

'And this was last Friday?'

His mention of the day brings home to me that a whole week has passed when, to me, it feels like barely seconds have gone by.

'Yes, I'm just concerned I haven't remembered anything by now. I thought it would come back to me.'

He starts tapping something on his computer, and I fight the urge to smack his hand away.

'Well, it's possible that the alcohol caused your memory loss,' he says, when he's stopped typing. 'But if you only remember having a couple of drinks then it's unlikely.'

'So do you think I could have been drugged?'

He places his hands together. 'I can't say for sure. Did you leave your drink unattended at any point?'

Lee was pouring my drinks. It would have been easy for him to slip something into one or all of them.

'Yes,' I tell the doctor. 'I did go to the bathroom a couple of times.'

He frowns. 'I see. And do you feel as if you were assaulted or anything like that?'

I shake my head. Whatever Lee and I did or didn't do, I can't think about that right now. This is about helping Rosie; that is all that matters. 'No, I don't think so, but it's just scary to have a huge chunk of time missing from my memory.'

'Yes, I can understand that. There is every possibility that bits and pieces will come back to you, if not the whole time, but I can't say when.' He turns back to his computer.

But I am not done. 'I was just wondering if you could test my blood or anything? To see if there are traces of any drugs. It's just really worrying me.'

He shakes his head. 'I'm sorry, but it's been a week so nothing would show up now.'

'Oh, I see.'

As I feared, I have left it too late. I thank him for his time and stand up.

'Mrs Logan, if you do think you've been attacked in any way, then you must go to the police.'

'I will,' I say.

But this is the last thing I intend to do.

Lisa is sitting on the doorstep when I pull up to the house, fanning herself with a leaflet. She stands up and rushes over to me. 'Where have you been? I was worried. I've texted you a thousand times.' Although she is firing her words at me, I know she isn't angry.

'Oh, Lisa, I'm so sorry, I forgot you were coming to talk to Rosie today.' And then I check my phone, and realise Rosie should have been home by now. 'Have you tried knocking?'

'Of course I have, nobody's in. Are you ever going to get that doorbell fixed? And aren't you usually home before now?'

I don't want to worry her by telling her I took a day off work, so I opt for a half-truth and tell her I had a doctor's appointment.

Lisa frowns. 'Are you okay? Is it serious?'

'No, no, don't worry, it was just a check-up.' I don't offer any more details; I haven't had a chance to think of a legitimate reason for seeing a doctor.

Lisa's frown remains on her face, but she lets it go. 'So where is Rosie then?'

I shrug. 'I don't know, but let's go in and I'll text her. I need to fill you in on what's happened, and it's too hot to be standing out here.'

Inside, I text Rosie then make us both a cold lemonade. The heat is unbearable so I open the patio doors, but it does nothing to cool down the room.

Leaning against the worktop, Lisa sips her drink, still fanning herself. 'Thanks for coming for dinner last night,' she says. 'I'm sorry about Harvey.'

'What do you mean?'

'Well, he was in a bit of a weird mood, I think. Kind of taking over.'

I try to put her mind at rest. 'I think he just loves you and was making himself at home, that's all. It's actually quite sweet.' I remember Noah's comments about him. Am I missing something here?

'Maybe,' she says, staring into her glass. 'I still don't know what I'm going to do about him, though. Anyway, forget that, tell me what happened with Rosie. Did you ask her about the initials?'

I repeat the conversation Noah and I had with Rosie this morning, and watch as Lisa's mouth drops.

'What a bastard,' she says, shaking her head. 'I can't believe it. Dead or not, that's just. . . I can't believe what a—'

'But how can I be sure it's true? Rosie's lied to us before, on a massive scale, so why not about this?'

Lisa considers this for a moment. 'I suppose. But let me try my best to find out when she gets here.'

I thank her, just as my phone pings and Rosie's name appears on the screen. I let out a deep breath I hadn't realised I was holding in; it is always a relief when I hear back from her.

'Is that Rosie?' Lisa asks.

I nod and tell her that she's on her way home. 'Apparently she had to see one of her teachers after school.'

'Why do you say "apparently"?'

'I don't know, Lisa, it's just hard to know whether I can trust anything she says. And then I feel guilty if I don't.'

Lisa steps towards me and pats my arm. 'This is exactly why I'm glad I'm not a mother. Hardest job in the world. And I'm too selfish.'

I tell her she's not, that her being here to talk to her niece proves that.

When Rosie finally gets home, she bounds in through the kitchen door, a scowl on her face, but it's quickly replaced with a smile when she notices her aunt is here.

'Hi, Lisa!' she says, rushing over to hug her. 'You're not leaving are you? I haven't seen you for ages.'

'Well, in that case, how about we go and grab a coffee in the park? Or a cold drink. Just the two of us.'

Rosie's smile spreads across her face, and it melts my heart. Why can't she be like this with Noah and me? 'I just need to go and change and I'll be right back.'

Once I hear her footsteps above us I whisper to Lisa. 'Thank you. I really think you might have a chance of getting through to her.'

'So you want to know about your neighbour, and this boy called Damien?'

'Yes, but don't push her too hard. Just see what you can find out.'

It still feels wrong to let Lisa talk to Rosie when it should be me, but I've tried and got nowhere, and desperation is forcing me to do something I would never normally consider.

The minutes pass too slowly once they've gone, and no matter how hard I try to distract myself, it is impossible to focus on anything. Outside, the news reporters have packed up for the day, the heat – and absence of Serena – forcing them to give up their vigil. For now, at least.

A knock on the door makes me jump; I am too used to it being bad news. But despite being prepared for the worst, seeing Mikey standing on my doorstep forces me to look twice. It is an incongruous picture; he has never been here before, and I would never invite him to my home. But he is here nonetheless.

'Hi Tara,' he says, as if this is the most natural thing in the world, as if I've been expecting him. And then he holds out the bunch of flowers I haven't noticed him hiding behind his back. 'I heard you had a family emergency and wanted to bring you these. I hope everything's okay?'

I don't take the flowers. 'How did you know where I live?'

'We were talking about it the other day, remember? About your poor neighbour. And once I got here it wasn't hard to work out. There are only ten houses and your car's parked in the drive.'

'Oh.' There is nothing more I can say.

'You'd better get these in some water,' he says, moving the flowers even closer to me, so that I have no choice but to take them. 'And how about a coffee? I don't fancy driving back right now when rush hour's about to start.'

My instinct screams at me not to let him in. Once he's been in my house, it sets a precedent for any other time he feels like turning up. But I glance across at Lee's house, and usher Mikey in.

'Nice house,' he says, once I've closed the door.

I thank him and take the flowers. Yellow roses. I heard once that yellow roses symbolise hate, so Noah would never buy me any.

In the kitchen, I tell Mikey to have a seat in the garden while I put the kettle on and hunt for a vase. But he doesn't move, instead choosing to stay where he is, his eyes inspecting every part of the room.

'It's got a nice family feel in here,' he says. 'My kitchen's nice, but it doesn't have a homely feel to it. Mind you, that's probably because I live alone.'

I have always wondered about Mikey's personal situation. I know he isn't married, but that doesn't mean he isn't seeing someone. Although his fixation with me heavily suggests otherwise. I am tempted to ask him now, but I don't want us getting into a personal conversation. So far in the time I've known him I've managed to avoid that. I don't even know his age, although I'm sure he's around his mid-thirties. Lee's age. He's not bad looking, but he would never be my type, even if I wasn't with Noah.

'Are you sure you don't want to sit outside? It will be a lot cooler under the tree.' I struggle to say this kindly, as if I'm doing him a favour, and it comes out as a command.

He looks out but shakes his head. 'Nope. I'm fine in here chatting to you. Shall I make the coffee? You don't seem to be having much luck finding that vase.'

'No, it's fine. Here.' I pull out an old cracked vase someone gave us as a wedding gift. I would never use it normally, but I don't want Mikey making himself at home.

'So do the police know what happened to your neighbour yet?' he asks.

Although I'm startled by his abrupt change in conversation, I try to keep my expression neutral, and my voice steady. 'No, not yet.'

I busy myself making the coffee, anything to avoid looking him in the eyes.

'Now that I've seen your road, it's hard to imagine nobody saw anything. I mean, from anyone's front window you must be able to see every house, because of the way the road curves.'

I knew it was a mistake to let him in, but I didn't think him talking about Lee would be the reason why.

'That's the funny thing,' I say. 'I rarely see any of the neighbours. It's very quiet around here.'

'It's a beautiful cul-de-sac, but I bet it feels a bit creepy now, doesn't it?'

I hand him a mug of coffee. 'I try not to think about it,' I say. And this is the truth.

Stepping outside, so he has no choice but to follow me, the air is no less stifling.

'Wow, this heat,' he says, pulling at his tie.

We sit down, and I silently plan how I can get him out of here as quickly as possible. Rosie and Lisa won't be back for a couple of hours, and Noah's not due home until after eight, so I struggle to think of anything convincing.

'So, is everything okay, Tara? It's not like you to take a day off work. In fact, you haven't missed a single school day in all the time you've been there.'

It is no surprise that he knows this. He has probably been keeping track of me since I started at the school.

'Just some family stuff I have to take care of.'

'Oh? Nothing bad, I hope?'

Most people would take the hint that I don't want to go into details, but not Mikey.

'Just stuff with my parents.' I only hope my lie doesn't come back to haunt me.

'Oh, well, I hope they're okay.' He seems bored with my reason, and starts looking around the garden.

It unnerves me that he is taking in every inch of my home, but I remind myself this is Mikey. We have worked together for years, and he's never done me any harm. Perhaps what happened to Lee has made me paranoid about everyone.

'It's funny, but you never think someone will be murdered on your doorstep, do you? I mean, we watch it on the news almost daily, but it's always so far removed.'

He seems pleased with himself for coming up with this theory, and I don't tell him that it is exactly what everyone has said when they've found out about Lee.

'How are your kids dealing with it?' he asks, when I don't respond.

I cannot take his comments personally. He knows nothing about me being there, he is only interested because it's so close to home.

'They're fine,' I say. 'In some ways kids deal with stuff a lot better than adults.'

'Not always. But I guess they are resilient. It's us adults who bear the scars of whatever happens to us, isn't it?'

I feel myself heating up. Every comment Mikey makes feels like it's being directed at me. But it is just guilt warping my view of everything. There is no way Mikey knows what I keep hidden.

Somehow he manages to make his coffee last for half an hour, but at least he has moved on from talking about Lee, replacing the subject with a long discussion about work.

'I really should be getting dinner ready now,' I say, when I can take no more of his moaning about students.

He looks at his watch. 'Oh, okay. Well, I really hope you sort your family situation out. Let me know if I can help with anything.'

As I see him out through our side gate and watch him head to his car, I wonder if I'm being too harsh on him. Coming here was a nice gesture, and he's gone without a fuss.

But inside the kitchen, I put the flowers in the bin. And then I wait for Lisa to come back and tell me what is going on with my daughter.

CHAPTER THIRTEEN

I am once again staring out of the living room window when Lisa's car pulls up. I scan the passenger side for Rosie, but she's not there. My stomach sinks as I realise they must have had an argument, and Rosie has stormed off somewhere.

Rushing to the door, I wait for confirmation.

'Hey,' Lisa says, when she steps out of the car. 'Have you been waiting there this whole time?'

But now is not the time for levity. 'Where's Rosie?'

'Long story. Can we go in and talk? It's too hot out here, and I've already been in the sun too long.'

When we're sitting in the living room, I fire questions at her, desperate to know what happened with Rosie.

'Okay, you need to stay calm, though, Tara. Don't fly off the handle.'

I make this promise, although I am sure I won't be able to keep it. And her assumption that I will lose control puts me on edge. 'Just tell me where she is first. Did you have an argument?'

Lisa leans forward. 'No. But she guessed that I was talking to her on your behalf and, well, I don't think she liked that. Anyway, she said she didn't want to be at home at the moment and that she was going to Libby's. She said you can call her mother and check if you want.'

But I won't do that. This time I will force myself to trust her.

'We talked a lot about your neighbour, and I really grilled her, Tara. But I have to say I think she's lying. She could hardly go into any details, and I don't know, I just don't believe her.'

'But we can't be sure, can we?'

As I say this I realise I would prefer Rosie to be lying. I don't want to believe Lee would have done that to her, because then the chances are more likely he had something to do with me ending up in his bed. Did he want something to happen between us? I search my mind, but in all the time I knew him he'd never made any suggestive comments or behaved inappropriately towards me. Never. But was it a way for him to get at Rosie for rejecting him?

'Tara, I can't tell you what's going on with her but I think. . . she might be heading for a fall again.'

This is Lisa's way of telling me my daughter is about to have some kind of breakdown. I love her for her tact, but it does nothing to ease my anxiety.

'Rosie's not a nasty person, Tara, and maybe in her head she does actually believe that Lee came on to her.'

Just like she thought she was in a relationship with Anthony. But this is far worse, because if Lisa is right, then Rosie is tarnishing a dead man's name.

'So, you think she developed an obsession with Lee? But we don't have any evidence, do we?' I need something palpable to take to Rosie before I confront her with this.

'You're right, Tara, but Rosie scribbled his initials on her notebook. What girl would do that unless she was interested in someone?'

I try to think of another explanation, anything else, but nothing else fits.

Lisa leans forward. 'Unless she was angry with him about something? Can you think of any other reason she might have for doing this?'

I shake my head.

Lisa pats my arm. 'I'm sorry I don't have all the answers, but I'm just telling you what I think. I know that whatever the truth is, it won't be easy for you all to deal with.'

It took months for Rosie to get Anthony out of her system. And that was straightforward. Lee Jacobs is far more complex.

'Did she say anything else?' I ask. 'What about Damien? Did she mention him at all?'

Lisa gathers her hair and pulls it away from her neck. 'Yes, I asked her about him, but she was a bit vague again. She just said it was going well with him. But Tara, there was something strange. At one point she called him Lee by mistake. I don't think she even realised she'd done it. But I couldn't help noticing.'

I consider this for a second. It's possible to mix up people's names when you've been talking about them both, of course it is. But Lisa clearly thinks it is more than this.

'What are you saying?'

'I don't know, Tara. It's just a bit strange this supposed boy-friend has suddenly come along. Did she ever mention Damien before your neighbour died?'

It is hard to remember the exact moment Rosie told me about him, but I'm sure it was after last Friday night.

'I'm not sure,' I tell her. 'But before I confront her I need evidence that she's lying,' I say.

There have been too many fights with Rosie recently, so I need to be sure I'm right before I potentially trigger another one.

'Tara, I think the initials scribbled on her notebook are enough. Because think about this: why would she write them if Lee Jacobs was just a sleazy neighbour who'd tried to sleep with her?'

Time ticks by too slowly as I wait for Rosie to come home. Al-though I had promised myself I wouldn't check up on her this time, as soon as Lisa left I texted Bernadette, and was reassured when she confirmed that Rosie was out with Libby. But this offers me little relief when I now have to face the possibility my daughter was involved with Lee in some way.

Spencer arrives home, and there is still no sign of Rosie and, with Noah still in a meeting at work, I have no choice but to focus on my son, and push aside everything else for now.

'People keep talking about Lee at school,' Spencer says, as he helps me peel carrots for our dinner.

'Oh? What do they say?'

'Just that I probably know the murderer, and he could live on our road.'

'Spencer, that's ridiculous. None of our neighbours killed Lee. And I hope you're not gossiping at school.'

'No, 'course not. But it's all they talk about.'

I remind myself this is natural, and that in a few days the kids will have something else to talk about. Lee will be old news. 'Just don't get involved,' I say, knowing this is easier said than done, especially for an eleven-year-old.

'Mum, I liked Lee, I don't exactly want all the kids talking about him like it's a TV programme or something.'

I give Spencer a hug then, because I love being reminded how mature he can be. And I realise that he is the anchor keeping this family grounded.

Rosie still hasn't come home by dinner time, but when I text Bernadette again she says she has just made the girls some food.

'It would be nice if Rosie actually bothered to tell you if she wasn't coming home for dinner,' Spencer says, when I report that it will just be us for dinner. 'She's really horrible sometimes. Sorry, Mum, but it's true.'

Once again the urge to defend Rosie kicks in, even against my son. 'She's just having a hard time at the moment. She'll be okay.'

'Well, it feels like she's always having a hard time, Mum.'

I smooth down his hair. Spencer is not being malicious when he says this; he is as sad as Noah and I are that Rosie never seems happy. That none of us seems to be able to help her.

It is past eight p.m. when Noah gets home. He looks exhausted as I hand him a glass of wine and report what Lisa told me earlier.

'So she's doing it again?' His hand clenches into a fist. 'But why Lee? He's far too old for her.'

'Obsession isn't about things being appropriate, is it? He was a nice guy, maybe she just fell for his charm.' It is hard to say this when I don't know how I ended up in his bed, but I do understand how Rosie might have developed feelings for him.

'I suppose. Where is Rosie now?' Noah asks.

'Still at Libby's, but she just texted to say she won't be long.'

Noah sits down to eat the dinner I have kept warm for him, and I join him at the table.

'So what do we do about this?' he asks. 'I'm at a loss here, Tara. Just when I think Rosie might actually be getting better. . .'

Again I must be her advocate. 'Remember we don't know for sure that she's lying, or that she was fixated on him. This is just what Lisa thinks.'

Picking up his fork, he digs it into his mince, but doesn't eat. 'True, but your sister's a smart woman, and it doesn't look good, does it? We just need to come straight out with it and ask her. Tonight. This is serious. She needs help.'

He is right, we are back to the ticking time bomb Rosie often is so we need to know what's going on before anything else happens.

'She'll be home soon,' I say. 'Let's sort it out then.'

The knock on the door comes just as Noah finishes his dinner. Thinking Rosie must have lost her key, I rush to get it before

Noah can; I don't want an interrogation to begin the second she steps inside.

But it is not Rosie. It is a man in a suit. A man it takes me a few seconds to realise I've seen before. The detective who was with Serena earlier; the one she claimed was nice.

He flashes his badge at me and introduces himself. DCI Hunt. 'We met earlier today,' he says, when I don't respond.

'Yes, of course, um, come in.'

He thanks me and steps into the hall just as Noah appears in the living room doorway.

I quickly introduce them, and Noah's face pales.

'Are you here to see me?' he asks. 'Because there's really nothing more I can tell you.'

'Actually, no, sir, I'm here to see your daughter, Rosie Logan.'

This is the last thing I've been expecting. I only thought he would be here for me or Noah.

'But. . . why?' I can't help sounding defensive.

'I don't want you to worry. One or both of you can be present while I speak to her. It's not formal at this point. I just have a few questions I need to ask her.'

I glance at the stairs, hoping Spencer doesn't appear. 'About Lee? But Rosie doesn't know anything.' I feel Noah's eyes on me; he will think I'm protesting too much.

DCI Hunt doesn't answer. 'Is she at home?'

'No,' Noah says, when I cannot speak. 'But she's due back any minute. Do you want to wait for her?'

'I think that would be best,' DCI Hunt says. 'Shall I wait in there?' He nods his head towards the living room. 'I assume that's your front room? All these houses have a similar layout and I've spent enough time across the road there to know my way around.' He doesn't wait for a response, as if he's talking to himself. 'And don't worry about getting me a drink or anything. I'm fine.'

I steal a glance at Noah, and he raises his eyebrows. There is something about this man, and I can see why Serena has put all her trust in him. He can't be older than his late thirties, and underneath his stubble and messy hair he is a good-looking man, somehow commanding respect without being rude or forceful. I will have to be on my guard with him, this much I know for sure.

'Is Rosie in trouble?' I ask, following him into the living room.

'All I can say at this point is that we have new information connecting her to Lee Jacobs, so I just want to clear up a few things. That's all.'

Serena. She must have reported everything I told her this morning. I know I have no right to be angry with her when I am keeping such a terrible truth from her, but I can't help feeling betrayed. She could have warned me she was going to talk to this detective. At least then I would be prepared, and I could have spoken to Rosie first.

But nobody can be trusted. I should know this by now.

The second I hear Rosie's key in the door I jump up. 'I'll just go and tell her you're here,' I say, trying not to run from the room.

I expect an objection, but DCI Hunt only smiles and tells me to go ahead. I close the door behind me, and hope that Noah distracts him for a few moments.

'Mum, what's going on? Who's in there?' Rosie says. She looks past me to the closed living room door and slips off her shoes.

'Don't panic, but there's a detective here, and he just wants to ask you a few questions.'

Her eyes narrow. 'Me? Why me? What's going on, Mum? What have you told him?'

'Shhhh, keep your voice down. He just knows what Lee said to you, I think, but don't worry, he says it's very informal.'

She folds her arms across her chest. 'Yeah, that's what they said to Dad, and he had to go to the station. I'm not going anywhere, Mum!'

I tell her to keep her voice down, and add that if he wanted to speak to her at the station we would already be on our way there.

This seems to appease her and she follows me into the living room.

'Hi, Rosie,' DCI Hunt says, standing up and holding out his hand. But I don't trust his politeness; it surely must be a tactic he uses to get what he wants.

When I turn to Rosie I expect to see fear in her eyes, but there is only defiance. It is a look I am all too familiar with, and I dread even more how this will play out.

'I'm sorry, but why do you need to talk to me?' she says, only briefly shaking his hand.

But DCI Hunt doesn't seem fazed. He must be used to people with attitudes far worse than Rosie's. 'It won't take long,' he says. 'I just have a few questions about your neighbour, Lee Jacobs.'

'Fine,' she says, taking a seat and crossing her legs. 'What do you need to know?'

'How well did you know him?'

She shrugs. 'I don't know, not that well, I suppose.' She glances at me. 'But we've lived here for years now and so have they.'

The detective nods. 'Six years, isn't it?' He has done his homework.

Rosie shrugs. 'I don't know. Something like that.'

'Yes, it's about six years,' Noah interjects, unable to keep the impatience out of his voice.

The detective nods. 'And the Jacobs moved here about two years ago?'

'Yes,' I say, before Noah can offend him again.

DCI Hunt turns to me, and smiles. 'That's very helpful, Mrs Logan, but I'd like Rosie to answer the questions as far as possible.'

But how can she be expected to keep track of when our neighbours move in or out? I almost say this, but bite my tongue. I don't want the detective to think we're being difficult.

'Two years then,' Rosie says, sighing heavily. It is only a matter of time before she erupts; I can feel it.

'Okay. So you would have been fifteen?'

'What's that got to do with anything?' Rosie says, and although I agree with her at first, I quickly realise where he is going with this.

'I'm just trying to create a picture of Lee Jacobs, Rosie. When you first met him you would have been fifteen?'

'Yeah, and Spencer would have been nine. So?'

'So why don't you tell me what happened a few months ago?'

She looks at me and scowls, and I wish I could tell her that it wasn't me who told the police, that I would have done anything to stop Serena doing so if I'd known what she was planning.

'He tried it on with me, and I turned him down. That's it. End of story.'

'I'm afraid I'll need to know more details than that,' DCI Hunt says.

After a heavy sigh, Rosie repeats the story she has already told us, almost word for word. It is just as difficult to hear this time around. Despite what Lisa says, I still need to hear an admission from Rosie, and I'm sure that with the right approach I can get through to her somehow. It worked with Anthony in the end. But despite my doubts, as she tells this story I can almost see it: Lee in his front garden, smiling up at her, hoping to seduce her with his smile.

'So, just for the record, you weren't having any kind of relationship with Lee Jacobs? Physical or otherwise?'

Rosie stares him straight in the eyes. 'No, of course I wasn't. Now can I go please?'

DCI Hunt doesn't get up once she has gone, so I know he hasn't finished with us.

But before he can speak, Noah says: 'Well, that was a waste of your time, wasn't it? Rosie could have told you all that on the phone.'

'Perhaps. But I like to be thorough. And I have to be honest with you, we're certain Lee Jacobs was having an extra-marital affair with someone, so I will be speaking to Rosie again. Because, although I need to check something out, right now the person we think Lee Jacobs was seeing is your daughter.'

CHAPTER FOURTEEN

When I wake from a fitful sleep the next morning, it is impossible not to acknowledge that it's been exactly a week since I woke up in Lee's bed. And seven days later, I still know nothing. The only difference is that now it is clear that Rosie is somehow tangled up in this.

After DCI Hunt left last night, she refused to speak to us, and knowing that Rosie will not be pushed, we retired to bed none the wiser. But I will speak to her again today. There are too many unanswered questions, and my family is falling apart.

'If he wasn't already dead, I'd kill him myself,' Noah had whispered, once we were in bed, his cheeks flushed with anger.

It is fortuitous that when he is irrational I manage to remain calm, and vice versa. It would do no good for us both to blow up right now. I reminded him that he has been the one saying we shouldn't jump to conclusions, and now he was doing just that.

'But it's a different thing altogether when the police are involved,' he said.

It hadn't gone down well when I'd responded that they had been wrong about him. And then I'd pictured Amelie, with her neat hair and clothes, and her insistence that she'd had a lucky escape.

But dealing with the Amelie situation has to wait. Rosie is more important.

Spencer is already in the kitchen, eating his breakfast, when I go downstairs, still in my nightclothes. The smile he usually greets me with each morning is thinner today, his expression downcast.

'Everything okay, Spence?' I ask, forcing my voice to sound cheery.

He looks at me but doesn't smile, which is unlike him. 'What did that policeman want last night?'

I should have known Spencer would hear the commotion last night, and of course he wants to know what's going on. I now have a choice to make: I can keep him in the dark as much as possible, or I can be honest, no matter how hard it will be. We are a family, and it's not fair that he doesn't know what's happening with Rosie.

'Okay, listen carefully. The police wanted to talk to Rosie about Lee.'

A frown appears on his forehead. 'Oh. Do they want to speak to me too?'

He is clearly nervous about this so I try to reassure him.

'Not at the moment, but they may do at some point. It's okay, though, they'll just want to find out as much as they can from the people who lived closest to him.' I pray Spencer will never need to be involved in this.

'But why did they want to talk to Rosie? Did she see something?'

'No, Spencer, but they think she was quite close to him, so. . .' There is no other way I can bring myself to explain this to him.

But he is smart, and within seconds he has worked out what I mean. He screws up his face. 'Yuk, you mean? No, forget it, Mum, don't even tell me. I don't want to know what Rosie does.'

'She hasn't done anything, Spencer, they only want to question her.' But I know this can't be true; DCI Hunt seemed very sure of himself yesterday, almost too casual about it.

'Okay,' he says, already letting it go, which only makes me feel worse for snapping at him.

'Are you talking about me?' Rosie says, appearing in the doorway. 'Because if you want to know something you can just ask me.'

Spencer and I both turn to her, and although I'm fed up that she keeps sneaking up on me all the time, I am pleased at her warm tone. And shocked.

'I was just asking Mum about the detective,' Spencer says, clearly wary of Rosie's pleasant demeanour this morning. 'Don't flip out.'

Rosie crosses to the table and sits next to him. 'I'm not going to,' she says. 'Of course you want to know what's going on. I get it. But just ask me, okay?'

'So why do they want to talk to you?' Spencer asks, making the most of this rare opportunity.

'Because Lee was scum, and he tried it on with me, that's why.'

Spencer's mouth hangs open. 'What?'

So she is sticking to this story.

'Listen,' I say, before she can tell him any more. 'Dad's going to take Spencer swimming today, so—'

'Is he?' Spencer squeals. 'Really? Just me and Dad?'

I nod. 'I know he's been working hard lately and hasn't had much time to do all the things you used to do at weekends, but all that's going to change now the summer holidays are coming up.' I shouldn't make this promise when I don't know what the next few hours, let alone weeks, will bring. But I will do my best to make it happen.

'I'm going to get my stuff ready,' Spencer says, rushing off.

'Rosie, how about we have a picnic in the park? Just the two of us?'

I wait for the accusation that I have an ulterior motive for wanting to do this, but this is a different girl who sits before me. The other Rosie.

'Okay,' she says. 'That sounds nice, Mum. I just need to get ready and do a couple of things first, though.'

I tell her to go ahead, and breathe a sigh of relief that Rosie is in such a good mood.

'So you might actually get her to tell the truth, whatever it is, today?' Noah says, his eyes wide.

We are in our bathroom, the door shut so that there is no chance of being heard. We quickly learned when we moved here that this is the only place that grants us a modicum of privacy.

'I don't know. But she was in a good mood this morning, so it's worth a try. I just want her to know that we'll support her no matter what.'

Noah picks up his toothbrush. 'It's awful to think she might have been. . . with Lee, but I don't blame her for any of it. I'm just sick of the lies, Tara. I'm tired of not being able to trust her, of not knowing where we are with our own daughter. I can handle teenage rebellion, but this is something else.'

I tell him I agree, and that maybe she has been spooked by DCI Hunt turning up last night. I don't add that I was too, because every second he was in our home I felt that he was judging and analysing all of us.

'Perhaps this is a blessing in disguise, then,' he says, squeezing toothpaste onto his brush. 'A wake-up call for her. Maybe it will put a stop to all the lies.'

'Let's see,' I say, because no matter how friendly she was this morning, I have learned that she can change by the hour.

Rosie looks like a delicate flower as we sit in the park. She is wearing a short white floaty dress I've never seen before, and a wide-brimmed sun hat. Her tanned legs are streaked white with sun cream, but I don't mention this because at least she's put some on. Despite her issues, Rosie knows how to take care of herself.

She lies back on the picnic blanket and closes her eyes. 'It's so peaceful here, isn't it, Mum?' she says.

Next to her, I too lie down, turning to face her. 'Yes. I think we both need a bit of peace, don't we?'

She mumbles agreement, and keeps her eyes closed.

'Rosie, I hope you know how much I love you, and that I'll do anything to protect you and keep you from harm.'

Her eyes open, and she stares at me, unblinking. 'I know. But do you love Dad?'

'Of course I do; what a question to ask. I love you all, and our family means more to me than anything. I know we're going through a tricky time at the moment with. . . everything that's happened, but we need to stick together, that's how we'll get through this.'

Although I mean every word I speak, even to me it sounds as if I'm reciting a self-help book on dealing with difficult teenagers. I wait to see what Rosie's response will be.

'I know why you've asked me here, Mum. You want to know the truth about Lee because you think I'm lying.'

'Yes,' I say. If I want Rosie to act like an adult then I have to treat her as one, and that begins with some honesty.

Her expression shows no surprise at this. 'I'll never escape all that Anthony stuff, will I? Nobody will ever believe anything I say.'

'Of course we will, but it takes time to shake off the past, Rosie. You have to earn our trust back.'

She turns at me and stares with her large, dark eyes. 'Because lies are what destroy relationships, aren't they, Mum? And families.'

I search her face to see if there is a hidden meaning in her comment, but find only sadness. I need to get a grip on my paranoia.

'Yes, that's true. But what I want you to know is that there is no need to lie – to either of us. Whatever has happened, we will stick by you.'

'Mum, it sounds like you're accusing me of something?'

'No, Rosie, I just want a fresh start. No more lies.' Once again I baulk at my hypocrisy, but remind myself why I am keeping things from my family.

'No more lies,' she repeats. 'Okay. A fresh start.'

This seems too easy. I know Rosie can almost be a different person from one day to the next, depending on her mood, but surely she hasn't changed overnight?

'Now can you be honest about something?' she asks.

A lump forms in my throat. 'Yes, I will.'

'Did you have a hard time with me when I was a baby?'

Her question comes from nowhere and catches me off guard. I have expected her to ask about Lee, or when Noah left, but not this. But I need to be honest if I expect the same from Rosie.

'Yes, I did. I was only twenty-one when I had you, and I had no clue what I was doing. Your dad was working all the time to support us, and my parents were still working so couldn't help much. I felt completely alone. But that doesn't mean I didn't love you.'

'But you didn't want me, did you? I was an accident.'

I have never told Rosie this, but somehow she must have sensed it.

'We might not have planned to have you that soon, but we still wanted you, Rosie.'

I can never tell her that every day was a struggle, that I resented having to give up my life when all my friends were out having fun, experiencing the world, while I was stuck at home with a baby who was never happy. Even then, Rosie was angry at the world. And, yes, I found it hard to bond with her for a long time. And I will always have to live with the fact that it is probably because of this that Rosie is the person she is.

'Right,' she says, shifting herself up to sit cross-legged. 'But it was different with Spencer, wasn't it?'

Again, she is right. Spencer came along much later, when I was older and more prepared. A lot more prepared.

'Rosie, I love you both and treat the two of you equally. But if you feel I don't, please tell me how that is and I'll do my best to change it.'

'Oh, never mind,' she says.

I watch a couple with two young children walk past us, all four of them smiling and laughing, and wonder what is beneath their surface of perfection. Because we all put on a face to the world, don't we?

'Why are you bringing all this up now?' I ask Rosie.

'Because I wanted to see if you could be honest.'

I tell her I have been, that she now knows how difficult I found her as a baby. But this will never be enough. 'And now I'd like some honesty in return,' I say. 'Is everything you've told us about Lee the truth?'

'Yes, Mum. But I can't prove it to you, can I?'

'And that's all there is to it. You weren't interested in him and the two of you never? . . .' I cannot say the words.

'No.'

Now is the time to tell her that I found her school notebook, and saw Lee's initials on it. So far, Libby seems to have kept her promise not to mention it, but as Serena also knows, it's only a matter of time before she finds out. And it needs to come from me.

'What the hell?' she says, when I admit what I've done. 'That was nothing, I was just doodling. I think I'd just found out about Lee being dead so it was on my mind. Mum, it's nothing!' And just as I prepare myself for a full-on verbal attack, she leans forward and gives me a hug. 'Look, I know you only did it because you're worried about me, and I appreciate you being honest.'

I wrap her in my arms and tell her I'm sorry. But all the time I can't help feeling I have got off too lightly. With everything.

When we arrive home, a crowd of reporters has gathered once again outside Serena's house. I drive past them and pull into our drive, ignoring their yells, and the cameras they point in our direction.

'What's going on?' Rosie asks. 'Why are they back?'

I tell her I have no idea, and then I see Layla marching down her driveway, Guy following behind her. At first I assume she has come out to tell the journalists to leave Serena alone, but I am soon proved wrong as she heads in our direction.

'Mum, what does she want?' Rosie says, and for the first time in years she seems nervous. 'Why does she look so angry?'

Before I can open my door, Layla is banging on the window.

'What's your problem?' I say, flinging the door open so she has to step back. I can no longer force politeness with this woman.

Guy grabs her arm and whispers something in her ear. 'Is it true?' he asks. He looks from me to Rosie then back again, and I'm not sure which one of us he expects to answer his question.

Rosie rushes round to my side, and I put my arm around her to try to lead her into the house, because suddenly I know what this is about.

'Just leave us alone,' I say, conscious that we now have an audience of reporters eagerly watching.

Layla's voice booms out into the street. 'You're a slut, Rosie Logan. How could you do it? He was a married man. You're a despicable human being.'

Rosie stops walking and turns around. 'I haven't done anything. Leave me alone.'

And she rushes into the house before I can catch up with her.

I take a step towards Layla. 'You're a nasty piece of work, spreading malicious lies around. Why don't you get a life?'

Guy puts his arm on Layla's shoulder, clearly afraid this will get out of hand if he lets her speak.

'But they're not lies, Tara,' he says. 'We know on good authority that Rosie was having an affair with Lee. It's disgusting. Did you know about it? Because if you did that makes you even worse than your daughter.'

I look past him to the mass of faces staring at us, their eyes eager for something new to report back. I will not give them, or Guy and Layla, the satisfaction. Without a word I turn around and head into the house.

Rosie is sitting on the stairs when I get inside, her head buried in her hands. 'Why are they saying those things?' she says.

This is because of Serena. Despite what DCI Hunt told us last night before he left, the police would not have told Guy and Layla anything, no matter what neighbourhood role they have bestowed upon themselves. In her desperation for answers, Serena has got it into her head that Rosie is the person Lee was having an affair with. Although it makes no sense, perhaps that is easier for her to accept than her husband simply being rejected by Rosie. Maybe she needs to remember him as desirable, not a predator preying on teenage girls. But if this is the case, doesn't she see that, either way, he is exactly that?

'They're just sad people with nothing better to do than gossip about everyone else. We've just got to rise above it. Don't respond to anything they say, no matter how tempted you are to defend yourself. The best thing you can do is stay silent.'

'But. . . but then they'll just assume I've got something to hide.'

'Do we really care what Guy and Layla think?' And the rest of the neighbours, by the time those two have spread the word. But, of course, I don't point this out to Rosie.

'I suppose not,' she says, pulling herself up. 'They're nothing to me.' And then, almost as if nothing at all has happened, she tells me she's going up to get changed because she is drenched in sweat.

As soon as she's disappeared to her room, I find my mobile in my bag and text Serena. I don't expect a reply, but it's worth a try. I struggle to find the words but then settle on telling her I'm sorry she's been hurt, but we need to talk. I end the message with two kisses, as I always do, in the hope that she'll realise I'm not angry with her.

As soon as I've put my phone in my pocket I see someone standing at the front door. Assuming it must be Guy and Layla again, I turn away before the knock comes. But before I reach the kitchen, I hear DCI Hunt's voice, calling my name and asking me to open the door.

He is not alone this time. Another officer in plain clothes stands on the doorstep next to him, her badge in her hand. This is serious.

'I said I'd be back,' DCI Hunt says. He gestures to his colleague. 'This is DS Aldridge. We have some more questions for Rosie.'

'I'm here,' Rosie says, appearing at the top of the stairs.

'Do you realise we're being harassed by the neighbours now?' I say to DCI Hunt, holding the door open for them.

They both step inside. 'I'm sorry,' DCI Hunt says. 'But that's not what we're here about. If you need to report any kind of harassment you'll have to go down to the station.'

'Mum, just leave it,' Rosie says, coming downstairs. 'I'll talk to them. I've got nothing to hide.'

'Fine, but let's all go in the kitchen,' I say, because the air is suffocating me. 'It's cooler in there.'

DCI Hunt is the first to speak when we get there. 'You see we have a bit of a problem, Rosie, and we really need your help.

We're looking at Lee Jacobs's death as a possible crime of passion. Do you know what that means?'

Rosie tuts. 'I'm not stupid.'

He smiles. 'No, of course not. So, anyway, one of the angles we're exploring is that whoever Lee was seeing had a motive to attack him in that manner. I don't know, say if, for example, he ended the relationship and refused to leave his wife.'

'But this has got nothing to do with me,' Rosie says.

DS Aldridge finally speaks. 'So you weren't having a physical relationship with Lee Jacobs?'

'No! I told him that yesterday.'

DCI Hunt turns to me. 'Then I'm afraid we're going to have to question Rosie at the police station.'

'Why?' Rosie and I both say simultaneously.

'To explain to us why you were seen rushing from his house on the night he was murdered.'

CHAPTER FIFTEEN

I hold Rosie's arm as we sit and wait. The interview room they've put us in is small and dark, with only a slit of a window, too high up to see outside. At least they have offered us tea, even if it tastes foul.

'Why are they making us wait so long,' Rosie says. 'It must be nearly an hour now.'

She taps her leg under the table, something she's been doing since we arrived.

It has only been ten minutes, but to Rosie the minutes must seem endless. For me, time is now a blur, my thoughts trying to comprehend how Rosie is mixed up in this. Part of me doesn't believe it, because if she'd been there she would have seen me, and Rosie would never keep quiet about that.

'Are you sure there's nothing you want to tell me first?' I ask for the third time. 'Whatever it is, we'll deal with it together.'

She shakes her head, but doesn't look at me. 'It's all a mistake. I wasn't there, Mum. This will all get sorted out quickly when they realise.'

'You told me you stayed at Damien's that night. Damien, who we've never laid eyes on.'

'Mum, what are you saying?'

'Only what the police will when they come in. You do know they'll want to speak to him, don't you? To confirm where you were.'

'That's fine. But he's not around at the moment.'

I stare at her, trying to keep calm. 'What do you mean?'

'His parents live in Australia, and he's visiting them for two weeks. He left yesterday.'

I let go of her arm. 'And you didn't think it was worth mentioning this, seeing as we'd asked to meet him?'

She gives her usual shrug, clearly not realising the seriousness of her situation. 'I did tell you he was busy. I just didn't think I had to give you his itinerary for every day.'

'But you must know where he lives, at least? You can tell the police.'

She shakes her head. 'I never went to his place, Mum. When we met up we were always out.'

Although I want to protest about this and tell her how untruthful it sounds this is not the time or place for an argument so for now I let it go. The police will track Damien down, if he exists, and soon we will have answers. But this doesn't look good. If there is a witness claiming they saw Rosie fleeing from Lee's house that night, then we are all in a lot of trouble.

The door finally opens, and DCI Hunt and DS Aldridge appear. I don't even give them a chance to speak before I demand to know who saw Rosie running from Lee's house.

'We can't give out that information,' DS Aldridge says, and I begin to wonder if they're just trying to test Rosie.

For over an hour they grill her about Lee, but she sticks to her story, insisting that she was nowhere near either Lee's house or our own. But when they ask for Damien's address, she says she doesn't know it. That they only met in public.

The detectives turn to each other, and I don't need to be a mind reader to know exactly what they're thinking: this girl is lying, and doesn't she realise we see straight through her concocted and convenient story?

Proving me right, DCI Hunt does not let this go. Ignoring Rosie, he turns to me, and I wonder if I can sense an apology in his expression. 'Mrs Logan, we're going to need to search your house.'

I am not prepared for this. 'What? Why?'

'Because your daughter was seen leaving Lee Jacobs's house, and this is a murder investigation.'

I know exactly what he's suggesting, but I just want him to say it. 'Are you arresting her?'

'If we have to, but I'm hoping not to have to do that. Now, we'll be getting a search warrant, but it would help us if you gave us permission to take a look around your home.'

This is a ploy. I know it is. But surely it's better if we cooperate. I turn to Rosie but she only looks blank: neither scared nor assertive.

'Fine,' I say. But something tells me I will live to regret this decision.

Noah is standing in the back garden when we get home. At my suggestion, he has dropped Spencer at my parents' house, because neither of us wants him witnessing this search.

'They're already here,' he says. 'They didn't waste any time.' But there is a reason for this: they didn't want any of us removing any evidence. 'I don't know what they think they're going to find. . .' But he trails off as he looks at Rosie, and I know he is struggling to accept that she might have something to do with Lee's murder.

'I'm going to sit in the back garden,' she says, and when she is out of view, I fill Noah in on her police interview.

'Do they actually think she killed Lee?' he asks, shaking his head. 'It's ludicrous. Rosie might be many things, but she's not a. . . a murderer.'

I recoil at his use of the word, but there is no other way he could put it. 'Well, they haven't actually come out and said that, but clearly it's what they believe. They at least think she was sleeping with him.'

He clutches the sides of his head. 'What a mess. I can't believe this is happening.'

I take his hand and suggest we join Rosie, who has been sitting alone at the table.

'I don't want to leave her on her own,' I say, because, whatever happens today, I already know our family is living on borrowed time.

'Are you okay?' I ask, as we sit at the garden table, all of us staring up at the house, picturing the uniformed officers rifling through our drawers, our possessions no longer private.

'I'm fine, Mum. It will be okay. There's nothing for them to find because I didn't do anything.' And then she grabs my hand, and reaches for Noah's. 'Are you both okay, though? I know this has shaken you up.'

I give her hand a squeeze and hope she knows it means we will get through this together. We have to.

'Don't worry about us,' Noah says, and we all go back to staring at the house. 'This will all be over soon.'

It is hard to judge how much time passes before DCI Hunt appears in the kitchen doorway. 'They said you were out here,' he says.

Noah jumps up. 'Is that it then? Have they finished?'

The detective walks towards us, his pace measured. 'They have finished, yes.'

'Right, so are you going to leave my daughter alone now?' Noah puts his hand on Rosie's shoulder.

'I'm afraid that's not possible,' DCI Hunt says, walking towards us.

'What's going on?' I ask, even though I already know.

'We've found something.' He leans down to Rosie and holds up a clear plastic bag. From where I sit, I struggle to see what's in it. 'Do you recognise this?' he asks her.

Rosie stares at the bag. 'No. What is it?'

'We've just had confirmation from Serena Jacobs that this is Lee Jacobs's wedding ring. Now can you tell me what it was doing in your bedroom, Rosie?'

I stare at my daughter as the ground falls from beneath my feet. She looks as shaken as I am and tries to grab the evidence bag from DCI Hunt. But he is too quick and whips it out of her reach.

'This is rubbish,' she says. 'I've never seen that before.' And for the first time since this all happened her eyes fill with tears. She turns to me. 'Mum, I don't know what they're talking about. That can't have been in my room. They're lying!'

I stand up and take her hand. 'Rosie, just stay calm.' I feel her grip tighten. 'None of this makes sense,' I say to DCI Hunt. 'How can that be Lee's ring when he would have been wearing it?'

'That's just the thing,' he says. 'According to Serena, Lee lost his wedding ring months ago. And she thinks it's possible he might have given it to the person he was seeing. I don't know, perhaps as some sort of promise that his marriage was as good as over.'

Noah takes a step towards the detective. 'That's just conjecture. Where's the evidence of this? I thought that's what the police dealt in, not just make-believe.'

DCI Hunt nods. 'Hmmm. Perhaps you're right, but the only other alternative is much worse, Mr Logan.'

I wait for realisation to dawn, just as it did for me the second I saw the ring.

'Wait,' Noah says. 'Are you saying Rosie took that after Lee was killed?'

'These are the two theories we've got to work with. So now do you understand why Serena's claim is better for Rosie?'

Noah and I stare at each other, and Rosie clutches my hand even tighter.

'So what happens now?' I ask. The sooner we get legal help the better. We are both out of our depth here.

And in answer to my question, DCI Hunt reads Rosie her rights.

At the police station they tell us they can hold Rosie for twenty-four hours, even though she's under eighteen, and then they can charge her if they have enough evidence.

They have her locked away for now, and my heart aches when I picture her alone and terrified, a shadow of herself. I still don't believe she had anything to do with this, but cannot think of any other reason Lee's wedding ring would have been in her bedroom.

With no air conditioning, the waiting area is stifling, and sweat pours from every inch of my skin, but I will not move until we've got Rosie help and I know she'll be okay.

Noah comes back in from phoning my parents. 'They said they'll keep Spencer tonight. I told them what's going on, but asked them not to let Spencer know. It has to come from us.'

He gets us both a cup of water from the machine in the corner of the room, but it is lukewarm and does nothing to cool me down.

'We have to face reality here, Tara. Rosie—'

'Don't say it. Just don't say the words. They haven't proven anything so far, so I'm not going to give up on her.'

But I cannot tell him the real reason I'm sure Rosie wasn't there. I would tell everyone now if I thought it would help her, but I can't prove she wasn't there when those hours are a huge empty hole.

Noah shakes his head. He will think I'm just in denial, that I cannot see any faults in our daughter, but he's wrong. It is no longer about innocence or guilt; it's about being there to support her. Being her mother.

'I spoke to Lisa and have called a solicitor,' I say. 'His name's Thomas Butler and he's on his way here now. He's someone Harvey knows, so we can trust that Rosie's in good hands.'

Noah nods. 'Okay, good. What did Lisa say?'

'She's shocked, like we are, but said she'll do anything she can to help.'

'How did we get here, Tara? How did things get so complicated? It's just one thing after another, isn't it?'

I don't tell him that it's called life, or that he doesn't know just how bad things really are. Instead, I reach for his hand and we sit and wait, because right now that is all we can do.

It is almost three hours before Thomas Butler arrives, striding into the waiting area. He is full of apologies for taking so long, but he is here now, and that's all that matters. He tells us to call him Thomas, and suggests we go outside so Noah and I can fill him in before he talks to DCI Hunt. We have both been cooped up in this waiting room for too long so are more than happy to do this.

But despite it being night-time, the air out here is not much better, and I still feel as if I'm suffocating.

'The main thing is they can't talk to her without a responsible adult present,' Thomas says, once I've brought him up to date. 'So in this case that's me or either of you. That means there's no way for them to manipulate Rosie into confessing to something she hasn't done.'

I don't point out that there would be little chance of that with Rosie.

'So what happens now?'

'I spoke briefly on the phone to the detective in charge, and he said they won't be speaking to her tonight. My guess is they're getting their evidence together before they talk to Rosie again.'

'Is that good or bad?' I ask.

'It's hard to say. It could mean they don't have enough, or it could just as easily mean they want to cover all their bases and make sure they don't make any mistakes.'

I let out a heavy sigh, but I am numb. This feels as if it's happening to someone else, not us. 'Why won't they let us see her?' I ask. 'Just to check she's okay. Please, Thomas, do you think you could arrange it?'

'It's doubtful, but I can try. Let me go in and speak to the detective in charge. Are you going to stay out here or wait inside?'

'We'll stay out here,' I say, and beside me Noah nods his agreement.

Once the solicitor has gone Noah pulls me into a hug and buries his face in my hair.

'I think Rosie did this,' he whispers, and I'm not sure I hear him correctly, or if it is my own thoughts echoing through my head, but either way, I think this may be true.

To my surprise, Thomas Butler appears again after only a few minutes. 'There's been a development,' he says. 'Rosie's asked to speak to DCI Hunt alone.'

Puzzled, I shake my head. 'No, that can't be right. Why would she do that?'

'I don't know,' Thomas says, 'but I've insisted on being there, and she's agreed.'

I nudge Noah. 'But one of us should be there too. I'm going with you.'

Thomas reaches for my arm. 'I'm sorry, Tara, but she's refusing to see you or Noah.'

'I can't believe this,' Noah says. 'What the hell is she playing at?'

'I'm going to find out, don't worry,' Thomas says, and then he is gone, and I am lost for words.

There is a wooden bench just beyond the car park, and Noah leads me to it.

'She's doing this on purpose, to spite us,' he says.

I tell him that at least she has accepted help from Thomas Butler, but it does little to pacify him.

'That girl is just something else,' he says.

But she's still our daughter.

'Noah, we can't fall apart here. Whatever's going on in Rosie's head doesn't matter. We just need her to be home with us and this mess to be cleared up.'

While we wait for news, I try to find comfort in memories of Rosie as a child. She was never a happy baby, but we had been close at one time, before Spencer came along. How did we end up here?

For over an hour Noah and I sit and wait, until finally DCI Hunt steps out of the building, scanning the car park. It takes me a moment to realise something is wrong, and that it should be Thomas Butler coming to find us. But then he appears behind the detective, and they both head towards us.

DCI Hunt reaches us first.

'Tara Logan, I'd like you to come inside to answer some questions.'

'Of course, anything I can do to help Rosie.'

'I'm coming with you,' Thomas says, frowning at the detective. He turns to me. 'Tara, I'm afraid Rosie's made an allegation.'

My chest tightens and I struggle to breathe. 'What do you mean? What allegation?'

Thomas glances at Noah then back to me. 'She's, um, admitted she was outside the victim's house that night, but she's saying she was only there because. . . she saw you enter his house, and when you didn't come out, she went there and. . . Oh, Jesus,

I'm sorry. She's saying she looked in the downstairs windows but couldn't see either of you. So she waited and you finally came out in the morning, running from the house.'

DCI Hunt steps forward. 'Which means you were the last person to see him alive.'

PART TWO

CHAPTER SIXTEEN
Three Weeks Later

It's been three weeks since I was arrested. Three weeks since my world collapsed. But in that time, somehow, I have found a strength I didn't know existed within me. I have lost nearly everything, so I no longer have anything to fear.

'I miss Dad,' Spencer says. He has barely touched his breakfast, and the glass of milk I've given him is still full to the brim. 'Everything's horrible now.' He looks up at me. 'I don't mean being here with you, Mum, I just mean it's—'

'I know, Spence.'

With Spencer's talk of Noah, it is impossible not to recall our last encounter outside the police station when they arrested me. How his face flushed red while he shouted barely decipherable words at me, and how he kept repeating the same thing.

'You lied about being in his house!' he had yelled, his face barely a centimetre from my own.

I had never known him capable of such anger, and even DCI Hunt looked shocked as he pulled him away from me and told him to go home, before he took my arm and led me inside. But Noah still continued with his outburst as we walked away, and I could tell, despite the circumstances, that the detective pitied me.

I reach for Spencer's arm. 'We just have to get used to this, and then we'll be fine. At least we're still in our home.'

'I'd rather not be,' he says.

I know what he means. We cannot leave the house without one of the neighbours – usually, but not exclusively, Guy or Layla – shouting accusations at me. Calling Rosie and me murderers, even though the police have no evidence, so couldn't charge either of us. Even with Lee's ring, they cannot prove murder. A connection between him and Rosie, yes, but not that she killed him. I can handle what people say about me – that I planted the ring to frame my own daughter – but when they bring Rosie into it my blood boils. Mum and Dad keep telling me to ignore them, that by blowing up at them their suspicions are confirmed, so I try to let their comments bounce off me. But each one leaves a dent.

'I even wish Rosie was here,' Spencer continues, before I have a chance to answer. 'She kind of brought life to the house, in a weird way.'

I have never thought of it like this before, but it's true. The house feels empty without her. She was a constant presence, even when she was elsewhere, but now the atmosphere is bereft.

'Do you want to see her?' I ask, my hopes rising that something good can come out of this mess. 'I can call Bernadette and arrange it.'

Since Rosie has moved in with Libby and her mum, she refuses to see me. But Bernadette, still as kind and helpful as she's always been, has taken pity on me and texts me updates on how she's doing.

Spencer shakes his head. 'No, I don't want to see her. Not after what she's done to you.'

And once again I marvel at how my eleven-year-old son believes my story when no one else will. Noah couldn't look me in the eye once he found out, and still can't now on the few occasions our paths have crossed. And even my own sister has her doubts, I can tell. She is different around me now, more distant, even though she has offered me her support. But other than our parents, Lisa is my only visitor, and I'm grateful for her presence.

'Just think about it,' I say. 'She's still your sister.'

'Maybe,' he says, finally picking up his spoon and digging it into his Weetabix.

With half the school summer holidays left, I am running out of things to do to keep Spencer distracted. It would be better if it was term time and he had lessons and homework to occupy him, but by his own admission, these days seem endless. It wasn't this difficult last year when we were all together. That summer flew by.

My mobile rings, and instinctively my stomach clenches when I see it is Noah. I will never give up hoping that he'll forgive me for my lies, but it is too soon; there is still too much hanging over us all.

'How's Spencer?' he asks, not bothering to say hello.

'He's doing okay. How are you? Are you still at the hotel?'

The bill for all these weeks will be eating into Noah's savings, but he would rather that than come home and try to work things out.

He mumbles a yes, and an awkward silence follows.

'Do you want to speak to Spence?' I say.

'Yes, in a second. I, um, we need to talk, don't we?'

'Probably,' I say, unsure whether this is a good or bad thing. 'Go on, then.'

'Not on the phone. And I'm not coming to the house. Can you meet me at my hotel this evening? I should finish work around six, so could you make it for seven?'

I tell him I'll take Spencer to my parents' and seven should be fine, and then without another word about it, he asks me to put Spencer on.

It is a mystery why Noah has picked a hotel in Putney when he works in central London, but I assume it's because he wants to be close to the children, without being too near to me.

Walking in here reminds me of the morning I visited Amelie at her hotel, a day that feels as if it was a million years ago. I spot Noah straightaway, sitting in the corner of the bar, a half-finished gin and tonic in front of him.

He looks different somehow, as if the weeks I haven't seen him have made him a stranger to me. I don't recognise the blue polo shirt he wears, or the loafers on his feet. I have no clue what he is about to say to me, so I take a deep breath and prepare myself for the worst.

'Thanks for coming,' he says as I approach his table. 'Can I get you a drink?' It is too formal, and somehow this is worse than if he would just shout at me and express some emotion.

'Just a black coffee,' I say, and he stands and heads to the bar.

'Why have you asked me here?' I say, when he returns. I don't wait for him to sit, because I've been kept wondering far too long already.

'I just want to hear it from you, because imagining things is twisting my mind. I'm going crazy. I just want the truth, Tara, whatever it is.' His words echo mine to Rosie not long ago.

But I will not make this easy for him. I tried to tell him my side of things at the police station that night Rosie was arrested, but he only walked away. It was only through Spencer I learned that he didn't believe me, that he is convinced something happened between me and Lee.

'Why now? For three weeks you've chosen to believe I was lying about Lee. So what's changed?'

He shrugs. 'I was too angry with you, and it clouded my judgement. But I'm ready now. Ready to hear it all.'

'Well, I'm sorry but it's too late. And do you realise what a hypocrite you are? You lied to me about seeing Amelie that weekend, yet I forgave you. I listened to your explanation and tried to understand it.'

'This is a bit different, Tara. Lee was murdered. And if Rosie did it, then it's because she saw you with him.'

So this is the conclusion he's reached after three weeks of space from me.

'You still think she's guilty?'

'Don't you?'

It is a good question, and one I have silently wrestled with since the police found Lee's ring in her bedroom. But the truth is I just don't know for sure. I want to believe in her innocence, though, so that is what I cling to.

'But the police let her go, Noah.'

'Only because they couldn't make anything stick. Serena said he hadn't worn his wedding ring for ages so he could have lost it, and Rosie could have picked it up from anywhere. That doesn't mean she didn't. . .'

'And her motive is because she found me in bed with him? And, what, couldn't bear the thought of us splitting up again?'

He nods. 'Remember how badly she took our separation last time? How destructive she became? How self-destructive? Wasn't it around that time she developed her fixation on Anthony? So tell me this – how is this any different?'

'Well, I'm not a detective, Noah, I don't have all the answers.'

He takes a long sip of his gin. 'Maybe. . . maybe she was seeing him after all.'

This has also crossed my mind, but again there is no evidence.

'Innocent until proven guilty,' I say. 'And that goes for me too. I did not sleep with Lee. At least not knowingly. I don't know if I was drugged, or if the alcohol caused me to blackout, but I would never have cheated on you.'

He searches my face, but I cannot read what conclusion he is reaching. And now that I'm sitting here in front of him, I no longer care. He should have stood by me, as I would have him. As I'm doing for Rosie. But instead he walked away. We are supposed to be a family, but he turned his back on me, on us, when we should be sticking together. So what is there left for us now?

'Have you seen Rosie?' I ask, although I'm certain he hasn't.

'No. What am I supposed to say to her?'

How ironic that the parent desperate to see her is the one she wants nothing to do with. This makes me even angrier with Noah for wasting an opportunity to bond with his daughter. It is as if he has given up on being her parent.

'You could start by telling her you love her. And that you'll stick by her no matter what.'

He reaches for his glass. 'Even if she's killed someone?'

'Yes, Noah, it's called unconditional love.' But it is easy for me to say this when I don't believe she did it.

'How did we get here?' he says. 'One minute we were fine, and the next. . .'

I don't point out that we were hardly fine. Getting there, maybe, but with a long way left to go.

'There's no point dwelling on it. We need to work together to help Rosie.' An impossible task when she won't even see me. 'You've got to call her, Noah. And see her. She won't talk to me.'

He sighs. 'Okay, fine, I will.' Reaching for his glass, he finishes his drink and looks towards the bar. 'I just need time, Tara. Everything's such a mess, and I can't think straight.'

'I'm not asking you for anything,' I say.

But Noah doesn't hear my words. He carries on mumbling something about things never being the same again.

I stand up and leave, without once looking back.

Approaching the house these days forces me to be on my guard, especially this late at night. Although the reporters and photographers disappeared some time ago, I never know when Guy or Layla will appear – or the shy woman whose name I still don't know – and launch a verbal attack. So when I see a figure sitting on the doorstep, clutching a mobile phone, I am ready.

It is only when I get closer I see it is DCI Hunt. I will never be able to see him without feeling my heart is stopping, and tonight is no exception. He can only be here because there is new evidence.

'Tara,' he says, standing up. 'I apologise for the late hour. Can we go inside?'

'Is Rosie okay? What's happened?'

'This isn't about Rosie. And as far as I'm aware she's okay. But you should know that better than I do.'

Can he really not know she won't see me? I thought it would be his business to know everything to do with the suspects in his case. But I have nothing to lose by being honest.

'I would know that if she'd talk to me, but she hasn't for the last three weeks.'

DCI Hunt frowns. 'Oh, I'm sorry.' But he doesn't admit he didn't know. Is this man playing games with me? 'Look,' he continues, 'can we just go inside?'

'You're asking me as if I have a choice,' I say, pushing my key into the lock.

'Very true,' he says. 'Sorry. You don't really have a choice, but it might be in your best interests to just go with this.'

Inside, I turn on the lights and tell him to go through to the kitchen. 'You've been here enough times to know where it is,' I say.

That produces a half-smile. 'Yes, I have, haven't I?'

'So what is it you need to say? What's going on? This must be serious if you're turning up here after ten o'clock at night.'

'Let's just have a seat, Tara.'

I sit at the table and tell him he's making me nervous by stringing this out.

'Okay,' he says. 'For three weeks I've thought of nothing but this case, to the point where I'm even dreaming about it. I swear, I don't get a second's respite from it.'

'Well, how do you think I feel? And Rosie? Don't try to tell me it's as bad for you. You're just annoyed because you haven't solved it and that won't look good on your record, will it?'

Instead of this angering him, though, he actually offers another thin smile. 'I wish it was just that. But it isn't. And that's why I'm here.'

He's not making any sense.

'Why exactly are you here? If nothing's happened, then—'

But he still doesn't answer my question. 'Do you realise the whole force thinks you're guilty? They're even suggesting you set up your own daughter by planting that ring in her room. Either that or you hid it there, never thinking we would find it.'

I'm not surprised to hear this. It is what I have lived with for three weeks now.

'So arrest me then. Because do you know what I've got on my side? The truth. So I'm not scared.'

He sighs, exasperated by my defiance. 'That's just it, Tara, if you'll give me a chance to speak, I'm trying to tell you that I believe you. I know you didn't kill Lee Jacobs.'

For a second I think I have misheard him. I stare at him, at the face that is too pleasant to be dealing with murder every day. 'What? What did you say?'

He repeats himself, and his words wrap around me, lifting me up.

'So. . . you believe me? I can't tell you how good that feels. But what's changed?'

'Three weeks of analysing every aspect of it, that's what. And it just doesn't make any sense. I've looked into your background, Tara, and I know you weren't involved with Lee. We checked your phone records, and know you got that text from Serena, as you claimed. It's not proof in itself that this is the reason you went over to their house that evening, but I'm trusting my instinct here.'

'What about Rosie? Please tell me you don't think she did it.'

He shakes his head. 'I'm afraid it's not as straightforward as that. Rosie's often been a troubled girl, hasn't she?'

'Yes, but don't try to tell me all troubled kids turn out to be murderers, because that's just laughable. And that can't be your reason to suspect her, surely?'

'No, but—'

'Do you have children, Detective Hunt?'

'No, I—'

'Then you will never understand a parent's instinct. A mother's instinct. I know she didn't kill Lee, just as I know we're sitting here having a conversation at almost eleven o'clock at night. Do you understand me?'

I haven't meant to take out my frustration on him, especially when it seems he's come here to help me, but everything I've been bottling up explodes, and he bears the brunt of it.

To give him credit, he remains calm and lets me have my say, even though I can tell it's killing him to be interrupted in this manner. But then he utters words I don't want to hear.

'I just don't know about your daughter, Tara. I'm sorry. But I promise you one thing – I will help you find out what happened, and I won't stop until we know who killed Lee Jacobs.'

CHAPTER SEVENTEEN

For the first time in over a month I have managed more than a few hours' sleep. DCI Hunt may have his doubts about Rosie, but I don't, and he will soon get to the truth. I trust in him. I can't explain why, perhaps he exudes confidence without being arrogant, and determination seeps through his pores. I am no longer alone with this.

It is tempting to knock on Guy and Layla's door and report this latest development, to see the smug smiles fade from their faces, but that will only let them know that their behaviour has bothered me. No, they will find out soon enough when my name, and Rosie's, are cleared.

Before I've even climbed out of bed I grab my phone and call Lisa, relieved that she sounds happy to hear from me.

'I can't imagine what you're going through,' she says. 'Are you okay without Noah?'

Aware that it makes me sound cold-hearted, I explain that I'm used to it after last time he left, and that it's Rosie's absence which leaves a gaping hole. Noah has gone before, but I have never been apart from my daughter.

'I understand,' Lisa says, 'it must be awful. But, I'm sure she'll come around, and Noah will to. You two are meant to be together. Tara. . . oh, never mind. I just hope you know I'm here for you. Let's meet up today. How about a shopping trip to take your mind off everything? We could go to Westfield.'

I almost laugh, taking her suggestion as a joke, because how can she think I can carry on as normal and go shopping when my family is in shreds? But when I don't say anything, she tells me she's serious.

'You need something normal in your life, something to show you that life will carry on. Trust me, you'll thank me for it after.'

I loathe shopping at the best of times, preferring the ease of doing it all online, but the anonymity of a huge shopping mall is surprisingly tempting. It might do me some good to escape for a few hours, to be surrounded by strangers who have nothing to do with Lee's death. Plus, DCI Hunt will be continuing to investigate, and it's not like I can help him.

'Okay, let's do it,' I say, also touched by her willingness to spend time with me with everything that's going on.

'Great. Meet me there at eleven. I'm hanging up now before you can change your mind.'

But I should know better than to think there will be any escape from this mess until Lee's murderer is caught. Now I am here, under the glare of bright artificial lighting, I realise I have made a mistake. I can't pretend I am just like everyone else here, because my world is as far removed from theirs as it's possible to be, but just as I'm about to text Lisa to ask if we can go somewhere else, she appears and wraps her arms around me.

I breathe in the smell of her perfume – one I haven't noticed her wear before – and squeeze her tightly.

'You'll be fine,' she says. 'Come on, let's get a coffee. I doubt you're in the mood to shop.'

Once we've sat down, Lisa pulls out her phone.

'I'm just texting Harvey. He doesn't know where I am and I don't want him to worry.'

'It sounds as if things are better between you both now?' I ask, hoping for some good news. Our family needs it.

She smiles. 'Oh, yeah. We're working things out. I want it to work and it's about time I settled down, isn't it? And, well. . . he's a good guy, Tara, and they're a rare species it seems.'

When she says this I think of Noah. How I felt exactly this way about him in the beginning. Why do people have to change, and let you down?

'And I've also been thinking that, yes, one day – not just yet, of course – but one day, maybe, I would like to be a mum. But that's a few years in the future.'

It is impossible not to think of Serena, and the baby she wanted so much, when Lisa says this, and of course that takes me right back to Lee, as everything does eventually. But I have become an expert at pushing these thoughts away when there is something I need to focus on.

'Well, I'm happy you want to put down some roots,' I say.

'Thanks, sis. But anyway, that's more than enough about me. Tell me what's happening with Rosie.'

The coffee shop is getting busier now, but this means louder background noise, so I don't have to keep my voice down.

'She still won't talk to me. I text her every day, morning and night to let her know I'm thinking of her, but she never replies.'

Lisa shakes her head. 'It sounds like she just needs some time and distance from you all. Perhaps she feels ashamed?'

'Of what?'

'Well, that she talked to the police about you to get herself off the hook.'

But this doesn't make sense – Rosie always knows exactly what she's doing, she is too calculated to have simply panicked. And if she regretted her decision then surely she would have contacted me to tell me this.

'That's true,' Lisa says, once I've explained this to her. 'Then maybe – and sorry to say this – it could be about you spending the night with your neighbour? That's got to have messed with her.'

I cringe to hear Lisa say this. 'But I've told her nothing happened.'

Lisa's eyes widen. 'Oh, so you have spoken to her?'

'No, she wouldn't see me so I had to send her a text explaining everything.'

'Give her time,' Lisa says. 'I think that's all you can do. But it's nice that you're texting her every day. It shows her you love and support her.'

I take a sip of coffee and watch Lisa do the same. 'I need to ask you something.'

'Go on. You know you can ask me anything.'

'Do you think Rosie had anything to do with Lee's murder?'

Lisa avoids looking at me now, and stares at a couple with a newborn baby who have just walked in. 'I. . . I'm sorry, Tara, I just don't know what to think. It just. . . doesn't look good. But it doesn't matter, because I'm still her aunt and I still love her.'

'It's okay,' I say, 'you don't have to be worried about telling me what you think. I asked you a question and you answered it. What about Mum and Dad? What do they say about it?'

'They adore Rosie, you know that, and never could see her as anything other than perfect.'

This is true, she is their first grandchild and they've always been sucked in by her, never able to see her behaviour as difficult, even when they are the ones she's making problems for.

'But,' Lisa continues, 'I think this time they might actually be worried. It's the wedding ring they can't get their heads around, and to be honest, that's what's bothering me too.'

And me, but I am determined to find an explanation for it. 'The police say that's not evidence of her doing anything,' I say.

And then I tell Lisa about DCI Hunt visiting last night, and the vindication he offered me.

'Well, that's good to hear, but I never doubted you,' Lisa says. 'Not once.'

'I really appreciate that. When everyone turns their back on you it's hard to believe there's anyone left in your corner.'

'It's so awful. I'm so sorry I haven't been there for you as much as I could have these last few weeks. It's just been a bit tricky, what with Harvey moving in and everything.'

I almost choke on my coffee. 'What? Harvey's moved in? When? That's great, Lisa. Why didn't you tell me?'

'How could I share such happy news when you were going through hell? I wanted to wait a bit.'

Tears form in the corners of my eyes. 'I'm sorry, you shouldn't have had to keep quiet.' I lean across the table and hug her. 'I'm really happy for you.'

'Well, it took me a while to work out what I wanted but this just feels right.'

'It's wonderful ne—'

But Lisa is no longer listening. She is staring at her phone, a frown on her face. 'Oh, Tara, I'm so sorry but I have to go,' she says, tapping away at the screen. 'It's an emergency and Harvey needs me. Um, I'll call you. So sorry.' She stands up and leans down to kiss me on the cheek. 'Please try not to worry about anything.'

Although I'm not too surprised by her early exit – Lisa is always on the go – I feel disappointed that she didn't tell me exactly what was going on. I still can't believe Harvey has moved in with her so soon, but it does sound as though they've worked things out.

Once she's gone, though, rather than head home myself, I decide to browse the shops, and buy a nice top for Rosie. I can drop it off at Bernadette's, and even though I'm sure Rosie still won't see me, she'll at least know I'm thinking of her.

But a couple of hours later, I am still finding my way around the gigantic mall, feeling out of my depth, with no clue what shop to look in, and there is no hope of me finding anything suitable for Rosie.

I'm about to give up and go home when I notice a familiar figure heading towards me. I recognise his walk long before he reaches me, but still I don't move fast enough to get away without being spotted.

Within seconds, Mikey Bradford is standing in front of me, beaming, as if he's just won the lottery.

'Tara! I can't believe you're here,' he says. 'What a coincidence.'

But I have lost my ability to believe anything just happens at random. Especially where Mikey is concerned. 'What are you doing here?' I ask, glancing around me as if I'll find something to help me get away from him.

'Oh, I always come here. It's far enough from the school to ensure I don't bump into any of the kids.' He laughs to himself. 'Hey, I'm sorry to hear about your husband.'

My insides turn cold. How does he know about Noah moving out? I don't answer, hoping he'll take this as a hint to drop the subject.

'I've got to go,' I say, but he reaches out his arm to stop me.

'Now that we're both here, why don't we get a coffee? There's a Costa not far from here.'

'No, I really have to go. Sorry, Mikey.' And I turn and head off as quickly as I can, feeling his eyes on me until I turn the corner.

Just as I'm getting my head around what's just happened, my phone rings and I'm surprised to see it's Lisa. 'I'm so sorry about rushing off,' she says. 'I feel awful about it. And I was the one who invited you out.'

'Oh, please don't worry, but are you okay?'

'Oh, yeah, sorry, Harvey just locked himself out and needs to get something urgent for work. His USB stick. He was in a huge panic so I thought I'd better get back quickly. Still took me nearly an hour, though.'

'Well, I'm glad it's all sorted.'

'Are you okay, Tara? You don't sound right.'

I tell her about bumping into Mikey, and what a shock it was to see him here. 'He's a colleague of mine, a science teacher, and just always seems to be following me around at school. He even turned up at the house a few weeks ago when I took a day off work. He's just a bit. . . intense?' I look behind me to make sure he's not still around.

'So let me get this straight,' Lisa says. 'He's stalking you or something?'

I have never thought of the Mikey situation in these terms, probably because he is nothing like how Rosie was with Anthony. 'I don't think so,' I tell Lisa.

'Well, it sounds like it to me. Hey, do you think he knew you were going there today?'

'No, that's impossible. How could he have known?'

'I don't know, it's just a bit weird, that's all.'

'But Westfield's a popular place. Loads of people come here from all over. Is it that strange?' I want her to reassure me, but the more we talk about this, the more I realise she could be right.

'What about his mentioning Noah? I find that a bit weird. It's a very personal thing to say, Tara.'

I explain to her that Mikey does sometimes overstep social boundaries, but he doesn't mean any harm.

'I hope you're right,' she says. 'Anyway, I didn't just call to apologise, I called to tell you you're coming for dinner tonight. I won't have you sitting around worrying on your own.'

I try to protest but she won't take no for an answer, so I am forced to agree.

And while I head to my car, I constantly glance over my shoulder, expecting Mikey to reappear at any moment.

* * *

It is strange to see Lisa's flat filled with Harvey's belongings. Every available space is now crammed with CDs, DVDs and books, so that I can barely spot Lisa's possessions in the midst of the chaos.

Harvey notices me eyeing his things. 'Looks a bit different in here now, doesn't it? Slightly more masculine I reckon.' He is cooking tonight, and smiles proudly, as if he is right where he's always wanted to be.

'I'm happy for you both,' I say, still not sure this is true. How did Lisa go from thinking things weren't working to letting Harvey move in? 'Something smells good,' I say, to change the subject. 'What is it we're having?'

'It's a chilli dish I love to cook,' he says, once again flashing that proud smile. 'Sit down, won't you? Here, try this, it's lovely.'

He tries to hand me a glass of wine but I hold up my hand to stop him. 'I, um, sorry, I don't really. . . feel like alcohol at the moment.'

He frowns. 'Oh, sorry, I didn't realise you don't drink.'

I feel the weight of Lisa's eyes on me, because she knows my reason, but I don't need to share this with Harvey. 'Sorry.'

Harvey holds up his hand. 'Oh, no need to apologise. It won't go to waste.' He pauses for a moment. 'I hope you don't mind me bringing this up but I hope Thomas is helping with your situation? He's a good man – his parents are friends of my parents so we've grown up together.'

As the solicitor is assisting Rosie, and I have my own solicitor now, I have heard nothing from Thomas. 'Well, I don't know because she won't see me.'

Harvey shakes his head. 'I know, Lisa told me. I hope you don't mind. But, please, if there's anything I can do – anything at all – don't hesitate to ask me.'

I don't know whether to be annoyed or pleased with this. I never told Lisa to keep anything to herself, but it's not like her to talk about personal family things. I glance at her but she is busy preparing a salad, and doesn't look up.

'Thanks, Harvey. I appreciate that,' I say. And then I change the subject and ask him about work, remembering that last time it kept him busy with Noah for most of the evening.

But tonight it only works for a short while, and by the time we've finished dinner, he is asking me about Noah.

'It's such a shame,' he says, ignoring Lisa shaking her head. 'You've been together such a long time, isn't it worth trying to work things out?'

It irritates me that Harvey is asking such a personal question, but for the sake of my sister I bite my tongue. They are just starting out and I don't want to cause any tension between them. 'I don't know. I can't think about that right now, there's too much else going on.'

'Of course,' Harvey says, taking a bite of his food.

'Let's talk about something else,' Lisa says. 'Tara seems to have acquired a stalker.' Her hand flies to her mouth as soon as she's said this. 'Oh, sorry, Tara.'

Until this moment I had almost forgotten about seeing Mikey.

'A stalker, eh?' Harvey says, grinning. 'Who's this, then?'

'Oh, he's not really a stalker, just a teacher at my school who just happened to be at Westfield at the same time as me. It's no big deal.'

'I'm still a bit worried, though, Tara,' Lisa says. 'Turning up at your house uninvited is just weird.'

'He did that?' Harvey asks.

'Only once,' I say. 'He was just worried because I'd taken a day off school and I never do that. But he did buy me flowers.'

'Oh, I didn't realise that,' Lisa says. 'That must make it worse.'

Harvey twists his mouth. 'You should be careful, Tara. I had a friend who was stalked and, I have to say, it was a terrifying experience for her. She was even scared for her life at one point. But the police didn't do much about stalking at that time so she just suffered in silence. They're much better now, though, I'm sure.'

'Actually,' Lisa says, 'Harvey has a good point. You should tell the police about him, just so they're aware.'

'But he hasn't done anything,' I protest.

'I just worry about you,' Lisa says. 'Especially now that Noah's not living there. It's just you and Spence, and what if he turns up again?'

'I can handle Mikey, don't worry about me. He's harmless.'

But for the rest of the evening I am on edge because, the truth is, how well do we ever know anyone?

CHAPTER EIGHTEEN

'I need to speak to you. It's important. Do you think you could you come over?'

There is a long pause, and my nerves are shattered as I wait for DCI Hunt's reply. What makes me think I can ask this of him when my daughter is a suspect in a murder case?

Finally, he speaks, his voice hushed. 'Is this about Rosie?'

'Yes. Well, not exactly, but it's important.'

Of course he won't come; he is a busy detective, trying to solve a murder, so he doesn't have time to waste on my unfounded fears.

'I'm tied up at the moment,' he says, 'but I can be there this evening. Around seven?'

And now it is my turn to fall silent because how can it be as easy as that?

But I thank him before he can change his mind, disconnecting the call, and hugging my phone to my chest. I hope I'm doing the right thing.

Spencer shuffles downstairs and finds me in the hall. 'Hi, Mum,' he says, his tone sad, much as it has been since Noah and Rosie left. He no longer bounds down the stairs to start his day early, and I can't remember the last time he asked to watch a DVD. I need to put this right.

'Hi, Spence.' I give him a hug, but he barely reciprocates. 'Shall we do something together today? Go swimming perhaps? Or to the cinema?'

His reaction is not what I've hoped for. 'That sounds nice, Mum, but remember Ryan asked if I could go out with them. They're going to Chessington World of Adventures. You said I could go, remember. Can I?'

Guilt swamps me because I have no memory of this promise. Once again I have been so consumed with Rosie that my son has suffered. My first reaction is to say no. I should be the one taking him to a theme park, not his friend's mother. But then I realise it would be good for him to have some space from me for the day. To not be reminded that our family has been ripped apart.

'I suppose that's okay. Is Ryan's mum picking you up or should I drop you at theirs?'

'They're picking me up at ten. I told you a few days ago. Mum? Are you okay?'

'Don't worry about me, Spence, I'm fine. I've just got a lot on my mind.'

'I know you miss Dad and Rosie. But it will all be okay, Mum.'

Later that morning, once Spencer has gone, I do what I should have done weeks ago and drive to Bernadette and Libby's house. There is a less than slim chance Rosie will agree to see me, but I can't let any more time go by without trying. Although I didn't manage to buy her a new top, I stop at the corner shop and buy her favourite chocolate bar. At least I won't be spoiling her with such a simple item.

Bernadette answers the door, and her face drops when she sees me. 'Oh, Tara, hi. Um. . .'

'I know I shouldn't be here but I really need to see Rosie. It's been three weeks and I miss her so much. Can I come in? I won't stay long.'

She makes no move to let me in. 'Rosie and Libby are out. They've gone out with a few friends from school. I'm sorry.'

I am about to turn away when she reaches for my arm.

'But why don't you come in anyway? I can let you know how Rosie's doing.'

Inside we sit in the living room and an awkward silence hangs around us. Although Bernadette has invited me in, she now seems reluctant to discuss anything.

'Thank you for having Rosie,' I say. 'Please let me give you some money towards her food and everything else.'

'No, no, I won't accept it. She's been Libby's friend for years so there's no need to give me anything. You've had Libby over at your house enough times, haven't you?'

Saying thank you just doesn't seem enough, but I do it anyway, and tell her if Rosie needs anything at all then I will provide it.

'How's she doing, Bernadette?'

She looks at me for a minute without answering, so I know something is wrong. 'To be honest, Tara, I don't think she's doing well. And I have tried to get her to call you, or even text, but, well, you know how stubborn she is.'

'What makes you say this, apart from the obvious, that is? Has something happened?' I hold my breath.

Bernadette sighs. 'I don't know how to explain this because it's not something I can pinpoint, but I've been getting the feeling the girls aren't as close as they used to be. Since this all happened.'

I consider this for a moment. Rosie was arrested for murder and, whether or not she's now free, it will still hang over her. Perhaps Libby is finding that hard to deal with.

But when I mention my theory to Bernadette she shakes her head.

'I don't think it's that. I've spoken at length to Libby about it, and she swears Rosie is innocent. But the other day I heard them arguing, and I didn't catch the whole conversation but I'm sure it was about a boy.'

That feeling of dread hits me again, one I should have become accustomed to by now with Rosie. But this time it's far worse. 'Tell me,' I say. 'What did you hear exactly?'

'Libby said Rosie was being selfish, and that nobody was her property, something like that. Then she said something about Rosie having no rights to him. The conversation ended after that because Libby stormed out and went to the bathroom.'

I try to make sense of this. Taken out of context, the words have little meaning, and I'm reminded of Noah's insistence on not jumping to conclusions.

'Did you ask Libby about it?'

'Yes, I did, but she said she didn't know what I was talking about.'

My head spins. Is there no end to all the lies? Libby has always been such a sweet, honest girl.

'So I just let it go,' Bernadette continues. 'But there is definitely tension between them, and today is the first time in days they've been out together. Rosie's just been going off on her own.'

This is the first time I've heard this. 'Where's she been going? I wish you'd told me.'

'Sorry, Tara, but I can't text you every time Rosie goes out. She's nearly eighteen, and my life is busy enough already. I've got twin boys to look after as well as Libby.'

And now Rosie. Quickly I apologise, because I have been unfair. Rosie is not Bernadette's responsibility, she is mine.

Bernadette leans forward, resting her elbows on her legs so she can cup her head in her hands. 'This must be really hard for you. I can't imagine how I'd feel if Libby had been arrested like that. What must go through your mind? It must be terrifying.'

'I can't even begin to describe it,' I say, and I'm being as honest as I can. All I have felt is a horrifying numbness.

She watches me and starts to open her mouth before closing it again. I know exactly what she wants to ask me.

'The worst part of all this is when I start to doubt her. It doesn't happen often, but I'd be lying if I didn't wonder, however briefly, if she could have done that to Lee.'

Bernadette lets out a small gasp. 'I had no idea what you were wrestling with. Of course you would wonder, especially given Rosie's. . . previous troubles.'

'How about you? You've taken her in when most people avoid her – and all of us – at all costs, so haven't you ever wondered?'

After a brief pause she answers. 'I'm going to be honest with you, Tara: yes, I have worried about it. Even when Libby was adamant that Rosie couldn't have done it, I've had my doubts from time to time. But I have to trust in the police, and they've let her go, so that's good enough for me.'

I thank her for her time and leave without mentioning that they have only let her go because the evidence against her wasn't strong enough to pursue a conviction, or that every minute they're working to try to prove she did it.

When I pull up to the house it is nearly two p.m. I am counting the hours until DCI Hunt gets here, and part of me wonders if what I'm most looking forward to is having some company. From anyone. The people who want to spend time with me these days are few and far between.

It is only when I get out of the car that I see her, heading up her driveway with two large suitcases. Serena is back. She never replied to my text all those weeks ago so I haven't heard from her since Rosie and I were arrested.

I should turn around and walk into the house, pretend I haven't seen her, and accept that we will never speak again. But even as I think this, my feet carry me towards her, out of my control. I know this is wrong. I should avoid her; this can only end in more trouble. But I have to explain. She has to know I did nothing with Lee, nothing I have any knowledge of.

She whips around when she hears me behind her, and drops her cases to the ground when she realises it is me. 'Get away from me,' she says. 'I've got nothing to say to you. Just leave me alone.'

But of course I can't do that. 'Serena, please, just hear me out. I need. . .' But what do I need? Her forgiveness for lying to her? Her to tell me that she believes Rosie and I are both innocent? Now that I'm standing here, on her property, I realise I have no right to ask her for anything.

But still I cannot let this go. Perhaps I am as stubborn as my daughter. 'I'm not leaving until you listen to me.'

She pulls out her mobile, but I grab her hand.

'Please, Serena. Call the police if you want to, it won't be as bad as when they questioned me before.'

Shaking free of my grasp, she shakes her head. 'Why should I give you even a second of my time? You're the last person I owe anything to. Why should I even listen to you after what you did? You came to my house and pretended to be there for me when all the time you'd. . .' She turns away from me, and swipes at her eyes.

'Don't you want to know the truth, or at least what I know of it? Please, just hear what I've got to say, and then you never have to see me again.' This is the best I've got. I don't want to give up but if it doesn't work I will have to admit defeat. I can't stand here all day harassing her.

She spits her words at me. 'Well, that's a bit hard when you live right across from me.'

This is good. At least she is talking to me now. 'Does that mean you've come back?' I glance at her cases.

'Why shouldn't I? This is my home, and I have the right to be in it.'

But how can she when her husband was murdered here? How can she walk in his footsteps every day, and wonder what happened, wonder who, other than me, came into their house that night? I know I could never do it.

'Of course you do. Look, I don't want to argue, I just want to tell you that nothing happened with Lee. I wasn't seeing him, or doing anything with him that night or any time before that. I'm not the woman he was seeing, Serena, if that's true.'

She hesitates. 'Of course it's true. I showed you the watch, didn't I?'

But I have learned that even evidence can't always be trusted. 'Well, I can't comment on that. All I know is it wasn't me. I don't know how I ended up in your bed, but I know I didn't kill Lee.'

'You can't know that!' she screams. Any second now faces will appear at the window next door.

'Serena, I had no blood on me, nothing. So, other than the fact I know I couldn't do that to anyone, yes, I do know.'

'If it wasn't you, Tara, then it was Rosie. But of course you will defend your daughter, even if you know she's done something this. . . this. . . horrendous. And that makes you as guilty as she is.'

'You can't make up your mind, can you? One minute you think it was me, then you're convinced it's Rosie. The police have let both of us go, Serena. That should tell you something.'

'We both know why that is, though, don't we, Tara? They just need more evidence. So your temporary freedom doesn't mean anything. Make the most of it, won't you?'

I understand her anger, so I take the bullets she fires at me. 'I know you miss Lee; I know how awful this is for you—'

'Miss him?' She throws her head back. 'You couldn't be more wrong. I'm glad to—'

'Serena? Are you okay? Is she upsetting you?' Layla's voice booms out and within seconds she barges past me to stand beside Serena, draping her spindly arm across her shoulder. 'You don't have to talk to her,' she says, 'let's go inside.' And in one quick motion she hauls Serena's suitcases to the front door and bustles her inside.

But before she follows her in, she comes back out, striding towards me until her face is barely centimetres from mine.

'Why can't you just leave her alone? Haven't you done enough already? What is wrong with you?'

Today has been a day of doing things I probably shouldn't, and right now is no exception. For years I have been holding back, forcing myself to be polite to this hideous woman who only cares about herself and her tiny world. But it stops now.

'I'm not the one with the problem, though, am I, Layla? Is your life really so sad that you have to get involved in everyone else's business? You're enjoying this, aren't you? The fact that Lee is dead so you can rush around rescuing Serena. There's finally something to give you a purpose. Well, it's disgusting.'

I could carry on, but the expression on her face changes, the assertive woman she usually is has gone, so I know my words have got to her.

She heads back inside, but before closing the door she calls out to me. Of course she does, because she will be desperate to have the last say. 'Come anywhere near her – or me – again and I'll call the police.' And then she slams the door, the vibration echoing into the street.

But this is okay. I have got more than I needed.

CHAPTER NINETEEN

'There's something not right about Serena,' I say, as soon as DCI Hunt has stepped through the door. He's dressed as he always is, in an expensive suit that contradicts his unkempt hair and stubble. I wonder if this look is a deliberate choice, or if he is just too busy to shave or get his hair cut. I also wonder if he knows he can get away with it because of his attractive features beneath all the hair.

'Of course there's something not right with her – her husband was murdered.'

He loosens his tie.

I recall the first time I saw DCI Hunt – he was with Serena at her parents' house, looking after her. They seemed close, and she spoke fondly of him, so how much can I trust this man with what I'm about to say?

'I mean apart from that.' I realise I'm not explaining myself very well. 'Come and sit down, and I'll tell you what I'm thinking.'

The living room, as usual, is too warm, but I am reluctant to open a window. Perhaps I am being paranoid, but I don't know who might overhear us. It would not surprise me if Layla or Guy had seen the detective arrive and were right now out in their garden, hoping to find out what's going on.

'It was something she said today,' I tell DCI Hunt. 'She said—'

'Woah, wait a minute. You spoke to Serena?'

'Yes, she came back today, and I ran into her.'

He frowns. 'You ran into her? Hmmm. And she spoke to you?'

Ignoring his disbelief, I tell him she only spoke reluctantly, but I managed to get a few words out of her.

He leans forward, once more pulling at his tie. 'So I'm not sure exactly what you're trying to say here, Tara. Can you be more specific?'

I try my best to articulate what I'm thinking without it sounding absurd.

'She hates Lee. But they were married for years, and trying for a baby for as long as I've known her, so how is it that she now can't even say a good word about him?'

DCI Hunt frowns again. 'I'd say her feelings are perfectly understandable given that he had an affair.'

'But even so, it was just what she said before we got interrupted by Layla Watts. I'm sure she was about to say she was glad he's dead.'

'Tara, I still don't think that's unreasonable, especially when someone's grieving. It changes you. But are you trying to suggest she did it? Because that's a stretch, and we've already checked out her alibi. There's nothing to suggest she had anything to do with it.'

I lean back, my head sinking into the sofa. 'I don't know. It was just a feeling I got. The thing is, she was at a hen-do but, once everyone went to their rooms, how do you know she didn't sneak out and come back here?' This has only just occurred to me, but now that I've said it, it makes perfect sense.

'There's no evidence of that,' he says. 'Her alibi checked out, Tara. Look, I understand why you want answers so desperately. You're doing this because you don't want to believe it was Rosie. I get that but—'

'What if Lee wasn't having an affair?'

He shakes his head. 'You know about the watch. I'd say that's pretty conclusive.'

'Hear me out. What if. . . I know this will sound far-fetched, but what if she made up that he was having an affair and got the watch engraved as evidence?'

There is a pause as he considers what I've said, and long seconds tick by. 'But why would she do that? Her husband having an affair would immediately make her a suspect.'

'But not when her alibi is watertight, as you've said. I have to be honest, I'm only just thinking out loud, but surely it's worth exploring? I'm not trying to tell you how to do your job, please know that. I just want the truth.' I have probably overstepped a line here, becoming too informal, too quickly, with the man who only weeks ago arrested me for murder.

But he doesn't seem angry or annoyed by my comments. 'You do realise this is all my job to figure out, not yours, don't you?' he says. 'This isn't some film or book where you can just solve a crime before the police do. That's not reality, Tara.' His tone is not unkind, but I sense the underlying warning to stay out of it.

'Can I just say one thing? By making it look like Lee was having an affair, Serena has given you a suspect. And right now, that's still my daughter.'

He sighs, and I sense I have worn him down. 'Okay, Tara, I'll tell you what I'll do. I will check out the hotel Serena stayed at again, but you have to know, every second I focus on her means whoever did this is another step further away. The trail has already run cold—' Suddenly he stops and stares at his shoes.

'What's the matter? What is it?'

He shakes his head, and a different expression crosses his face. 'I shouldn't be telling you all this. You're still not completely out of the clear as a suspect yourself, and your daughter certainly isn't.'

'Then why are you?'

He shrugs. 'Call me crazy, but I've always trusted my instinct, and you are not a murderer.'

And for the first time in weeks I smile, a real smile that spreads from inside and travels through my body. 'Don't they only say that in books or films?' I say.

He laughs. 'Well, you've got me there. But like I said, I will check out Serena's alibi again, but don't get your hopes up. It's a real shot in the dark, Tara.'

I thank him and offer him a drink.

'No, I'm all coffeed out, and I need to get going. So is this all you wanted to talk to me about?'

Mikey. I have almost forgotten about him since talking to Serena. 'Actually no. There was something, but it's unrelated to this.'

'Oh? I'm intrigued.'

For the next few minutes I tell him all about Mikey, and Lisa's suspicions about him, adding that I don't share the same concerns. And as I speak, his expression is impassive, so it is hard to tell whether he thinks worrying about Mikey is an over-reaction.

'Well, it's difficult to make a judgement just on what you've told me, but if you like I can check him out for you?'

'You would do that for me?' Suddenly I am filled with doubts about DCI Hunt. Why would he help me in this way when it is nothing to do with him? 'But it's probably not something someone of your rank would normally get involved in, is it?'

'That's true.' He stares at me for a moment. 'But I'll do it anyway. In my own free time, though, so it could take a while. But let me know if he does anything worse.'

For now, I will put my misgivings aside. 'Thank you so much, DCI Hunt, I really appreciate this.'

He offers a thin smile. 'It's a bit of a mouthful to keep calling me DCI Hunt. Maybe you should just call me Holden.'

* * *

When Spencer comes home, he is surprised to find me in a better state. 'Has something happened?' he asks. 'Are Dad and Rosie coming home?'

My heart aches at having to let him down again. 'No, it's not that. But I think things will get better, Spence. Just hang in there.'

He doesn't reply, so I know he's not convinced. The best thing I can do is distract him by asking him about his trip to Chessington.

'Oh, Mum, I get what you're doing, and you really don't have to. Like you said, things will get better. Anyway, can I watch a film in my room on Dad's iPad?'

There is no reason for me to say no. It's the summer holidays and Spencer has no homework, plus it's not too late. But more than that, I am pleased he seems to be getting back to his old self. As far as that's possible.

'Yes, you can. But it's not going to be a habit, okay?' I add in this last bit to demonstrate a sense of normality. It is what I would have said before all this happened.

He thanks me and rushes off, and I am grateful to hear his footsteps pounding on the stairs. For now, at least, he is happy enough.

I have come to realise it is rarely a good thing when someone knocks on your door this late, so when I hear the thud, I am tempted not to answer. But then I realise it could be DCI Hunt – Holden – and that maybe he's forgotten to ask me something important. Besides, it's been a while since any of the neighbours set foot on our property and, after my confrontation with Layla, I'm hoping she wouldn't dare again.

The one person I'm not expecting to see when I open the door is Rosie. Somehow she looks older, taller even; a different girl to the one I last saw the day we were both arrested. I open my mouth but no words come out.

'Hi Mum,' she says. 'I don't have my key.' Next to her is a huge travel bag I've never seen before. This can only mean one thing.

'Are you. . . coming home?'

'Can I?'

'Of course you can. This is your home.'

It is not the reunion I have imagined. I inch forward, desperate to reach out and hug her, but something stops me. My instinct. She does not want me to do it. So instead I lean down and grab her bag, hauling it inside.

She follows me in without a word, staring around her as if she's never been here before. 'It seems different,' she says. 'What's changed?'

'Nothing's changed, Rosie.' But really, everything has. Neither of us are the same people we were the last time we stood together in this hallway.

'I'm ready to talk now, Mum. About everything. I'm going to be honest for once because I'm sick of all the lies. My lies. And yours.'

Once I'm sure Spencer is occupied with his film, I join Rosie in the kitchen. She has made me a coffee, and the mug sits alone on the table – strangely out of place when she hasn't got herself a drink.

'Are you glad I'm home?' she says. She has already made herself at home, and sits with her feet up on the opposite chair.

Fighting the urge to comment on this, I tell her I've wanted nothing more for all these weeks, and wait for a smile, or anything, to show she is glad to hear me say this. But her expression remains unreadable.

'Even though I could be a murderer?'

'Don't say that.'

'But it's true, Mum. How do you know I didn't kill Lee?'

'I don't know what to tell you, Rosie. I know because I'm your mother. That's how. It's probably not what you want to hear, but it's all I've got.'

She fans out her hands on the table, and I stare at her bright pink nail polish.

'Fair enough.'

'So tell me everything, Rosie.'

She leans back and takes a deep breath, giving me the first inclination that she is nervous tonight. 'I've done a lot of thinking since I moved out, and, well, I like to think I've grown up a bit. It's about time, isn't it?'

Can she really expect me to believe she has changed in a matter of weeks? I don't respond, but wait for her to continue. I have heard promises like this from her many times before.

She examines her hands. 'I've never admitted this before but I was obsessed with Anthony. I know it was obvious to everyone, but I just couldn't bring myself to admit it, because I felt ashamed. So it seemed easier to keep up the pretence that we were together.'

For months I have wanted to hear her say this, to have confirmation that Rosie can see reality. There are a million questions I want to ask her, but I will let her finish first.

'I think I just needed someone, Mum. It felt so good that he liked me, was interested in everything I had to say, even if it was only for those few days. I don't know what I did wrong, why he lost interest, but something put him off.'

When she says this I want to reach for her and hold her tightly, because in this moment she seems so vulnerable. But I still don't know how she would react to a hug.

'Rosie, if a boy doesn't like you, it's not because there's anything wrong with you, or you've done anything wrong, it's just the law of attraction. You just weren't right for each other. It has nothing to do with looks, or personality even, it's just about whether two people are meant to be together.'

'Mum, that sounds—'

'I know how it sounds, but it's true.'

'Anyway,' she continues, 'I've been thinking about why I needed him, or someone, so badly, and. . . I'm sorry to say this but I think it's because of you and Dad.'

My chest tightens as she says this, but I need to stay calm. 'How is that?'

'I don't want to sound like a spoilt brat, who claims to never have any attention, because that's not what I mean, but since Spencer came along, I've just felt so. . . inadequate. It's like he can do no wrong, and I'm just the troublemaker. Well, I think that just made me live up to that role even more.'

As much as it hurts to hear this, I need to try to understand. 'Why didn't you talk to me before? If I'd known how you felt I could have done something about it.'

She shakes her head. 'I just couldn't. I couldn't even acknowledge it to myself, so how could I have told you? But I'm telling you now. That's the important thing, isn't it?'

It is difficult not to defend myself, but I don't want Rosie to shut down, not when this is the most I've ever got out of her. 'Okay, I'm listening.'

'Anyway, it didn't stop after it all blew up with Anthony, and the police warned me to stay away from him.'

Although I am desperate to hear this, part of me wants her to stop talking because suddenly I fear what she's about to tell me. 'You mean you didn't leave Anthony alone?'

She shakes her head. 'No, I did leave him alone. But my focus moved to someone else.'

We both stare at each other, neither one needing to hear his name. Lee. It couldn't be anyone else.

'Tell me what happened.'

'It started at the barbeque. I told you that Lee was flirting with me, but he wasn't.' She looks away from me. 'It was me who was flirting with him.'

'And. . . he didn't respond?'

'No. He wasn't interested at all. I was just a stupid kid to him.'

Relief floods through me because it has been destroying me to think he might have done something with my daughter, or even that he wanted to. 'So he never invited you upstairs to his bedroom?'

She looks away. 'No. I invited myself. But he said no way.'

Something niggles away at me: the conversation I had with Spencer where he almost said something but stopped himself. 'Did Spencer know you felt this way about Lee?'

Rosie shrugs. 'I don't know. He's never said anything but he might have overheard me talking to Lee once and guessed.'

I don't know whether to be annoyed with Spencer that he didn't tell me about this or pleased that he respects people's privacy.

'What about Damien?' I ask. 'How does he fit into this?'

'He's just company, Mum. I was never really that serious about him. How could I be when Lee was all I could think about?'

I shake my head. 'Why did you lie, Rosie? After Lee died, why did you turn him into a monster?'

There are tears in her eyes now, and I am torn between wanting to shout at her and comfort her.

'Because I was angry with him. Not just for rejecting me, but for you being with him that night. You were drinking together, and you both just looked so happy. I knew you were together. . . well, I thought you were. That's what it looked like.'

'Rosie, what are you trying to tell me? Just say it.'

'I ran, Mum. I was so upset and angry with you both so I just ran. Damien was waiting for me in the car. He parked up on the next road, by the nursery school. I swear to you I didn't do anything to either of you. I don't know what happened to you, but it wasn't me.'

'Are you saying you spent the whole night in a car?'

She nods. 'I think I fell asleep, though, and Damien too, because I don't remember it being that long. And then we just drove around for ages before I could bring myself to come home. Please, Mum, you have to believe me.'

Rosie has asked me this too many times. She has begged me to believe her, only for me to find out she has lied, sooner or later. But this time I do believe her. Reaching across the table, I grab her hand and hold it in mine. I have forgotten how small and delicate her hands are.

'I do. This time, I really do. But we need to find Damien, Rosie. He is your proof.'

Her tears flood out then, dropping onto the table like rain pelting the ground, and her 'thank you' is barely a whisper. Minutes pass before she composes herself, dabbing her cheeks and rubbing at her eyes. 'I know. But, Mum, I'm really scared.'

'I know you are, but we'll be okay. We just have to explain all this to the police.'

'No, it's not that. It's the ring. Lee's wedding ring. I didn't take it, Mum. I swear to you. Which means someone deliberately put it in my room.'

CHAPTER TWENTY

The next morning, I watch Rosie and Spencer sitting together on the sofa, watching a cartoon that must have been Spencer's choice, and my spirits soar. We are still in a lot of trouble, and Noah's absence continues to leave a gaping hole, but for the first time I am convinced this will all work out.

'Does this mean Dad's coming home too?' Spencer asks. His eyes are wide and eager, and I hate to let him down.

Rosie glances at me, then leans in closer to Spencer. 'I miss him too, but I don't think that's going to happen, at least not right now. Isn't that right, Mum?'

I don't know how she's reached this conclusion when I haven't even mentioned Noah, but there will be no more lies.

'I'm afraid so, Spence. But you can see him whenever you want. In fact, why don't I call him this morning to see if he can take both of you out after work?'

Rosie nods her agreement while Spencer remains silent, turning back to his cartoon.

Later, when Rosie is upstairs, I sneak to Spencer's room to check on him. I find him sitting on his bed, playing a game on Noah's iPad. It has completely slipped my mind to take it back.

'I don't trust her, Mum. She's being weird.'

'What do you mean?' I ask, clearing a space at the end of his bed so I can sit down. 'You were both watching TV together earlier. I thought you wanted things back to normal?'

'I do, but this isn't the normal Rosie. She's being too nice. It's not like her and it's freaking me out. I want. . . the old Rosie back.'

Spencer doesn't know what Rosie revealed to me last night, but I won't tell him now; I need to make sense of it myself first. He has already had to hear far too much for an eleven-year-old.

'She's just trying to make an effort,' I say. 'But don't worry, I'm sure in a few days she'll be back to normal, fighting and arguing with us.'

'Okay.' He flings his legs over the side of the bed and pulls on his trainers. 'Can I go to Ryan's?'

It hasn't escaped my notice that Spencer seems to be spending more time at his friend's house than here at home, but perhaps it is for the best at the moment.

'Yes, that's fine. But be back by five because your dad's finishing work early to pick you both up.'

He smiles at this, and as I leave his room I feel a wave of remorse that I've had to book in a time for the children to see their father.

It is when I am alone in the house that the doubts find a way to creep in. Rosie's insistence that she didn't take Lee's ring only leads me to come to worse conclusions. Why would somebody frame Rosie for his murder when I would have been the more obvious choice? Unless someone is targeting her on purpose, and right now that is exactly what it looks like.

Once again I think of Serena, and it is the only thing that fits. Perhaps she saw Rosie flirting with Lee and misinterpreted it. But then how do I fit in? Somebody left me alive in his bed, and I can think of no reason why.

Except if it was Rosie. Even in a deep rage, she wouldn't have wanted me dead.

My mobile rings, and I am grateful to be interrupted from this thought.

'Tara?' The female voice is familiar, but I struggle to place it.

'Yes, who is this?'

'It's Amelie. I'm sorry to bother you, but, well, you turned up at my hotel when you needed to speak to me, so I think the least you can do is meet me when I need to see you.'

But I hear nothing she says, other than her name, because I am too shocked that I am speaking to her, that she has dared to call me.

'Tara? Are you there?'

'Yes. What exactly is it you want, Amelie? I thought we'd said everything there is to say.'

'I need to talk to you, Tara.'

Perhaps it is her use of my name that softens me towards her. 'Okay, I'm listening. But if you're just going to repeat your claim about Noah then I'm not interested.' As I say this, I wonder if she has heard about Rosie and me.

'No, it's not that. But I can't talk now. Can we meet somewhere later? I'm rushing back to a meeting in a minute.'

Only then does it dawn on me that she was supposed to be here for only a few days. She should be in New York now, far away from me, and far away from Noah.

'Why are you still here?'

'I'm living here now. Work has given me a permanent transfer. I'm staying with a cousin in Hammersmith until I find my own place. So can you meet me or not?'

It should bother me that she's decided to make London her home, and that she's living in Hammersmith, walking distance from Noah's hotel, but I only feel numb, as I do with everything to do with Noah at the moment. But still, I will not make this easy for her.

'Meet me this afternoon in Richmond Park. I'll be there at one o'clock.'

'Thanks,' she says, but I detect she is anything but grateful.

* * *

Amelie looks different as she walks towards me; her hair is now short, cut closely to her head, and although not many women could carry this style off, it suits her, and if anything, she looks even more attractive.

Reaching me, she probably doesn't know whether to smile or not, given how bizarre this meeting is, and she keeps her expression serious. But she does thank me for meeting her.

'Shall we walk or do you want to find somewhere to sit?'

I stare at her shoes – three-inch stilettos – and am tempted to say I want to walk, but there is no need for me to be cruel. 'There are benches a bit further along,' I say.

Once we're sitting down, I start to wonder why I agreed to this. There is nothing Amelie can say that I need to hear, not now. I have barely spoken to Noah for weeks so cannot understand what she wants from me. 'So tell me why we're here,' I say.

She pulls a bottle of water from her bag and takes a sip, clearing her throat before she speaks. 'I know that Noah's moved out,' she begins. 'And I saw him a couple of nights ago.'

This is not what I have expected, but I try to remind myself that what Noah does is not my concern any more, as long as it doesn't adversely affect Rosie or Spencer.

Amelie watches me, waiting for an answer, but I don't say anything.

'We had a long talk about everything,' she continues, in the absence of a response, 'and—'

'So he's forgiven you for lying about him, has he?'

'Tara, I didn't lie. I didn't see him that night, but you don't have to believe me because that isn't the point.'

She is taking too long to get there, and I'm quickly losing patience. 'Then what exactly are you trying to tell me? Because I really don't have time to—'

'Do you love him?' She stares directly at me as she asks this, showing no shame that she, of all people, is asking such a personal question.

'That's none of your business, is it?' And then I realise why I'm here. 'You're here because you want Noah back. Please don't tell me you're actually asking my permission?'

Amelie stares into the distance. 'No, of course not. But I need to know if things really are over between you this time. I know I have no right to ask you that, but. . .'

'You love him.'

She nods, and when she turns to me I see her eyes are awash with tears. 'I've tried not to. So many times. But he's just. . . under my skin, I suppose. I know I shouldn't be talking to you about this but, please, just put me out of my misery.'

Listening to Amelie, everything becomes clear, and although there is no need for me to explain anything about my marriage to this woman, I suddenly pity her. She deserves the truth.

'I don't know how I feel about him at this moment. I'll always love him, but I don't know in what way. He's the father of my children, and that comes first, but right now I can't think straight where Noah is concerned because he let me down. And I let him down. Everything's blurred. But none of this should matter to you because the truth is, Amelie, he doesn't love you and I think you know that.'

I don't know what reaction I'm expecting once I've finished speaking, but the tears, which moments ago pooled in her eyes, have now dried up.

'Then why did we spend Sunday night together?'

I stare at my mobile, the screen sticky from my sweating hands, and fight the urge to call Noah. I will see him in a couple of hours when he comes to pick up Rosie and Spencer, but I won't confront him while the kids are present. But when I scroll through my recent contacts to find his name, I spot DCI Hunt's name at the top of the list. It is a missed call from earlier I hadn't heard or noticed on my mobile.

Quickly, I call him instead, relieved that he's stopped me from doing something I might regret.

He answers straightaway. 'Tara. Glad you called back. I've done some checking on Serena and Mikey, and I was going to come over this evening to fill you in. Are you around?'

I try to stay calm. 'Yes, any time after five.' It is only an hour away, but how can I wait even that long? 'Can you tell me anything now?'

'I shouldn't be telling you anything at all, but, well. . .' He hesitates. Clearly he is still not sure why he trusts me, and I can't blame him for that. But does he realise I feel the same about him? 'I'll see you at six,' he says. 'Got to go.'

Noah doesn't even get out of the car when he pulls up in the drive. He beeps the horn and sits drumming his fingers on the steering wheel, even though I am standing at the door, clearly in his line of vision.

'Aren't you going to say hello to Dad?' Spencer asks, passing by me to step outside.

'Not this time, maybe when he drops you off. He's probably in a rush so he can make the most of his evening with you.'

He shrugs, clearly too excited about spending time with Noah to care too much about my decision.

Rosie comes downstairs and gives me a kiss on the cheek before following Spencer to the car. Her show of affection would fill me with happiness if everything weren't such a mess.

I watch them jump in the car, the whole time Noah refusing to look at me, and in that moment, if I didn't already know, I am certain my marriage is over.

* * *

DCI Hunt – it is strange to think of him as Holden – seems on edge this evening. He's been here for no more than five minutes, but has already checked his phone numerous times. I am tempted to ask him who he is waiting to hear from, but I am already pushing my luck with him. If he is genuine. If he doesn't have an ulterior motive for helping me.

'Are you okay?' I ask.

He slips his phone in his pocket. 'Yep. Fine.'

I'm far from convinced, but he clearly doesn't want to talk about whatever it is that's bothering him. 'So you said you had some things to tell me?'

As soon as I've said this, he seems to return to normal, the tension from a moment ago fading away.

'I've had a long think about Serena Jacobs, and I double-checked every part of her story, but, Tara, there are no holes in it. She was at that hotel off Oxford Street, in the restaurant and bar until at least midnight, and then she went up to bed. The hotel receptionist once again confirmed that he saw her heading upstairs, and that she didn't come down again.'

I think about this for a moment. 'But what if she found another way out? One that meant she didn't have to walk through the reception area? It wouldn't have taken her long to get home from there. The timing fits, Det. . . Holden.'

But he shakes his head. 'There is no other way out, except for the fire exit, but that would have meant setting off an alarm. Plus, she would have probably had to get a cab, and we've checked all the cab firms that took any bookings in that area on the night. A lot of work has gone into this, Tara. I'm sorry, but I just don't think she had anything to do with it.'

Disappointment surges through me, because I dared to get my hopes up, even though I knew it was too easy. But that doesn't mean it wasn't her. She might just have covered her tracks thoroughly.

'But you think Rosie did?' I say.

He stares at me for too long, and I hold my breath while I wait for a reply. 'I hope not,' he says eventually. 'I really hope not.'

'But you don't think it was Serena, so who does that leave?'

He shakes his head. 'Stop trying to do my job, Tara. I've said this before: that's what I'm here for so you don't need to try to be a detective.' His tone is not unkind but I'm still hurt by his words.

'I'm just trying to—'

'I know. And I get it, I really do. Otherwise I wouldn't be here, but just let me worry about solving this case.'

I study his face, then glance at the untouched glass of water in front of him. 'So why are you here exactly? You could have told me this on the phone.'

'That's a question I keep asking myself, but let's just say I have my reasons. Now, I make it just about dinner time, so are you going to offer me anything to eat?'

'Oh, I suppose I could rustle up some pasta quickly.' He hasn't answered my question but I don't think I'll get any more out of him.

'Tara, I was kidding. You don't have to cook for me; that would just be weird, wouldn't it?'

But his mention of food reminds me I haven't eaten since breakfast.

'Why don't I just do it anyway? Weird or not,' I say.

All the while I'm cooking, I feel his eyes on me, and wonder again if I can trust him. He is surely risking his job being here, and I can't see any benefit for him in talking to me, especially when Rosie is still under suspicion, but perhaps, as he claims, it is as simple as wanting – or needing – to solve Lee's murder.

'Tell me something about you,' I say. 'I feel like I'm about to eat dinner with a stranger. All I know is that you're a detective and your name is Holden.'

'Yeah, and I can blame my mother for that. It's a character in one of her favourite books apparently. You can imagine what it was like for me at school.'

'Actually, I like it. It's different.'

He smiles then, and I realise it's the first time I've seen a full smile on his face.

'Can I ask you a personal question?' he says.

'Well, you haven't told me anything about you yet, but go on.'

'Did your husband leave because of all this?'

Of all the questions he could ask me, this is one I least expect. 'We were probably heading for a crash anyway. It's a long story but we separated a while ago and I guess it just wasn't the same when we got back together.'

'I'm sorry.'

'Don't be. What's meant to be is meant to be, isn't it?'

He sighs. 'Possibly. But I'm not sure I believe in all that. It's too easy, isn't it? An excuse for criminals not to accept responsibility for their actions.'

'Maybe. But we all choose what works for us, don't we? And I need to believe things happen for a reason.'

He doesn't reply, but watches me intently.

'Are you married?' The question leaves my mouth before I've realised I was about to ask it.

His mouth twists, and I can tell he's wondering how much to tell me. 'That's a bit of a long story too. I'm divorced. Well, about to be. Cassie and I are separated, and she's with someone else.' He snorts. 'Has been since we were still together.'

And now it is my turn to say I'm sorry.

'Don't be, I'm well rid of her.'

I wonder if this is what Noah will be saying about me. No matter what has happened, I hope he doesn't feel this way. 'Let's change the subject.' The pasta is almost ready and my appetite is dwindling away at the thought of Noah.

At least throughout the meal we manage to talk about anything other than the state of our marriages. And even Lee's murder doesn't come up for a while, and by the time we've cleared our plates I feel as though I know enough to reach the conclusion that he's a man whose job is his life, and he has little time for much else.

'Has anything happened with your colleague from school?' he says, out of nowhere.

'No. Why? Did you find something?'

'I haven't had a chance to check yet, but I just wanted to make sure you're being careful. With your husband no longer living here, it just makes you a bit more vulnerable.'

And Mikey knows Noah is no longer here. Just as he probably knows everything about me.

'I'll be fine,' I say.

Not long after we've finished eating, Holden tells me he has to leave. I have told him that Noah will be bringing the kids back soon, and he probably doesn't want any of them to see him here and wonder what he's doing.

At the door, he says goodbye, but then he mumbles something so quietly I cannot be sure I've heard it correctly.

'I really hope you're not lying to me, Tara.'

CHAPTER TWENTY-ONE

'Why didn't Dad come in last night?' Spencer asks the next morning. 'He's talking to Rosie, so why not you? You haven't done anything, Mum. I believe you so why won't he?'

'That's obvious,' Rosie says. 'Because—'

'Rosie,' I say, before she can go into any detail. Spencer already knows about me being in Lee's house; he doesn't need to hear it all again.

'I wasn't going to—'

'What are you both going to do today?' I ask, changing the subject before anything else comes out. 'I don't want you just sitting around here watching TV all day.'

'It's not even on, Mum,' Spencer says, glancing at the television. 'Can Ryan come over here?'

'Yes, that's fine. What about you, Rosie?'

'I'm meeting someone this afternoon,' she says, avoiding eye contact.

I still don't know whether Damien is really her boyfriend or just another fixation. Despite her assurances that he is, and her honesty about Lee, I'm still wary of what she says. The police still haven't been able to track him, or his parents down. Not asking who she is meeting would show her that I trust her, but I can't stay silent.

'Anyone I know?' I ask, in an attempt to make my question light-hearted.

'Just a girl from school.' She doesn't offer up a name, but I choose to let this one go.

'Going anywhere nice?' I am pushing my luck but it's worth a try.

'West End. And I might see Dad after that.'

She looks up at me now, and there is a flicker of defiance in her eyes. Does she expect me to be annoyed that she's seeing Noah? This couldn't be further from the truth; despite my issues with him, I am thrilled that he's spending so much time with the kids.

'It's a great idea,' I say.

'I'd like to see Dad too,' Spencer says.

'Maybe tomorrow.' I lean across the sofa to give him a hug. 'Let this be time for Rosie and Dad. Now, why don't you give Ryan a call and tell him he can come over.'

'I'd rather go to his house, if that's okay? He's got an Xbox.'

'I suppose that's fine. But I don't want you playing computer games all day.'

Spencer runs off, and I breathe a sigh of relief that he didn't make a fuss about Noah seeing Rosie without him.

'Thanks, Mum,' Rosie says, once he's gone.

But I'm not quite sure what she's thanking me for.

My plan for the afternoon was to catch up on all the work I've got behind on, so that once September is here I have a head start. But now, as I sit at my desk, paper scattered all around me, I find myself writing names on a sheet of A4 paper. 'Serena'. 'Rosie'. The woman Lee was supposedly having an affair with. This is all I have so far. But then, without thinking, I add Noah's name to the list.

What if he came home that night and saw me with Lee? It would make sense that he wouldn't want me dead, but he would have been furious enough with Lee to end his life.

But do I really think Noah could have done it? He has never shown a violent streak, but in the heat of the moment, more than anything else, it would have shocked him to find me in Lee's bed.

My phone rings before I have a chance to develop this thought, and I answer it, even though I don't recognise the number.

'Tara? Is that you?'

It is unmistakably Mikey's voice I am listening to, and I pull the phone away from my ear, tempted to disconnect the call.

'Tara,' he says again, 'are you there?'

I don't have the heart to cut him off when he sounds so harmless. 'Yes, I'm here.'

'It's Mikey. From school.'

'Hi.' I keep my words to a minimum, as I don't want him to think it's okay for him to call me like this when I have never given him my number.

'How are you doing? I've been worried about you. Are you okay?'

'Mikey, I'm fine. But thanks for your concern. How did you get my number?'

He mumbles something about Kirsty in the office giving it out, but I'm sure she wouldn't do this without checking with me first.

'Actually, there's another reason I called,' he says, before I have time to question him further. 'And I hope you don't mind, but I need to ask you something.'

He wants to know about the murder investigation, or what it was like being arrested. Or having a daughter under suspicion. None of which are things I'm prepared to talk about. I stay silent and wait.

'I was wondering if you're busy this evening? If not, would you like to have dinner with me? I could cook for you, or we could go out to eat somewhere, whichever you prefer, I—'

'I can't. Sorry.' But I'm not sorry. In fact, I'm angry that he's now made things awkward. At least before I didn't have to acknowledge that he was interested in me.

'Oh, you're busy. How about tomorrow? Or any other day this week?'

Now I have no choice but to be cruel. I need to stamp this out before it can go any further. 'Mikey, I'm not saying I can't because I'm busy, I'm saying it because I don't want to have dinner with you. I'm sorry. You're a great person, but. . . I'm barely separated and not even divorced, and I don't have time for anything like this. Not with you. I'm sorry.'

The silence that follows is painful. I have no idea how he will react to my rejection, but this pause is worse than anything he could say.

At least this is what I think until he finally speaks.

'You're making a huge mistake,' he hisses into the phone, before cutting me off.

After everything that's happened in the last month, Mikey's words shouldn't have shaken me up this much, but they have. I have been so wrong about him, my instinct letting me down, and if I'm mistaken about him being harmless, then what else have I been wrong about?

'It could have been a threat,' Holden says, when I call him, 'but not necessarily. He may just have been letting off steam after your rejection. It's important to stay calm about it.'

'I am staying calm. I'm not some hysterical woman. But, I can't ignore the fact that my neighbour was murdered, which means anything is possible. What if Mikey?—'

'Don't say it. He's never exhibited any violent or aggressive behaviour before, has he?'

'Not to me. And not to the kids at school. But. . . well, there's a first time for everything, isn't there?'

'Let me do some digging and I'll call you later. Where are you?'

I tell him I'm at home, but after Mikey's call it's the last place I want to be.

'Are you alone?'

'Yes. The kids are out and won't be back until this evening. But I'll be okay.'

'I'm sure you will, but why don't you pop out for a bit?'

I'm about to tell him that I won't be chased out of my own home because of a vaguely threatening phone call, but then I think of Lisa, and how it would be nice to pay her a visit. And hopefully Harvey won't be there so I can grill her more about what's going on between them. She was vague last time I spoke to her, and I'm still confused about her U-turn with him, so it will be a good distraction for me.

'Actually, I might just do that.'

'Good,' Holden says. There is a pause before he speaks again. 'Where are you thinking of going?'

'To see my sister, Lisa.'

He tells me that's a good idea, and that he'll call later with an update.

There is no answer when I try Lisa's mobile and she doesn't pick up her house phone either, but I decide to drive to her flat anyway. Anything to get me out of the house, and she might still be at home, or if not, she could be there by the time I arrive.

I try not to think about anything as I drive, and turn up the radio to drown out the thoughts crashing around in my head. Lee. Serena. Mikey. Rosie. I just need to escape from it all, even if only for a few hours.

Her car is outside her flat, parked haphazardly, as she always does, inches from the kerb. I smile to myself because this is Lisa all over.

But there is no answer when I press her buzzer, and no sign of life when I stare up at her window. I'm about to give up and drive home when the door beeps and clicks, allowing me to go inside.

When she answers her flat door, the first thing I notice is that she's still in her pyjamas. I open my mouth to tell her how lazy she is, but then I see her face. The deep red and black under her eyes and covering half her cheek.

I rush forward, taking a closer look. There is no mistaking the severity of her bruises.

'Lisa, what happened? Are you okay?'

She stares past me and then ushers me inside, locking the door behind us. And then she is falling into me, tears gushing from her eyes and soaking my top.

Before she's even said a word I know that Harvey did this.

'Where is he?' I ask, pulling back so I can see her face.

'At work,' she manages to say.

Still holding Lisa up, I double lock the front door. 'Have you been to the police?'

She shakes her head, and looks like a lost little girl, not the strong, vibrant woman who is my sister. The one who would stand up to anyone.

'Well, we're calling them. But tell me what happened first. And don't leave anything out.'

I lead her to the sofa and ask if she wants anything to drink, but once again she shakes her head.

'It happened last night,' she says. 'I just couldn't take any more so I told him I wasn't sure about my feelings for him, and that him moving in was a mistake.'

This comes as no surprise. I sensed something was wrong, but I was so wrapped up in my own problems I didn't push the issue with Lisa. I have let her down, and once again guilt wraps itself around me like a shroud.

'Carry on,' I say. I need to know everything, and then we will deal with that man.

'At first he just wouldn't listen to me. He kept telling me I was being irrational, not thinking things through. But I told him all

I've done lately is think about the situation, and that being with him just didn't feel right.' She brings her hand to her cheek. 'And then he did this. Out of the blue. It completely stunned me so I didn't even feel anything. But I fell to the floor and smacked my head, and I think that hurt more at first.'

I lean across and put my arm around her, close to tears myself. 'I'm so sorry, Lisa. I haven't been here for you.'

She dabs at her eyes. 'This is not your fault, Tara. It's mine. I should never have let him move in. I should have ended the relationship ages ago. I just never knew how controlling he was until he moved in.'

Had I sensed this? It is easy now to look back and find it obvious, but there was something about the way he made himself so at home here, even before he'd moved in. But I will not say this to Lisa.

'Has he done this before?'

'No, never. We have argued in the past, and he does have a temper, but he's never hit me before. Although. . .'

'What? What is it?'

'He's thrown things. A few times. Not at me, but at the TV.' She points to the television stand, and I see the dent at the edge of the black glass. 'He threw his coffee mug. But that's very different from actually hitting someone, isn't it?'

'Yes, that's true.' But Noah has never done anything like that, despite his faults. 'I'm calling the police,' I say, already thinking of DCI Holden Hunt. 'In fact, the detective investigating Lee's murder, well. . . he. . . we talk quite a bit, so I'm thinking we could tell him about Harvey.'

Lisa perks up. 'What do you mean you "talk quite a bit"?'

'I don't know. I suppose I'm starting to think of him as a friend.' But is that what we are? Whatever is between us has developed so quickly I cannot get my head around it.

'Just a friend?' she says, squeezing my hand. 'I'm sure that's what you called Noah when you first met him.'

'Just a friend,' I repeat. 'But this isn't about me, let's focus on you.'

'I know, I just felt so sad when you told me Noah walked out. You've been through so much together it would be nice if there was the possibility of someone else.'

'Well, there won't be for a long time, Lisa. Anyway, I'm going to call this detective now, okay?'

'Tara, I really appreciate all your help, but I think I should do this myself. I need to make the call, and I'll do it to my local station. Is that okay?'

'Of course it is; you don't need to ask me that. I just want you to do it so he gets what he deserves and can't hurt you again.'

Sadness crosses her face. 'I'll do it now.'

While she makes the call I start clearing Harvey's belongings off the shelves and units, throwing all his DVDs onto the floor. Several times Lisa looks up to see what I'm doing, but she doesn't object to my cull.

'They've told me to go down to the station,' she says, once she's finished on the phone. 'The sooner the better.'

'Right, let's go then. I'll drive.'

'Wait, can we just pack up all his stuff first? I don't want it here any more. I want a fresh start.'

'Get me some bin liners,' I say, and together we clear Lisa's home of every sign that Harvey exists.

On the way back from the police station, Lisa barely says a word. I imagine she is thinking of Harvey and what will happen now, so I need to put her mind at ease. 'You've done the right thing,' I say. 'The police will make sure he doesn't go near you.'

She stares out of the passenger window. 'Will they? They can't even find your neighbour's murderer. . .' She turns to face me. 'Oh, Tara, I'm sorry, I shouldn't have said that. I'm just. . . scared,

I suppose. What's to stop him turning up in the middle of the night?'

'Well, it won't matter, because you're coming to stay with me. Until all this is sorted out and Harvey is out of your life for good, my home is your home.'

Lisa hesitates to answer. 'That's so kind of you to offer but. . . I need to be at home.'

'No you don't. You need to be safe.'

But the truth is: is my home any safer than hers? Especially now that Mikey has escalated his fixation on me. Still, I won't leave Lisa on her own.

'But you've got enough going on,' she says. 'And what about the kids? They won't like me staying with you. It's your home and you don't need me intruding.'

'You are my family too, Lisa. Spencer adores you, you know that. And Rosie—'

'Hasn't spoken to me since she was arrested. I've tried to call and text her, but she never replies or answers her phone.'

'I think she was just too ashamed to talk to you. But she's fine with me now so there's no reason she won't be with you. Anyway, I'm not taking no for an answer – you're coming to stay with us. Even if it's just for a couple of days. We'll go back to yours, pack some things and dump all of Harvey's stuff outside the door. He can get it whenever he wants, but he's not setting eyes on you.'

Lisa shakes her head. 'I'm not sure, Tara. Don't get me wrong, I'd love to stay with you, it's just, I hate putting you out.'

I assure her she isn't and eventually she agrees. 'But we probably shouldn't put his things outside the door, otherwise someone could steal them then I'll have to replace it all.'

I agree with this, and we make our way to Lisa's flat.

'But it's only for a couple of days,' she insists.

* * *

Rosie and Spencer are both pleased when I tell them Lisa is staying with us for a while. They don't even ask why, and Spencer tells us all at least the house will be more lively now. Rosie gives her a hug and apologises for not returning her calls or texts.

'Don't worry about it,' Lisa says. 'As long as you're okay, that's all that matters.'

'I just hope you're okay,' Rosie replies.

Both she and Spencer know what happened to Lisa, because I need them to be vigilant, and to call the police if they see any sign of Harvey.

Later, when the kids have disappeared upstairs, we sit in the living room and I pour Lisa a glass of wine.

'Are you still not drinking anything?' she says, when she notices I have only brought in one glass.

'I can't face it. Not after. . . that night. But you definitely need one.'

'I don't blame you,' she says, 'but there's no harm in having just one, is there? You can't stop living your life because of what happened.'

'I know. And I'm not. But I just can't bear the thought of it. Maybe once I know what happened. I just feel like I'm stuck in limbo.' It must be a thousand times worse for Serena – if she is innocent – despite her insistence on hating Lee.

'What if you never know?' Lisa says, after taking a long sip of wine. 'Murders go unsolved all the time, I'm sure, and this might be one of those times. I just don't want it to stop you. . . being you.'

'I could say the same about you,' I say. 'Don't let Harvey get the better of you.'

'I won't,' she says, but her hand rises to her cheek again. I wonder if she even knows she is doing it.

We both retreat upstairs to bed soon after that, and for once I fall asleep quickly.

But it doesn't last long, because I'm soon woken by Lisa opening my bedroom door and whispering my name.

I spring up, assuming Harvey must have turned up, and that I need to call the police. 'Are you okay, what's going on?'

She tiptoes over to my bed. 'I'm fine, but I couldn't sleep and I heard Rosie creeping downstairs so I followed her to see what she was doing.'

Lisa doesn't trust her. She won't say it outright, but this proves it.

'What are you trying to tell me? Where is she?'

'Tara, she's across the road at your neighbour's house. The one who died. A woman I assume is his wife just let her in.'

CHAPTER TWENTY-TWO

So many times I've stood by the window, staring at Lee and Serena's house, reliving that moment. But I never thought I'd be waiting for my daughter to walk out of the door.

'What do you think she's doing in there?' Lisa whispers.

I have no idea why we're whispering, though, when Rosie won't hear us.

'I don't know. But it doesn't look good, does it? So you say a woman definitely let her in? Was it Serena?'

Lisa nods. 'I've seen pictures of her on the news, and it was definitely her.'

There is no reason for Rosie to be there. The last time I spoke to Serena she was accusing Rosie of being a murderer, so why would she let her into her home in the middle of the night?

'Tell me again everything you saw.'

Despite looking exhausted, Lisa joins me by the bedroom window, and repeats what she witnessed.

'But did she look surprised to see Rosie? Or did it seem like she was expecting her?' It is essential for me to know which one of these is true if I'm to make any sense of this.

'Oh, Tara, I couldn't really tell from this far away. Rosie knocked on the door, then a few seconds later the woman opened it. They spoke for a moment then she let her in.'

This tells me nothing, other than Serena is not angry with Rosie. If I know Serena, it would have taken Rosie a lot longer than a moment to convince her to let her inside. So Serena must have wanted Rosie to be there. But that doesn't make sense, not after everything she said the other day. And she was the one who told the police about Rosie.

'What are you going to do?' Lisa asks.

I keep my eyes fixed on the house. 'The only thing I can. Wait for her to come back and ask her what the hell's going on.'

'Don't jump down her throat, though, Tara. There could be an innocent explanation for this; it doesn't have to be anything sinister.'

But nothing Rosie ever does seems to be innocent. 'I won't,' I promise my sister.

Lisa stays with me for a while longer, but I can see how tired she is.

'Go to bed,' I say. 'I'll wait for Rosie. You need to get some rest, and it's probably not a good idea if we're both awake when she comes back.'

Once she's gone, I decide to wait downstairs. That way I have a good chance of catching her before she rushes to her bedroom. So I drag an armchair over to the window and sit alone in the dark, staring through a slit in the curtains, fighting to stay awake.

But eventually exhaustion overcomes me and I fall asleep.

'Mum? What are you doing down here?'

Rosie's voice rouses me, and my eyes flick open, squinting from the sunlight streaming through the window. So it is morning, and I have no way of knowing how long Rosie was across the road. She is wearing pyjamas, and her hair is tied back in the way she always has it to sleep, so she must have come home. And I slept right through it.

'What the hell is going on? Why were you at Serena's in the middle of the night?'

'Oh.' She sits on the sofa, staring at her feet. 'I'm not going to lie, Mum. I went over there to apologise. For all the things I said about Lee.'

Anger builds inside me. 'In the middle of the night? Do you know how unbelievable that sounds?' I shouldn't be harsh, but I have had about all I can take of lies and secrets. Of not understanding anything that's going on around me.

She nods. 'Yes, maybe. But it's the truth. You can ask her if you don't believe me. Call her right now and she'll tell you exactly what I've said.'

But of course I'm not going to do that, and Rosie knows this.

'Why would she let you in? She thinks one of us killed Lee, or that we were having an affair with him.'

Rosie tugs at her hair, pulling the clip she has held it back with. 'And that's exactly why I wanted to go over there. To set her straight. I couldn't sleep and saw a light on in her front room, so I went over there. And it wasn't the middle of the night. Not really.'

After Rosie's track record, it's hard to know what to think, but, as always, I want to believe her. 'So what did she say?'

'She wouldn't hear a word I said, at first, but I told her everything I told you, and I think by the end of it she believed me. Or at least it made her think twice. I'm just sick of the way everyone looks at me, Mum. At us. As if we're. . . I don't know. . . tainted or something. As if we've got something catching that will spread to them. I hate it.'

As she speaks I am already making up my mind to talk to Serena. Not just to check Rosie's claim, but to make my own peace with her. I tried the other day, to no avail, but if she let Rosie into her house then perhaps she is starting to accept we had nothing to do with Lee's murder.

'Things will die down,' I say. 'People will soon forget, especially when the police catch his killer.'

'But what if they don't, Mum? Do we have to live with this for ever? We should just move away.' As soon as she says this, she grows excited. 'Yes! That's what we need to do. Let's just go. Dad will come with us, I'm sure he will.'

It is moments like this I realise how much Rosie still has to learn.

'We can't just run away. Especially not when. . . you know. The police may still need to talk to us.' An image of Holden appears in my head.

'But then we have to be stuck here with people like Layla. It won't ever go away.'

This is something I've thought about since it happened, and I can't find a solution. The only thing that will help us get our lives back is Lee's killer being caught. But until that happens, I will do what I can to spare Rosie and Spencer any more pain.

'Let's not worry about that now. We have to trust in the police.'

'Hmmm. That doesn't make me feel much better.' She turns to face me. 'Mum, is Aunty Lisa okay? I can't understand why she'd let that man do that to her. She never takes any shit from anyone, does she?'

I ignore her language. 'It's not as simple as that. Life isn't always black and white, Rosie.'

'You don't need to tell me that, Mum. It's just that, well, I've always looked up to her. She always seemed so cool. So free. Travelling the world, working for herself. I just don't know how she got trapped by him.'

Rosie is echoing my precise thoughts, but I don't tell her this. I have to protect Lisa's privacy as much as possible. 'Perhaps she just thought it was time to settle down. I suppose there comes a time for everyone when you just want to put down some roots.' This is exactly what Lisa told me.

Rosie doesn't seem convinced of this argument, but she lets it go. 'Shall I see if she wants to do something tomorrow? Maybe it will cheer her up? We could go shopping.'

I tell Rosie she'll love that idea, and she heads upstairs to get dressed. But Rosie's mention of shopping puts another thought in my head. Remembering the other day, when Lisa and I went to Westfield, I am now convinced that she rushed back home because she was scared of Harvey. She must have been. I no longer believe her excuse of him locking himself out of the flat. This only makes me loathe him even more.

A while later, when Lisa comes down for breakfast and I mention Rosie's plan, she is less than enthusiastic.

'I don't know, Tara. I think I should stay here. What if. . . Harvey finds me?' With her folded arms and wide eyes, she is once again unrecognisable. It is just another way in which Harvey has hurt her.

I try to convince her she will be fine. 'The police will have arrested him, so I'm sure he won't want to get in any more trouble. This is serious, Lisa, and I'm sure he wouldn't jeopardise his career. Plus, you'll be in a very public place.'

But my words barely register and she stares into space.

'Is there something you're not telling me? Has he done something worse?'

She shakes her head. 'No, I just don't want to take any chances. I don't want to see him, Tara.'

'And you won't. But remember you said you didn't want to stop living your life? If you don't go then that means he's won. Don't let him do that to you.'

'It's just a shopping trip, Tara. It's not that important that I go.'

I spend the next few minutes trying to convince her it's not about shopping, it's about her freedom, and eventually I get through to her.

'When you put it like that,' she says. 'Okay, I'll go out with Rosie. But I'm scared, Tara. Really scared.'

I grab her hand and tell her she's got nothing to be afraid of. And I only pray that I'm right.

* * *

Once Rosie and Lisa have left, and Spencer is occupied on the computer, I head across to Serena's house, checking first that neither Layla nor Guy is visible.

'What the hell do you want?' she says, as soon as she realises it is me at her door. 'I told you to leave me alone.'

'You made peace with Rosie,' I explain. 'I'm only asking for the same.' This is it. I am about to find out whether or not my daughter has lied once again.

'You're unbelievable. Rosie's not the one who went to bed with my husband, is she? Perhaps I can forgive some stupid schoolgirl crush, but what you did was something else.'

It takes me a moment to digest what Serena is saying. 'So you don't believe Rosie did it? I'm so glad—'

'No, I don't. I think it was you, Tara. And so do the police so it won't be long before they prove it. Enjoy your freedom while you can. I hear prison's a pretty awful place.'

The door slams in my face.

'I need to see you,' I say, whispering into the phone so that Spencer doesn't hear me. 'Now. Please.'

He sighs down the phone, perhaps fed up that I'm making a habit of demanding to see him. 'Tara, I'm at work. It's difficult to get away at the moment.'

'Please, Holden. I wouldn't ask if it wasn't important. Just an hour of your time.'

There is a long pause. 'Okay, give me time to get there, though.'

I thank him profusely, then give him instructions to come around to the back of the house and text me when he's there. I don't want Spencer seeing him and worrying about what's going on.

* * *

With Spencer engrossed in a film on Noah's iPad, I manage to sneak Holden into the house, and I lead him through my bedroom to the en-suite.

'Is this really necessary,' he says, but at least he speaks in a whisper, and there is a thin smile on his face.

'I don't want Spencer getting worried and wondering why there's a detective in the house,' I explain, and I'm relieved to find he happily accepts this.

Once we're inside I lock the door, and he chuckles. It is a strange sound, coming from a man who is always so serious.

'I feel a bit like a naughty school kid,' he says. But then his smile vanishes when he notices I'm not finding this amusing. 'But it's fine, whatever we need to do. So what's going on?'

I take a deep breath and tell him about Rosie sneaking off to Serena's house, and my subsequent visit there to find out what was going on. 'She thinks I killed Lee,' I say, trying to control my anxiety. 'And she was adamant that the police think so too. Is this true?'

'I have to be honest, Tara, you haven't been ruled out. By your own admission you woke up next to his dead body, so that immediately marks you as a suspect. But you knew this.'

'I know, but. . . it's just since you've been coming here, I kind of feel like we're. . . friends or something. And I thought you believed me.' I must sound needy and pathetic, and any second now he will tell me I've been wrong all along.

'Tara, I do. I've told you before that I wouldn't be here if I didn't think you were innocent.'

'So what's Serena talking about?'

'I have no idea. There are no new developments, and I'm still the detective in charge of the investigation, so everything comes through me. I would tell you if we had anything to go on.'

Unless you can't be trusted.

'Thank you. Sorry. I'm just on edge. There's so much going on, and I hate not being in control. I've always been so. . . together, and now I feel like I'm hanging by a thread.'

He stares at me for a moment, and I know I am being analysed. Perhaps he is doubting his instincts and is no longer sure what to make of me.

'Tara, I. . . haven't exactly been honest with you.'

I almost stop breathing. There is something else. I was right not to trust him.

'There's another reason I've been coming here so much.'

'What?' I say, backing away from him. 'What reason?'

It feels like an eternity passes, with both of us standing in silence, before he takes a step closer to me.

'This reason,' he says, pulling me towards him and kissing me.

CHAPTER TWENTY-THREE

I pull away from him after a few seconds, even though I don't want our kiss to end.

'What was that?'

'I'm sorry,' he says, offering that thin smile. 'I've just wanted to do that from the second I saw you. Well, once I was convinced you didn't kill your neighbour.'

'I'm sure you could get in all sorts of trouble for this.'

'Yes. But I'm willing to take that risk.' He leans in to me, but I gently push him back.

'Not here. Not with Spencer at home.'

'Then you're meeting me for dinner tonight. Somewhere out of London.'

I tell him I'm not sure I can, and find myself explaining all about Lisa.

'What a jerk,' he says, once I've finished. 'She's done the right thing reporting it, though. Let me look into it and see what's being done.'

His offer of help touches me, and it feels different this time, after our kiss, as if he's doing this for me as well, not just to put the world to rights. Now I understand why he's been helping me so much, and putting his career at risk in the process.

'I hope that kiss was worth all this trouble?' I say. I might be making light of things, but I want this to be true.

'Of course.' He looks at his watch. 'Now I better get out of here before we're caught. Meet me at the station at seven.'

'I really can't leave my sister. How about you come here? My parents are taking the kids out tonight, and Lisa will understand. I can just say we're friends.' That is what I've already told her, and she didn't believe me then, so what will she think now?

The frown on his face tells me he's not comfortable with this, but he agrees. 'Okay, I'll be here at eight.'

And I am left wondering if I will ever be able to read him correctly.

'Just a friend?' Lisa says, when I tell her the plan for the evening. My parents have only just picked up Spencer and Rosie, so this is the earliest opportunity I've had to tell her the plan for tonight.

'Hmmm,' she continues, 'come on, this is me you're talking to. Maybe a battered version of me, but I'm still your sister and I know you. So are the two of you really together?'

It feels strange to be discussing this in the midst of Lee's murder, but I am grateful for the tiny glimmer of hope it provides me. Hope that things will work out. I tell Lisa this and she smiles sadly.

'I'm happy for you, Tara, I really am. And please don't feel bad about me.'

I cannot tell her it will be impossible not to. Until she has her fighting spirit back I will constantly worry about her.

'Holden's really nice, Lisa. You'll like him. And hopefully he will find out who killed Lee and then we can all move on.'

'I hope so,' she says. 'I'm just worried it—'

'Don't say it. It's not her, I know it's not.'

She smiles but there is sadness behind it. She doesn't believe this. 'Anyway, you could have at least given me a chance to get ready. I'm a mess and I'm not meeting your new. . . whatever he is, looking like this. Come on, help me fix my face up at least.'

* * *

Holden arrives on time, and when I answer the door I'm surprised to find him in jeans and a T-shirt. I have only ever seen him in suits, but he looks just as good in casual clothes. In fact, he looks better, and I flush inside. It is a feeling I've not felt since I met Noah. It's hard to label my feelings for him because I can't focus on anything but Lee's death at the moment, but I have quickly grown fond of this man.

Noah. Thinking of him now saddens me, and then a rush of guilt hits me, until I remember that at this very second he could be with Amelie.

'Hi,' I say, pulling him inside before he is spotted. 'Come and meet my sister.'

'Not until I've done this.' He leans down and plants a brief kiss on my mouth.

In the kitchen I make introductions, and while I serve our chicken casserole, I watch as Lisa's hand touches her cheek the whole time she speaks to Holden. We've done our best to cover the bruising with make-up, but it is still obvious underneath the mask we've created.

'I'm sorry about what happened,' Holden says to her, as they both take a seat at the table. 'You are pressing charges, aren't you? It's just that so many people don't want to go through the stress of it, but that only means men like him get away with it.'

'Don't worry, I fully intend to,' Lisa says. 'He's not going to do this to someone else.'

Holden nods. 'Good. I know it can't be easy. I hope you don't mind but I checked into him and his record is clean. He doesn't even have any traffic offences.'

'I don't know whether to feel better or worse about that. Are you saying you think it was a one off?'

'In my experience these things never are. I just think either he hasn't been caught, or it's the beginning of something for him. Either way, it doesn't matter, he's still in a load of trouble for this.'

Lisa visibly relaxes and she takes a sip of wine. 'I feel such a fool,' she says. 'I mean, why did I not see how violent he was? Thinking about it now, the signs were all around me. He was a control freak, but it was so subtle, if that makes sense? It was nothing I could put my finger on.'

But demanding she return home immediately when she's out shopping should have been a sure sign.

'This isn't your fault,' I say. 'None of us saw it.'

Holden leaves his wine untouched, but reaches for one of the glasses of water I have placed on the table. 'That's the thing,' he says. 'People don't wear signs pointing them out as a wife beater or murderer. They're often the complete contrast of what we'd expect.'

I think of Rosie, now, and wonder if his comment is a veiled reference to her. But why is he here with me if he thinks my daughter is a murderer?

'I'm sure that's true,' Lisa says, and for the first time I notice she seems more relaxed.

I'm amazed that Holden can so effortlessly put her at ease, and it makes me warm to him even more.

'This is good,' Holden says, taking his first bite of food. 'I'm impressed.'

But after only a few minutes, Lisa places her knife and fork together. 'I'm so sorry, Tara, it's lovely, but I just don't have much of an appetite. And I know it's early but would you mind if I went to bed?' She turns to Holden. 'Please don't think I'm being rude, but—'

'No, not at all.' He holds out his hand. 'It was good to meet you, and like I said before, don't let that man get to you.'

Once she's gone, we finish our dinner, and Holden tells me how his day has been. He makes no mention of Lee's case, and I am grateful that, for an hour at least, I can pretend this is a normal situation.

But the bubble can only last so long, and when I serve cheese-cake for dessert he says we need to talk about what happened earlier.

'I don't do things like that lightly,' he says. 'And I don't think you do either. So when I do. . . you know. . . it's kind of a big deal.'

'But it's complicated, isn't it? How can we start something in the midst of all this chaos? And what about your job?'

'The truth is when Cassie left me I decided I'd had enough of the force. Don't get me wrong, I love my job, but it killed my marriage and seriously made me take a long hard look at my life.'

This is a shock to me. I can't imagine him as anything other than a detective. 'So what are you saying? You're going to quit your job?'

'After this case is solved, yes. And I'm setting up an investigation agency with an old friend of mine who left the force years ago. Ha, it's such a cliché, isn't it? But, hey, at least I'll be working for myself, and I can pick and choose the cases I want. I'll only have myself to answer to. So if you think about it, I'm really not risking much at all. Whatever happens with us, I'm out of there.'

'It sounds as if you've got it all worked out. And it explains why you've taken such risks to see me, and told me so much you shouldn't have.' I am a bit disappointed at this, but also relieved. It is one less thing to worry about.

'It means, if you want to, we've got a chance at starting something here. I don't want to push you – I know you've only just separated from Noah, but I sense there's something between us, and life's too short to let it pass us by.' He takes my hand, and I am surprised by how soft his skin is. 'I can't make you any promises and I don't know if this could turn into something serious or not, but I'd like to take the first step at least.'

I think of Noah, and how, before I do anything with this man, I need to be sure it really is over between us. For the kids' sakes as much as ours. 'Just give me time,' I say to Holden. 'I need this all sorted out before I can think of anything else. I'm sorry.'

'Nothing to be sorry about,' he says. 'But it's just even more incentive for me to catch a killer.'

My phone beeps with a text message and I apologise before checking it. It is Mum, texting to say Rosie has gone out with a friend, but she doesn't know where or who this friend is. I immediately text back telling her not to worry, but now that is exactly what I'm doing myself. Where has she gone this time? An image of her knocking on Serena's door flashes through my head.

'Are you okay?' Holden asks, a frown appearing on his forehead. 'Has something happened?'

But I don't want to tell him about Rosie. He already doubts her innocence so I won't give him further cause to suspect her. 'No, everything's fine. It's just my mother telling me what time to pick up—'

My phone rings. Mikey. The last person I want to hear from. 'It's him.'

'Who?'

'Mikey. My colleague. I'm not answering.'

We both stare at my phone, and when it stops ringing, wait to see if he'll leave a message. Sure enough, the voicemail alert pings a few seconds later, and with the phone clasped to my ear, I listen to Mikey's desperate voice.

'What's he saying?' Holden asks.

'He says he needs to see me, and that it's urgent. But there's no possible reason he would need to see me. It's the summer holidays so if it's school related then it can wait. And after what he said to me last time we spoke he must be crazy if he thinks I'll let him come here, or meet up with him anywhere.'

Holden falls silent. 'Hmmm,' he says eventually.

'What does that mean?'

'You've just made me think of something. When you said he must be crazy.'

I have no idea how Holden's mind works, so I am completely lost. I ask him to explain what he means.

'Tara, let me tell you something. I don't believe in coincidences. Not when it comes to a murder case.'

I tell him he still needs to elaborate, reminding him I'm not another detective he's talking to.

He stares at me for a long time before he tells me what's on his mind. 'You having a stalker at the same time as your neighbour ends up dead after being in bed with you. There could be something there.'

'Are you saying Mikey murdered Lee? But that's just. . .'

'What? Far-fetched? Too hard to believe? Are you telling me it's easier to believe your daughter did it?'

'No, I've never believed that. But. . . Mikey?'

'I'm not saying he did it, but it's a line of enquiry I need to check out. It's not unusual for stalkers to become violent, especially if they see the source of their attention in bed with another man.'

'But I'm married. I slept in the same bed with another man every night.'

'True. But you were already with Noah when you met Mikey. It would be easier for him to ignore that than a new love interest.' He holds up his hands. 'Not saying Lee was, but Mikey could easily have thought that. And it could have tipped him over the edge thinking you'd have an affair with someone, but not him.'

I think about this and wonder if it could be true. But, despite his threat the other day, it is still hard to imagine. 'I don't know. . . anything's possible, but—'

'I need to get back to the station. Check this out.'

And before I can say anything, he stands up and plants a kiss on my forehead before rushing out of the house.

Even though I can't believe Mikey is connected in any way to Lee's murder, I need to cling to this idea; it would finally clear Rosie's name, and mine. Being consumed in these thoughts makes me lose track of time, and when I realise I need to pick up Spencer, I'm already half an hour late.

Thankfully my parents haven't noticed either, as Spencer has kept them busy with a film, but it means I don't have time to stay and talk for long.

'We're worried about you,' Mum says, as I'm bustling Spencer into the car. 'You don't talk to us any more, and we don't know what's going on in your life. We have to hear snippets from the kids to keep up to date.'

I try to reassure her as best I can, but she won't be pacified.

'Well, at least Lisa's okay,' she says, and I turn from her and jump in the car before she gets the truth out of me, because somehow that's what she always manages to do.

'I promise I'll come over for a long chat as soon as I can,' I say, turning the key in the ignition. 'It's just that things are a bit crazy at the moment.'

'That's what I'm worried about,' she says.

When we get home, Spencer rushes to his room to have some time on his computer before bed, and I'm about to go upstairs myself when I hear voices in the kitchen.

I recognise Lisa's, but the other one – a male voice – is too muffled for me to recognise. Thinking it must be Harvey, I rush in there, my hand reaching for my phone, ready to call the police.

But it's not Harvey I'm staring at when I push through the door. Lisa sits at the table with Rosie, and beside my daughter is a young man I've never seen before.

'Hi, Mum,' Rosie says, smiling up at me. 'This is—'

'Damien? I'm pleased to meet you,' I say, heading over to him and holding out my hand. Finally I get to meet him.

He looks at Rosie then slowly lifts his hand to meet mine. 'Um, no, I'm Ewan.'

The room falls silent, and I try to digest what I'm hearing. 'Ewan? I. . .'

'You'll have to ignore Rosie's mum,' Lisa says, 'she's terrible with names.'

'Ah, okay,' Ewan says. 'Don't worry, Mrs Logan, my mum's the same. She gets me and my brother, Sean, mixed up all the time. We are twins, though, so I suppose I have to let her off a bit.' He smiles to himself more than any of us, as if he is proud of making this joke.

Lisa stands up. 'Can I have a quick word, Tara?' She turns to Ewan. 'It was lovely meeting you, and I'm sure we'll see you soon.'

'What the hell's going on?' I say, as soon as we're in the living room with the door shut.

'Shhhh, keep your voice down, they're only next door.'

'Lisa, just tell me. Who is that boy in my kitchen?'

'I was in bed trying to sleep when I heard someone come in. I thought it might be you bringing the kids back, but then I heard a boy's voice, so I went down to see what was going on. That's when Rosie introduced me to Ewan.'

'But who did she say he was? Just a friend?'

'She didn't say, but the fact that I found them kissing would suggest he is.'

Now I am even more confused. 'But. . . what about Damien?'

'Oh, Tara, I don't know, and I couldn't exactly ask her in front of him. I don't know what it all means.'

'So if he's her boyfriend, did she make up this Damien? But the police have been checking into him.' But they can't find him, I remind myself. And if he doesn't exist, where did Rosie spend that night Lee was murdered? She said she slept in Damien's car, and that they were parked further up the road. She promised me this.

Lisa shrugs. 'I'm as confused as you are. And Rosie just keeps on doing the strangest things, Tara. I think it's time you confronted her.'

But I have, many times, and just when I think we've got somewhere, she goes and does something else. But this does not make her a murderer.

'I need to talk to her now,' I say, more to myself than to Lisa, and I head back to the kitchen, because enough is enough.

'Ewan, I'm sorry, but it's getting late and I need to have a chat with Rosie, I hope you don't mind?'

Rosie jumps to her feet. 'Mum! What are you doing?'

'But it was lovely meeting you,' I say, ignoring her protest.

Ewan slowly stands. 'Oh, um, yeah.' He squeezes Rosie's shoulder. 'I'll see you tomorrow,' he says.

I hadn't noticed Lisa following me into the kitchen, but once again she helps out.

'I'll see you to the door, Ewan,' she says, mouthing good luck to me as she ushers him out.

'I can't believe you did that, Mum,' Rosie says. 'That was so embarrassing. I'm not a kid any more.' Her voice is measured, even though her words are angry.

'What is going on?' I say. 'Is Ewan your boyfriend?'

'I just can't win, Mum. You said you wanted to meet the person I'm seeing, but now when I introduce you, you're having a go at me.'

It is hard to keep calm when Rosie is ignoring the issue here. 'I wanted to meet Damien, Rosie. You know, the boy you were seeing. The boy you spent the night with when Lee was murdered. The one who can confirm everything. That boyfriend.'

She sighs, and begins picking at her chipped nail polish. 'I thought you believed me, Mum. But now I need to prove it?

Well, I can't, because Damien and I are over. It ended weeks ago. And then I met Ewan. I like him. Do you think he's nice, Mum?'

Rosie is doing this on purpose. She has to be. But I have to keep calm.

'Tell me exactly what happened with Damien. Why did it end?'

She tuts. 'Because he moved to Australia to be near his parents and isn't coming back. Bit hard to make a relationship that long distance work, isn't it?'

She's lying, she has to be. It is too convenient, once again. 'But when did you last speak to him?'

'I don't know. Weeks ago. By text.'

'Show me the texts.'

'Mum, what is this? Why are you interrogating me? You're worse than the police! I deleted the texts. Why would I keep them when we're not together any more?'

She storms out before I have a chance to respond, and I am left with no choice but to once again question everything she has said.

CHAPTER TWENTY-FOUR

It is only five a.m. when I tap on Noah's hotel room door, but he has agreed to see me, albeit reluctantly. It was a relief to find he was alone when I called, but now I wonder if Amelie was here, and he told her she had to go. But if that's true, at least it means his family comes first.

He answers the door in a white hotel dressing gown, his feet bare, and the room still shrouded in darkness, even though the sun is already up.

'Sorry,' I say.

He will have to leave for work in a couple of hours, probably for a day of meetings and presentations, and I know how much he values his sleep.

'It's okay,' he says, shutting the door behind me. 'What a bloody mess, though.'

As soon as I step inside his room, I wonder if I've made a mistake coming here. Perhaps it should be Holden I talk to about this, but something has drawn me here to Noah. Even if we've moved apart from each other, we are still both Rosie's parents: a bond that can never be broken.

'I'm starting to question her, Noah, and it makes me feel sick to think I'm doubting her. But everything she comes out with or does just seems so. . .'

'I know. There's no word for it, is there?' He gestures for me to sit in the only chair in the room, while he perches on the edge of the bed. 'So this boy is not Damien. And she's claiming she's no longer with Damien?'

'Yes, but it doesn't make sense. She said she slept in Damien's car on the night Lee was murdered, on our road, but there's no proof he even exists, is there? And if he doesn't then that means everything she said about that night is a lie. Other than seeing me at Lee's? What are we supposed to do about this? We can't shake the truth out of her, or even reason with her.'

Noah nods his agreement. 'But have you seriously only just considered this? Surely you can't be so blind to Rosie? She claims she never went to his home and doesn't even know where it is. It just sounds so implausible. Now even more so. He's the only person who can apparently back up her claim that she left Lee's immediately after seeing you there, and now he's conveniently in Australia. Untraceable. And their relationship is supposedly over.'

Of course I had thought about this, but until Rosie said they were no longer together, it didn't seem as far-fetched. Now, though, I don't know what else I can believe. 'I'm her mother,' is all I can manage to say.

'Actually, there may be a way to get to the truth,' Noah says. 'We get her to turn her phone in to the police. They'll be able to check whether she received texts from Australia a couple of weeks ago.'

It is so simple – I can't believe I didn't think of it. 'Yes, I'll do that as soon as I get home,' I say.

There is more I need to tell Noah, so that he gets the full picture, so I explain what has happened with Mikey, and Holden's theory about him somehow being involved in Lee's murder, although I don't mention who put it forward.

'That's hard to believe,' he says. 'Until the other day, Mikey had done nothing to you. He's just been a bit of a joke, hasn't he?'

'I thought that to start with, but perhaps he's sick of being thought of as a joke? People can snap, Noah, and then who knows what they're capable of?'

Noah's face scrunches as he thinks about what I've said and, for just a second, I almost forget that he has moved out, because it feels as though we are a team, in this together, no matter how bad it gets. He seems like the Noah I have always loved.

But all that changes when he utters his next words.

'Is this what you think or is it your new boyfriend's idea?'

I am stunned into silence. There is no way he can know about Holden. Not even the kids have seen him at the house, and I know Lisa wouldn't say anything.

'What are you talking about?'

'That detective.' He snorts. 'I know he's been sniffing around you. Bit unethical, isn't it? I'm sure he could lose his job for that.'

'There's nothing going on.' For the most part this is true. 'Why do you even think that?'

'Because I've seen him at the house. A few times. Three to be exact. And don't try to tell me he's just been interrogating you. Just cut the shit and be honest.'

He stares at me as if he's desperate for the truth, but I know he doesn't want to hear it. He will only want to hear denials. But there is a more important matter to address.

'So you've been watching the house? Watching me? Why, Noah? Why would you do that?'

'Spencer and Rosie are my kids, so I need to know they're okay. That they're safe.'

'Rubbish! This is not about them. This is about me.'

'You think too highly of yourself, Tara.'

I shake my head. 'No. I'm right, aren't I? You've been keeping an eye on me, checking what I've been up to. That's just creepy, Noah. It makes you no better than Mikey.'

He stands up and begins dressing, as if it is perfectly normal for me to still see him half-naked. I turn away, and try my best to suppress my rising anger.

'The difference is,' he says, 'you're my wife. So I have every right to know who you're involved with.'

'We're separated, Noah. And it wasn't just my decision, was it? You saw to it that our marriage died. And how dare you do this after you've been seeing Amelie again?'

He stops pulling on his trousers. 'What? What are you talking about? Of course I'm not.'

'Stop lying!' I can't help but raise my voice. 'I know for a fact you are because she came to see me and told me you'd been together again.'

'But that's impossible. She's back in New York.' He sits on the bed, his trousers around his legs.

'Wrong. She told me she'd moved back here to be near you. She's living in Hammersmith, apparently. How convenient that it's so close to this hotel.'

Noah finally pulls up his trousers, and continues dressing in silence. Only when he's put on his tie does he speak again.

'I don't know what game she's playing, but she's lying.'

And then I lose it. Any moment now they will kick me out of this hotel for disturbing the peace.

'Everyone's always lying, aren't they? I can't trust anyone, not even my own husband or daughter!'

Noah steps towards me and grabs my arm. 'Calm down, Tara. It's five in the morning and people are still sleeping. Look, we shouldn't be fighting with each other; we need to stick together on this. Rosie could be in a load of trouble and we need to help her. Isn't that what you've been saying all this time?'

He is right. I cannot think rationally when I'm boiling up inside.

'So what are we supposed to do?'

Noah sits back down on the bed and pulls on his socks.

'If she won't tell us the truth then there's nothing we can do except pick up the pieces when it all comes crashing down. Because that detective thinks it's her, and he won't stop sniffing around you until he's got the evidence he needs to arrest her.'

I shake my head. 'That's not what he's doing.' But how do I know this? Isn't this the suspicion I've had from the day he came to the house to tell me he believed me?

'What do you see in him, Tara?'

'That's none of your business.' I stand up. I'm getting nowhere here. Why did I think Noah could help? 'I thought you didn't want to fight?'

'I don't. But it makes me angry that you're. . . involved with him. Really angry.'

There is no point replying to Noah's statement. I was foolish to think we could work together on this. Walking to the door, I head out to the corridor without a glance back.

'I'll talk to her,' Noah says. 'Get her to go to Dr Marshall again.'

But I still don't turn around. It is too little too late.

'Don't trust that man,' Noah says, right before I slam the door behind me.

The house is still and peaceful when I arrive back home. It is early, and the rest of the houses on the road are yet to show signs of life. I have no idea what today will bring, but I'm convinced it can be nothing good.

But even with this strong sense of foreboding, I am paralysed with fear when I step out of the car and an arm reaches out and pulls me backwards, towards the side gate. I can't see who has got me in their grip, but it's a male arm, that I'm sure of.

And just as I try to recall how to squirm from an attacker's grasp, he speaks, leaving me in no doubt who it is.

'Tara, I need to talk to you. I'm not going to hurt you, please believe that, but when I let go you have to stay calm and promise not to scream. I just need to talk to you, that's all I want.'

'Okay,' I say. 'I won't scream. Just let go of me.'

Mikey loosens his grip, and I spin around to face him.

'What the hell are you doing?'

'I've just had a detective questioning me for hours, Tara. About your neighbour's murder. But I had nothing to do with it. Why did he want to talk to me? What have you been saying?'

I search his eyes and am surprised to find he looks scared. 'You threatened me, Mikey. On the phone the other day. The police take these things seriously, you should know that. As will the school when they find out.'

He shakes his head. 'It wasn't a threat. I was just. . . but what I said has got nothing to do with your neighbour. Why am I suddenly being questioned as a suspect?'

'Were you arrested?'

'No, but—'

'Then what makes you think you're a suspect?'

I back away from him, and glance towards the house, desperately hoping Lisa will have heard my car and be waiting for me to come in. When she doesn't hear me, she is bound to check what's going on.

'Because that detective as good as said it when he came to my house last night,' Mikey says. 'He wanted to know what I was doing that night, if I was with anyone who could verify where I was. So don't try telling me I'm not a suspect. And this has got nothing to do with me, has it, Tara?'

So Holden turned up at Mikey's alone. Something tells me that he has done this unofficially, that he hasn't gone to his superiors with this idea that Mikey is involved. I don't answer Mikey's question, but take another step back, hoping he won't notice.

But of course he does.

'You're scared of me,' he says, his eyes widening. 'Why are you scared of me, Tara? I've never done anything to you.'

Because you're crazy, I want to say. Crazy and creepy and I want you to get away from me. But instead I tell him I'm not now, and never have been, scared of him, hoping he won't see how afraid I am.

'Then you know I would never harm you. Never.'

My hand reaches into my pocket and I feel the cold glass of my mobile phone.

He takes a step closer to me. 'Do you know how much it hurts me that you would even consider. . . when we've known each other so long? How could you even think I could do. . . that to your neighbour.'

I pull out my phone and start dialling. 'I'm calling the police, Mikey, don't come any closer.'

Now there will be no doubt in his mind that I'm terrified of him. Of the man I thought was harmless, someone who was simply a bit over-friendly.

'Oh, Tara, put the phone away. You're making a big mistake.'

'Tell that to the police when they arrive,' I say, holding the phone to my ear, ready to run if necessary.

'Okay,' Mikey says. 'Right after I tell them that I saw your daughter that night, running from that house over there with blood on her clothes.'

CHAPTER TWENTY-FIVE

I disconnect the call and grab hold of Mikey's arm. I must have heard him wrong. There is no way he said what I think he did. I ask him to repeat it.

He doesn't seem troubled by my fingers digging into his flesh.

'You heard me correctly, Tara. I was here that night because I knew Noah was away, and that you were alone. I just came to see you, but then I noticed you heading over to your neighbour's house, so I sat in my car and waited for you to come back.' I know what comes next; I almost don't need him to say it. 'But you didn't come out,' he continues. 'Your daughter did, though, around about midnight, and her clothes were blood-stained.'

He's lying, he has to be. This is a sick joke, a form of revenge for my rejection. I tell him as much, but he shakes his head.

'You don't really believe that, do you? She's your daughter so you must have had suspicions. Where's her alibi?'

But as I always do, I will defend Rosie to the bitter end. 'So you're the one who told the police? But they never mentioned blood on her clothes. You're lying. Everyone knows Rosie ran from the house. She's admitted that. What was she wearing?'

'A white cardigan. And I haven't gone to the police. If I had, I wouldn't be telling you all this now, would I? They obviously don't know about the blood, as they would definitely have kept her locked up.'

I'm confused; as usual, nothing about this makes any sense. I tell him once more that he's lying, and that every woman owns a white cardigan.

He smiles. 'And she had on patterned black-and-white shorts, or a skirt that looks like shorts. I'm no expert on women's fashion – I can't tell you which it was. And there was something shiny in her hair. Again, I don't know what it was, but I know it was your daughter.'

It's hard to recall what Rosie told the police she was wearing that night, but I know they checked all her clothes and couldn't find any trace of blood or other DNA belonging to Lee. But surely Mikey is being too specific to be lying. And if it wasn't him who initially went to the police, then who was it?

I let go of his arm. 'Why didn't you tell the police this?'

'Up until now, for two reasons. Firstly, I knew what it would do to you and, despite what you might think, I'm not a nasty person, Tara. I couldn't hurt you like that. And secondly, I didn't want to place myself at the crime scene and get tied up in all this. Because, as I've admitted to you, my reasons for being on your road at that time aren't exactly. . . orthodox? I don't want to lose my job, Tara, it's all I've got and I love teaching. But now, it seems, I am in trouble with the police already, thanks to you, so I've really got nothing left to lose.'

'What do you want from me, Mikey? Just spit it out, because there's obviously something, isn't there?'

His eyes widen. 'How can you think so little of me, Tara? What have I ever done to you? Except be a friend, offer you company at school, an escape from the students.'

But I would rather deal with a thousand students all at once than Mikey on his own. I don't say this now, instead telling him that friends don't threaten each other, don't stalk one another.

'Stalking's a bit of a strong word, isn't it? I came to your house once, and bumped into you at Westfield once. How does that constitute stalking?'

'You're also everywhere I turn at school. Morning, afternoon, any time, you're always there.'

He sighs. 'I told you, it's a nice break from the students. And I do it because I like you, Tara. I thought we were friends. So of course I want to be around you.'

I glance at the house. But now I am glad there is no sign of Lisa. 'Mikey, you asked me to dinner. Anyway, I don't care about any of this. What do you want? And what are you going to do?'

'The police need to stop sniffing around me, Tara. I don't have an alibi for that night, because I was here, but I won't lose my job when I haven't done anything.'

'I can't do anything about that. They know about you now so what do you want me to do? Why would they listen to me, especially after I was. . . in Lee's house?'

But Mikey will not give up. 'You're the one who spoke to that detective. Hunt, is it? So call him off. Tell him you were wrong about me stalking you. If I'm not a stalker, then I have no motive so they'll leave me alone.'

'You're asking the impossible.'

'I'm sure you'll find a way. I'm sure he'll listen to you.' Mikey knows about Holden, he has to. 'It's not as bad as what I have to do,' he continues. 'Keeping your daughter's awful secret makes me an accessory in some way, doesn't it? Oh, what a mess, Tara.'

'So that's all you want? Me to try to put them off?'

'Yes. Try your best, though. Don't just try, and then tell me he wouldn't listen.'

Mikey is deluded if he thinks I can have any sway over Holden, or any other police officer.

'And that's it? That's all you want?'

'No. I'd like a bit of respect too.' The smile he offers is more of a smirk. 'That's not asking too much, is it?'

* * *

As if I haven't already had to make the most difficult choices of my life, I am now faced with the hardest yet. I watch Mikey walk off, then I walk into the silent house and head upstairs to Rosie's room. It is still early, so of course she will be fast asleep, but there is no time to lose.

She doesn't wake up when I walk in, so I sit on the edge of her bed and give her a gentle nudge. 'Rosie, wake up.' But it's not enough to rouse her, so I do it again, repeating the action until she stirs.

Rosie has never been a morning person, and her eyes don't seem to want to open.

'Mum? What's going on? If you've come to apologise for last night then—'

I get straight to the point. 'Someone else saw you, Rosie. The night Lee was killed. And they're claiming you were running from Lee's house with blood-stained clothes.' I haven't planned what I will say, the words fall from my mouth like a fountain.

Now her eyes pop open, and she pulls herself up to a sitting position. 'What? What are you talking about, Mum?'

I repeat what I've just said, my voice sounding as if it belongs to someone else. 'There's no point lying any more, Rosie. This person is ready to go to the police.'

'But the police already know everything. Who is it? They're lying! I did run from his house but there was no blood on me. I told you what happened. I didn't kill Lee, Mum!'

'Shhhh, keep your voice down or Lisa and Spencer will hear.' I press my finger to my mouth to reinforce this message, and wait until I'm sure there is no sound from the hallway. 'What were you wearing that night, Rosie?'

She swings her legs over the side of the bed. 'I can't remember. I told the police that. But they checked all my clothes, Mum. Everything I own. And none of them had any blood on them.'

This is true, but the chances are she would have got rid of what she wore that night. If she is guilty.

'Could it have been black-and-white patterned shorts or a skirt?'

She frowns. 'I don't know. Maybe. I've got so many clothes, Mum, you know that.'

When I saw Rosie later that day she had on a clean pair of jeans, despite the heat. But what does this mean? Did she change into the first thing she could find that night, or were her jeans already in her weekend bag?

I fight back tears. I need to be strong for her. 'I can't protect you from this, Rosie. I will be there for you, but there's nothing I can do to help you now. We've got to go to the police, okay? It's the right thing to do.'

She backs away to the other side of the room. 'No! I didn't do it, Mum! I'm not going back there, not again. I didn't do it!' She bursts into uncontrollable sobs.

I go to her and pull her towards me, wrapping my arms around her and rocking her back and forth to try to soothe her, as if she is still a baby. My whole body aches at the thought that Rosie could be capable of taking someone's life, and I know I will never be able to accept it.

'Can you prove it to me, Rosie. Anything at all. I just need proof, and then I'll do whatever I can to stop this.' Please let there be something. She can't have done this.

But she shakes her head. 'How? I don't know how?' Her cries grow louder, despite burying her head in the crook of my arm.

'Anything, Rosie. Anything. There's got to be something.' I whisper this, but I really want to scream it. I need so desperately for her to prove her innocence. 'What about Damien? He's the answer to this, isn't he?' And then I remember that I was going to ask Holden to trace her texts on her phone. 'Your phone,' I say.

'What do you mean?'

'We can get the police to check your texts and then they'll find Damien's, won't they? Even if you deleted them, there will be a permanent record of them.' Because nowadays nothing is ever truly erased.

But when she pulls back and looks me in the eye, I know exactly what she's about to say.

'He doesn't exist, does he?'

She looks away. 'I. . . I'm so sorry, Mum. I made him up because you would have found out I wasn't with Libby that night. But I didn't kill Lee, Mum. Everything else I've told you about what happened is true.'

'Where were you that night then? You said you slept in Damien's car, but where were you really?'

She pauses. 'Look, you won't believe me but I caught a night bus to Oxford Street and walked around there for ages. Then when the shops opened I just tried to take my mind off everything until I could bring myself to come home.'

Does she realise how unbelievable her story is? A strong sense of déjà vu overwhelms me; we are going around in circles and getting nowhere. I have lost count of the number of conversations I've had recently with her where she's insisted she's telling the truth, and begged me to believe her. But the words that leave her mouth are anything but the truth. But at least she has finally come clean about Damien.

Although I am seething with anger, I won't take it out on her, and I need to be mindful that Spencer and Lisa are still asleep down the hall.

'Didn't you think the police would check your alibi, and even if they didn't realise to start with, they soon would?'

'But they can't prove anything either way, can they?' This makes her sound cold and calculated. Perhaps she realises this as she quickly adds: 'I didn't think I'd be a suspect, Mum, otherwise I would never have said it because now it just makes me look even more guilty.'

I remember something then, a detail I had forgotten about with everything that keeps happening. 'What did you and Libby argue about?'

'What? What do you mean?'

'Bernadette said she heard you and Libby arguing about a boy. What was that all about?'

There is a long pause while she considers my question. 'Oh, that was about Ewan. Libby kind of liked him too. Mum, that's got nothing to do with anything!'

I don't reply, because I don't know if I'm just being fed more lies.

Rosie grabs my hand. 'Please help me, Mum. Please.'

And now I must face what I need to do.

Fifteen minutes later we are in the car, and I don't know how we've managed to leave the house without Lisa or Spencer waking. But I have left a note to say I had to take Rosie somewhere, and will be back soon.

In the passenger seat, Rosie still sobs, but her cry is more of a whine now, as she accepts her fate. My heart breaks for her, but right now there is nothing I can do to comfort her. Before we got in the car I told her to trust me, that the truth always comes out in the end, and if she is innocent then she has nothing to worry about, but it is clear this did nothing to ease her mind, and that she is petrified of what awaits her.

We've only been driving for a short time when she falls asleep, exhausted from all her crying, but I am relieved at this. Sleep will be an escape for her, and for a while, at least, she won't be scared.

Finally, we arrive, my heart pounding in my chest as I scan the car park for him. He has promised to be here, to help me with this as much as he can. And I trust him with this. I trust that he will look after Rosie.

After a few moments, he appears from the shadows, and walks towards us, but I need to get out of the car quickly so that I can talk to him first. Leaving Rosie to sleep in the passenger seat, I gently shut the door and meet him before he reaches the car.

'Thanks for coming,' I say.

He reaches for my hand. 'She's my daughter, of course I'm going to help. But, Tara, I don't think you've thought this through properly. This is serious. And I'm not exactly happy about doing it.' He glances at the car. 'Tell me again what your plan is?'

I kiss Noah's cheek then turn back to check Rosie is still asleep.

'We need somewhere safe for her to hide out for a while, because the police are bound to find out Damien doesn't exist, if they haven't already, and then they'll have more questions for her. I know she didn't do this, but I just need time to try to prove it. I need to do this for her, Noah, even though it seems like an impossible task.'

He nods. 'It will be, Tara, because you're not a detective, and they can't even find the person who did it. And they haven't been able to prove anything about Rosie, either way.'

'Oh, Noah, I don't know. I have no idea what I'll do, but I don't want them taking Rosie, not yet, and it's only a matter of time before they come for her.'

'This is crazy,' Noah says. 'She might be. . . We're breaking the law, Tara.'

But I have thought hard about this. 'No, we're not. Because Rosie hasn't been arrested again, and they haven't even asked to talk to her. Mikey hasn't said a word to anyone but me so far, so if I can just keep it that way then it buys us some time. So we're not breaking any laws.'

'It's still dodgy, though.'

It will take more than this to fully convince Noah, despite his willingness to help.

'Are you saying you don't want to help?'

Once more he glances through the car window. 'Of course I'll help. Despite everything, I trust you. And if you say Rosie didn't do this, then. . . she didn't do it.'

The feeling of relief it gives me to hear him say this is too great for words. I lean into him and hug him tightly. 'Thank you. That means a lot to me.'

We stay like that for a moment before I pull away. 'Where will you take her?'

'Remember my friend, Robert Hayes? I met him in New York? Well, I don't know if I told you but he moved back to the UK a few months ago and is now living in Manchester. We haven't spoken for a while so he knows nothing about Lee, but I called him this morning. I told him Rosie needed somewhere to stay in Manchester so she can check out the area and see if she wants to go to university there. It was the first thing I could think of. He's a nice guy and he readily agreed, so I'll drive her up there this morning. It's a long way, but she'll be well looked after with Rob and his wife. I'll stay there tonight with her and drive back tomorrow.'

I am impressed that Noah has managed to get all this arranged in the last hour.

'Okay, but remember she'll need a new mobile. A pay-as-you-go one would be best. We have to be careful the police can't trace her calls, just in case Mikey changes his mind and they try to find her. I'll keep her old phone at home.' Saying this makes me feel like a criminal, but I'm doing this for my daughter.

'I'll get her a new phone,' Noah says. 'Now we'd better get going. It's a long drive and will be rush hour soon.'

We head over to the car and I open the passenger door and gently wake Rosie, leaning down to her to whisper her name, almost in tears as I watch her rub her eyes and look around her. She turns to stare at me as she gradually focuses and takes in her surroundings: a deserted car park in the middle of a field, instead of a police station.

'Where are we?. . . what's going on?' she says. 'This isn't the police station.' And then she notices Noah standing right behind me. 'Mum? What's happening?'

'You're not going to the police, Rosie. Dad's taking you somewhere safe. Just for the time being until we can work out what to do about all this.'

I help her out of the car and she flings her arms around me. 'Thank you so much for this, Mum. And I promise you, I didn't kill Lee.'

I neither agree nor disagree but usher her into Noah's car, handing her the bag I'd told her to pack for the police station. She stretches the seatbelt across her and looks up at me, and the gratitude on her face is all I need to know I am doing the right thing.

But watching them drive away, I wonder what the hell I'm going to do now.

CHAPTER TWENTY-SIX

Spencer is having a bath and Lisa is up and making coffee in the kitchen when I get home. She watches me as I come in and throw my bag on the table.

'Tell me,' she says. 'And don't try to fob me off because I know you're not okay. Something's happened, because it's not like you to just leave a note with no explanation. I'm really worried, Tara. What's going on? Is this about Harvey?'

I reassure her it's not, and she listens as I tell her about Mikey turning up here last night to talk to me. I almost don't want to explain that Mikey saw Rosie running from Lee's house, but how can I leave out such an important detail? And even if Lisa believes she is guilty, I know she will stand by her, just as Noah is doing.

She shakes her head when I've finished, and her eyes are filled with sadness. 'Oh, Rosie,' she says. 'I just can't believe it. Not Rosie.'

'But that's just the thing, Lisa – I don't believe it. And it's not just about me being her mum and not seeing any bad in her, because I do. There's plenty of bad in Rosie. But not murder. No way.'

She studies my face for a moment. 'Well, I suppose you can't trust what Mikey says. And it's a bit scary that he just turned up like that. Maybe he's lying just to get to you? Why wouldn't he just go to the police?'

This is exactly what hasn't made sense to me. 'It's because he wants something to hold over me. He wants to hurt me. That's it.'

Lisa nods. 'I'm so confused, Tara. Is it as simple as him lying? Or is it that we don't want to think it could be Rosie, the little girl we've seen grow up to a young adult. Is our judgement clouded by this?'

'I've had weeks to get my head around the idea that Rosie might have done it, but it's never fitted. Never made sense. And, as I said before, that's not just because I'm her mother, I'm trusting my instinct.' The instinct that has let me down before.

'I understand,' Lisa says. But I wonder if she really does, or whether she is simply doing her duty as my sister, standing by me no matter what. 'So what are you going to do?'

I tell her about Noah taking Rosie to Manchester to stay with his friend.

Her eyes widen in surprise. 'Oh, Tara, is that a good idea? Rosie could get into all sorts of trouble. So could you. There has to be a better way. If you just tell the police everything.'

'No, I can't offer her up to them on a plate. We'll bring her back only if they want to arrest her. And if Mikey keeps his mouth shut then that shouldn't happen. They still don't have any evidence, so he's the only way they would arrest her again. In the meantime, I have to hope they find out who killed Lee.'

'Do you trust this man to keep quiet? How can you be sure he will?'

'I can't. But what choice do I have? I just have to make sure I keep him on side. All he wants is the police to leave him alone.'

Lisa's phone rings, but she lets it go to voicemail. 'Can I do anything? I need to help.'

Looking at her face, at the purple bruise that doesn't seem to fade, I marvel at her kindness. She has got enough on her plate without having to help me with my troubles.

'No, just your company is enough. You don't have to do anything.'

'Actually, I was thinking maybe I should get back home. I've put you out long enough.' She picks up her phone. 'Let me just check my message.'

While she's doing this, I text Noah to see how their drive to Manchester is going. I am deliberately vague in my message, and leave out any mention of Rosie. He won't be able to reply while he's driving, but hopefully they'll stop soon for a break, so he can update me.

'That was the police,' Lisa says, placing her phone on the worktop. 'I need to call them back. Oh, Tara, it must be about Harvey, mustn't it?' Her voice becomes shaky.

'Don't worry, it will be okay. They'll have found him and that's good news, isn't it?'

Before she can reply, Spencer appears in the doorway, his hair still damp from his bath. He seems unsure about coming in; perhaps he has got too used to the adults whispering in corners, but I tell him to get his breakfast.

'I'll return their call upstairs,' Lisa says. She won't want Spencer hearing any details of what happened.

When she comes back down, she stands in the doorway of the kitchen but doesn't come in.

'I'll be back in a sec,' I tell Spencer, but he's too engrossed in his football sticker album to pay any attention.

'What did they say?' I ask, once Lisa and I are out of Spencer's earshot. But one look at her swollen red eyes tells me this can't be good.

'They can't find Harvey!'

'What do you mean they "can't find" him?'

'They've been to his work but nobody's seen him since Tuesday. And he has no other address as he gave up his rented flat when he moved in with me.'

'They'll find him. He's probably just scared of being arrested for assault so he's staying with a friend somewhere.'

She shakes her head. 'They've checked with all his friends and nobody's seen him. They're checking with the airports now to see if he's left the country.'

This seems a bit extreme, but then so do many other things that have happened over the last couple of months, so there's no point writing it off.

'Well, if that's true then it's a good thing in a way. It means you're safe. Do you know if he took his passport with him?'

She frowns. 'I didn't think to check. I don't even know where he keeps it. Oh, Tara, what a mess! And with everything that's going on with you too, it's just. . . what the hell is happening to our family?'

At least our parents know nothing of Lisa's troubles. They have enough to worry about with me and Rosie, and Noah moving out. But I'm determined to show them we will all be okay.

'It will all work out,' I say. 'They'll find him.'

But this does little to pacify her.

'I've never been this terrified in my life, Tara. In fact, I don't think I've ever been scared of anything before now. I never thought I was this kind of person. I wasn't before he did this to me. I don't like it, but I feel powerless to stop it.' She touches her bruise again.

This is something I can relate to, although I am not going to stand back and let fear win. Someone out there knows what happened to Lee, and it's only a matter of time before it catches up with them. The clock is ticking.

I wish I could pass my determination onto Lisa, but it is something she needs to find in herself. All I can do is help her get there. 'You're not alone,' I say.

She tries to smile, but it seems to take a huge effort. 'I need to go back home, Tara. I've already been here too long. I'm running out of clothes and underwear.'

'You're not going home, Lisa. Not until they find Harvey and make sure he can't come anywhere near you. Give me your key and I'll go and get your clothes for you. I'll bring whatever you need.'

She opens her mouth and I can tell she wants to protest, but then gives in and reaches into her bag, taking a key from her key ring and handing it to me. 'Thank you,' is all she can manage to say.

Back in the kitchen, Spencer asks if Ryan can come over for lunch. There is so much I need to sort out, and having his friend here will only make things difficult, but Spencer's wide, shiny eyes silently beg me to say yes, and I can't bear to let him down.

Lisa steps in. 'I can watch the boys. I know you've got things to do today.'

'Thanks Aunty Lisa,' Spencer says, and before I say anything he is rushing off to tell Ryan the good news.

'Are you sure about this? Babysitting two boys might be a bit of a handful.'

'It will be fine. Spencer's no trouble so I'm sure his friend won't be either. Now, go and do what you need to do.'

The first thing I do is text Holden to tell him we need to talk. My phone beeps seconds after I've sent it, but it's not him replying, it is Mikey. And all his message says is good morning, with a small kiss at the end.

My first reaction is to delete it without replying, but this is a bad idea. Mikey has me backed into a corner, where he can see to it that he gets his own way. If I cooperate. I shudder to think where this will all end, but for now, I will play his game, and pray that Holden gets to the truth quickly.

Reluctantly, I start typing *good morning* back, without a kiss, and quickly send it before I can change my mind.

The second I put my phone down, Mikey texts again.

'Meet me for dinner at my place. Seven p.m. Just as friends of course.'

His words fill me with horror. I thought he might try to meet up, but inviting me to his flat is far worse than that. I know he lives close to the school but I've never been there before, and I would be well out of my comfort zone. Vulnerable. He would be in control.

I'm about to tell him there is no way that is happening, that he will have to meet me somewhere public, when I realise how I can use this situation to my advantage. Being at his flat means I might get an opportunity to look around, and if he had anything to do with Lee's murder, and setting up Rosie, then there might be something there to prove it. The chances are practically zero, but it's worth a try. And it's better than sitting back and waiting for Lee's killer to be caught. I will do what little I can.

'Fine. But text me your address. I have no idea what it is.'

I want to add that this is because I'm not a stalker, but refrain. I need to keep Mikey on side for as long as possible.

It feels strange walking into Lisa's flat, knowing she isn't here, knowing what happened to her within these walls. The place is exactly how we left it; the black bin liners with Harvey's belongings still occupying the hallway, untouched. He still has a key to Lisa's flat, but it doesn't appear that he's been here, so that's something good at least.

I rummage through the bags, looking for his passport, but there is no sign of it, and nor are there any other personal items or documents. No driving licence or birth certificate. No bills with his name on them. Only clothes, DVDs and books. He could have come back to take some things; I can't recall how many bags we filled, and I'm willing to bet neither can Lisa. There is no other explanation for how he moved into her flat with no personal documents. This is just one more thing I need to tell Holden.

Thinking of him reminds me he hasn't yet replied to my text, so I check my phone, just in case I missed it driving here. But there is only a message from Noah, telling me he got to Manchester with no problems.

It crosses my mind to text Holden again, but I don't. I will not harass him; there has been too much of that from too many people lately. He'll get back to me when he can.

Finding a suitcase in Lisa's built-in wardrobe, I throw clothes into it as quickly as I can because I don't want to spend a second longer here than necessary. Harvey could turn up at any second, and even though I double locked the front door, there is only one way out, and he could easily be waiting outside.

By the time I've finished there is still no reply from Holden, but there are two texts from Mikey reminding me about dinner. I don't reply, and it is an effort to stifle my anger, but I need to stay focused.

Lisa rushes out in bare feet the minute I pull up at home. 'What happened? He didn't turn up did he? Are you okay? You took ages and I was getting worried.'

Pulling her suitcase from the boot, I reassure her it all went well. 'It didn't look like he'd been there, but when I checked through his bags I noticed there was no personal documentation there. No passport, bank statements. Nothing like that. Do you know where he kept that stuff when he moved in?'

Lisa shakes her head. 'I've never thought about it. I just gave him a couple of drawers in my dresser and didn't notice what he put in there. But when we cleared all his stuff out I didn't see anything either. But to be honest, I wasn't really looking.'

'It doesn't matter,' I say, as we head into the house. 'I think it's worth mentioning to the police, though.'

'Which police, mine or yours?' she says, nudging my arm.

Despite the circumstances, I'm pleased that she's able to make light of this when it's causing her so much pain.

'Yours,' I say, but I have every intention of telling Holden when he finally gets back to me. I won't yet worry that I haven't heard from him; he is a busy man, and if that means he's doing all he can to solve Lee's murder then that's all that matters.

'Lisa, would you mind watching Spencer this evening as well? I hate to ask but there's something I need to take care of.'

'Of course I can. It's the least I can do after you letting me stay here. Is it anything to do with Rosie?'

'Yes. But I'll tell you about it later. I need to make some calls and then get ready.'

She assures me Spencer will be fine, and offers to make him dinner. And despite everything, I feel lucky to have my family. Even Noah has shown his support for us all, regardless of our marital situation.

But my spirits flag again when I think of where I have to go tonight.

Mikey's flat comes as a surprise. I have always imagined him living in a dark, old-fashioned property, a lonely place that needs modernising and brightening up, but I find myself standing in a new, pristine home, that is obviously well cared for.

'What's the matter?' he says, sensing my bewilderment. 'Besides the obvious, of course.'

'Nothing. You have a nice flat,' I say, but the minute I've said it I hate that I've offered him a compliment after what he's doing to me.

He beams and looks around proudly. 'Yes, it is nice, isn't it? It means a lot to me that you like it, and home is where the heart is so it's important to love where you live. Don't you think?'

I stand where I am, reluctant to move further from the front door.

'Actually, Mikey, what I think is that you're blackmailing me, forcing me to be here, so if you think I'm going to spend the evening making small talk with you then think again.'

He looks affronted. 'There's no need to be like that. Look, just come and have a drink. I've got wine. Do you like red?'

'No. Or white. Or any alcohol. I'll just have water.' But I have already decided I won't touch a drop of anything he gives me.

He seems disappointed at this, and I wonder if he was hoping to get me drunk. When I look at him, I cannot believe he would do that, but he is already doing something far worse. And he killed Lee. He must have done, because if he didn't then it was Rosie, and I refuse to believe that.

'Fair enough,' he says. 'Come to the kitchen and keep me company while I finish preparing dinner. That will be cosy, won't it?'

There is no way I want to touch any food he gives me, but I have to humour him.

'What are you making?' I ask. Distracting him is the only way I'll be able to get a good look at anything in his house. I have to make him believe I might actually be enjoying myself.

'Oh, don't worry, it's something you like. You've told me many times how much you love spaghetti bolognese. Well, I'm confident you won't be disappointed. I have a special recipe for it.'

He is right, it is one of my favourite meals, but I don't recall ever mentioning this to him. But how else would he know? It shows how much attention he's paid to our conversations over the years, while I cannot remember a single personal detail about him, other than how much he loves coffee.

'Why are you doing this?' I ask, as I watch him prepare a dinner I won't eat. He is clearly at ease in the kitchen, and I feel a surge of pity for him that he doesn't have anyone to cook for.

'Doing what?'

'Inviting me here. Cooking me dinner. Why are you doing this when you think my daughter is a murderer? That should make you want to stay away from me, and not trust me.'

'Because you're not your daughter, and you're not responsible for what happened.'

Neither is she, I want to shout, but I keep my mouth shut.

'And because I think of you as a friend,' he continues. 'And friends don't just turn their backs on each other when things get tough. Look, I know you're not interested in me, I've always known that, and I'm sorry if I've been a bit. . . full on.'

I study his face, and he seems genuine, but still I cannot trust him. 'You have, and it makes me uncomfortable.'

He dishes the spaghetti onto plates. 'But worth it, I hope?'

'What do you mean?'

'I know why you're here, Tara, and it's not just to keep me quiet. You think I killed your neighbour, and set up your daughter, so you're here to check out my flat, see if you can find anything.'

My whole body turns cold, and automatically my hand reaches for my bag. My phone is inside and I need to be able to reach it quickly.

'Well, go ahead, Tara. Feel free to take a good look around, anywhere you like. I won't even come with you. But maybe we could just eat first? Seeing as I've gone to all this trouble.'

'I don't need to look around,' I say.

He has clearly made sure there is nothing incriminating here, and I am convinced now, more than ever, that Mikey killed Lee. Why else would he have even thought that's why I am here? It is surely the sign of a guilty mind. I urgently need to speak to Holden.

'I need to text someone,' I say, fully prepared to run for the door when he tries to stop me.

His smile is a grimace. 'Go on then, Tara, I've got nothing to hide.'

There is a catch, there has to be. Mikey will wait for me to get out my phone then try to take it from me. But he doesn't, and I text Holden as quickly as I can, telling him where I am. But my finger pauses over the word 'send'. I cannot do it, because firstly, I don't need rescuing, and secondly, now that I'm here, I will get Mikey to admit the truth.

CHAPTER TWENTY-SEVEN

'We've known each other a long time, haven't we, Mikey?'

He places our plates on the table and, despite my determination not to touch his food, it does smell good.

'Six years this September,' he says. 'I remember the day you first started. You were so confident, even though you were new to the school, and I admired that in you. It doesn't come naturally to a lot of people, but you had classroom control down to an art.'

Regardless of the bizarre situation, I am flattered by his compliment. But not enough to be fooled by him. 'So let's be straight with each other,' I say.

'That's all I've ever wanted,' he says, twisting a strand of spaghetti around his fork, while my food remains untouched.

'I just want the truth. You admitted earlier you've been a bit intense—'

'Actually I said full on, but I suppose it amounts to the same thing.'

At first I think he must be making a joke, but there is no smile on his face, just a deadpan expression. This is Mikey all over.

'Whichever, it doesn't matter. The point is you admitted that. And I just want the truth about everything, Mikey. You're going about this the wrong way, trying to force my friendship by essentially threatening my daughter. But there is an easier way.'

He puts down his fork and folds his hands together as he stares at me. 'Oh yeah? And what's that?'

'Just tell me the truth and we'll take it from there. I won't tell the police. All I want is Rosie's name cleared, even if only in my mind. I don't want this question mark hanging over her.'

He picks up his fork again. 'I'm sorry, Tara, but I can't help you because there's nothing to admit. I didn't kill your neighbour. What reason would I have? I didn't even know him.'

'But you were waiting for me that night. You saw me there with him. Maybe you got jealous. That's motive enough for the police, isn't it?'

'Oh, Tara, I understand how desperate you are to believe this. You're a mother and it's got to be the worst thing to think your precious child is capable of extinguishing someone's life. But what I told you was the whole truth. I saw your daughter running from that house with blood on her clothes.'

So, he is going to stick to this story. I try a different approach. 'What did you do when I first went into the house? You said you were waiting for me, but what did you do exactly?' Catching him out may be the only hope I have now.

'I sat in my car and waited. I thought you might be a while, but after a couple of hours I wondered what you were doing. But I waited until it got dark and crept round the back of the house.'

My body freezes. He didn't tell me this last time. 'And. . . what did you see?'

He looks away from me then and picks up his glass of wine. 'Are you sure you want to know? Because once I tell you, what I say can't be unheard.'

'Just tell me!' I shout.

'You were both sitting on his sofa, drinking wine.' He holds up his glass. 'Nothing wrong with that. I watched you for a while and you just talked. He must have been a funny man because you kept laughing. I couldn't hear the words through the double or triple glazing. But you do look beautiful when you laugh like that. With your head thrown back. Your whole face lights up.'

'Get to the point, Mikey!'

'I was angry with you, Tara, I'll admit that now. Angry because your husband was away, and there you were flirting with your neighbour, drinking his wine. I lost count of how much you both had, but it was multiple bottles, I know that much.' He lets out a heavy sigh. 'I was angry that it wasn't me.'

Angry enough to kill him. I need to keep Mikey talking, but I fear where this is going.

'Is that. . . all we did? Drink wine, I mean? We didn't. . . take anything else?'

'You mean drugs? Not that I saw.' He still holds his empty fork in his hand and makes no move to pick up any food with it. 'Can you really not remember anything?'

'Not really. I remember going inside and drinking wine and, the next thing I knew, it was morning and I was waking up next to him.' Mikey is the last person I want to be talking to about this, but if it gets the truth out of him it will all be worth it.

'You don't need to say any more,' he says. 'I know the rest because it was all over the news. I've just had a thought – are they actually letting you back to work?'

'Of course. I haven't done anything.'

'But you were arrested; isn't that enough for them to suspend you? I hope they don't. It wouldn't be the same there without you.'

I don't know why Mikey is trying to unnerve me by mentioning this when he's doing a brilliant enough job of that already.

'Can you. . . look, just tell me what else you saw.'

He digs his fork into his spaghetti, wrapping a long strand around it and placing it in his mouth, so it is a few moments before he can answer. 'Okay, well, don't say I didn't warn you. Eventually he moved closer to you on the sofa. Too close. I thought you would push him away but you didn't. You just kept laughing at his jokes, playfully nudging him once in a while. That kind of thing.'

It sickens me to hear this, but I remind myself not to trust Mikey. This will all be part of his game. 'Then what?'

'He leaned towards you and kissed you, but you pushed him away.'

Relief floods through me. I did the right thing and stopped it before anything happened. I can tell Mikey is enjoying this, but he has only proved me right.

'I knew it,' I say.

'Oh, no, Tara, I haven't finished. You pushed him away at first, but he soon tried again and you gave in to him.'

I shake my head. 'You're lying. I would never have done that. Never.'

Mikey chuckles. 'You were so drunk, Tara, I don't think you knew what you were doing. In your defence, I think you were trying to resist him, but, well, even I could see he was a good-looking man. It would have taken a lot to resist that temptation.'

I shake my head. 'No. I don't believe it.'

'Well, there's nothing I can do about that. Anyway, it might surprise you to hear this, but the minute you started peeling each other's clothes off, I got out of there as quickly as I could. So I really didn't see. . . the act itself.'

Just hearing these words brings bile to my throat. This is all wrong. He's doing it to get to me, because he will never have me.

'See, I'm not as bad as you think. I could have stayed around, but I didn't want to, and not just because it hurt to see you with him like that. I am actually a decent person, Tara.'

There are no words I can say to this. He has rendered me speechless.

'I'm sorry, Tara, but it's true. And you mentioned drugs earlier, but it didn't seem as if you'd taken anything; you were just acting like someone who'd had too much to drink. You didn't seem completely out of it.'

And then I realise that something doesn't add up. 'But if you left, like you claim, then how did you see Rosie running from the house?'

'Because I came back. A bit later. I'd driven off, but after a while I was so angry with you that I came back to confront you. You see, before all this, Tara, I really admired you. I could live with the fact that you didn't want me, because it meant you were a good moral person. But when I saw you with him, it just destroyed the image I held of you.'

Again I am lost for words.

'And that's when I saw Rosie. When I noticed the blood, I got the hell out of there. I wanted no part of whatever had happened.'

I stand up. 'I'm leaving. You're full of shit, Mikey. I don't believe a word you've said, and I'm not listening to any more.'

Before I've reached the kitchen door, Mikey delivers a final blow. 'If I'm lying, then how do I know about the birthmark on your breast? Shaped a bit like a heart, isn't it?'

I park in the drive but don't get out to go in the house. I can't face Lisa, Spencer or anyone else until I've got my head around Mikey's revelation. I don't remember driving home just now, my mind crushed by the weight of his words, and the thought that he saw me with Lee like that. And worse than that, the realisation that I most likely slept with Lee.

I try to work out if there is any other way Mikey could know about my birthmark, but unless he's actually been in my house when I've been dressing or undressing, there is no way. So now I am left questioning everything I've ever believed about myself and my morals.

And the more I think about it, the more Mikey's story makes sense, because an undisputable fact is that I was naked in Lee's bed, and the most logical reason for that is if I slept with him. I shudder at this thought. Somehow having no knowledge of it makes it even worse.

But I need to pull myself together. What's done is done and I can't change any of that now. All I can do is make things right by protecting my daughter, because even if Mikey is telling the truth about me, I do not believe he saw Rosie with any blood on her.

Lisa is waiting for me when I open the front door, concern etched on her face.

'I've been worried about you! Why were you sitting in the car all this time? I saw you pull up ages ago, but thought you must be on the phone or something so I didn't want to come out.' She frowns. 'Tara? You look awful. What's happened?'

I shouldn't burden Lisa with this, but I need to tell someone, and Holden still hasn't replied to me. So I sit her down and tell her where I've been, and what Mikey claimed he saw.

'No way,' she says. 'Why do you believe him? He's lying, Tara, don't fall for it. He's just trying to get to you.' She points to the living room. 'Let's go in there. You don't want Spencer hearing this.'

But how will I stop him knowing about this when it all comes out? Which it will, eventually.

I follow her in and sit on the sofa opposite her. 'But he knew about my birthmark, Lisa. There is no way he could have unless he's telling the truth.'

She falls silent for a moment. 'Remember he's been following you everywhere? Who knows what he's seen. Sorry to make you think of this but he could have been standing in your back garden every night, watching you get undressed. Ughh, what a vile man.'

'I can't explain why, Lisa, but my instinct tells me he's not lying. I just feel it, if that makes sense. He's lying about Rosie but not this. It all fits, Lisa. And there's no escaping the fact that I was naked in Lee's bed.'

Lisa stands up and sits next to me, taking my hand. 'I know you, Tara, probably better than anyone, and I'm telling you, there is no way you slept with him. At least not with any knowledge of what you were doing.'

This only makes me feel slightly better. Even if it were true, I should never have sat down to drink with him.

'I know you've thought about this before, but if you were drugged that would explain things. Lee could have easily—'

'No, he wouldn't have. . .' But how do I know this? According to Serena he was already having an affair, and that didn't stop him doing what he did with me. Nausea overcomes me when I think of this, but better me than Rosie. At least, if he did do anything like that, he had the decency to stay away from her.

Lisa looks at me with pity. 'So what are you going to do now?'

'I just want to clear Rosie's name, so she can get on with her life with a clean slate. I'm not worried about me, or what people think I have or haven't done; they can all go to hell. It's Rosie I need to protect.' But as I say this I feel a flicker of doubt. What if there's even the tiniest chance I am wrong in my defence of Rosie? Quickly I shove this thought aside before it can take root.

'Of course. I get that.' Lisa lets go of my hand and touches her cheek again.

'You think she did it, don't you? Tell me the truth.'

She gives a barely perceptible nod, but then tries to mask it with her words.

'I just don't know, Tara. I don't know anything any more. I'm sure I've said this before, but it doesn't look good, does it?'

It is nine p.m. before Holden gets back to me. I almost don't answer my phone because I haven't worked out how I will tell him what Mikey claimed he saw. But I will need to tell him everything if it helps him work out what happened to Lee. I am done with secrets and lies.

'I'm sorry it's taken me so long to call you today,' he says. 'New case came in and I've been working on it all day without a break.' He pauses, and I wonder if he wants to talk to me about the case, but has stopped himself just in time. 'Anyway, forget that, are you doing okay?'

'Not really.' I debate how much to tell him on the phone. 'But can we talk in person. Are you free now?'

'Yes, shall I come there?'

But there seem to be eyes and ears on this house constantly, so we need to be somewhere public. 'No, meet me by the river in Putney, we can walk along there and talk in private.' Plus, it is dark outside now so there is less chance of being seen, and that's better for both of us.

He is already there when I reach the river, sitting on a bench facing the water. He's still dressed in a suit, so he must have come straight from work to get here quickly.

'Hi,' he says, standing up to kiss me on the cheek. As an afterthought he looks around us to make sure nobody is watching, but it's too late if they are. 'What's happened, Tara?'

I tell him everything that happened with Mikey, other than his claim of seeing Rosie. It is a huge risk, but one I have to take. I avoid eye contact when I repeat his story about what Lee and I did. And even when I finish, I can't bear to look at Holden.

But the silence is worse than confronting his reaction, and eventually I give in and face my fear. 'Well? Say something.'

He takes a deep breath, and I prepare for the worst.

'I spent a lot of time talking to that man. Asked him a lot of questions. Made him squirm. But he's not Lee's killer. I'm sure of that. However, I do think he's a bit unhinged and could quite easily be lying. He's trying to get under your skin. You can't just take his word for it that you cheated on your husband, Tara.'

For a man whose job it is to listen only to evidence, he seems very sure of himself.

'How do I know that any more? Look what I'm doing with you.'

'Tara, that's not the same thing. We've had one kiss, that's all, and you're separated. But, even if you did. . . sleep with Lee Jacobs, I can live with that. We've both got a past, haven't we?'

I recall what he's told me about his wife having an affair, and it helps put things in context. To him, nothing, other than murder, would seem as bad as that.

'Okay. But why do you think he's innocent? He's got a motive, hasn't he? And he's admitted he was there that night.'

'Not to me. So it's your word against his if it all comes out.'

'Holden, I need to ask you something and it might be difficult for you to answer, but I really need to know.'

He looks wary as I say this. 'Go on.'

'Who was the witness who said they saw Rosie running from the scene? Please tell me.'

There is a long pause, and I don't look at him, but stare at the river while I wait.

'Sorry,' he says, 'I just don't think—'

'Please, Holden. I will never ask anything of you again. Who was it?'

'Knowing won't help you,' he says.

But I will not let this go without a fight. 'Why won't it? If I can prove they're lying, then Rosie will be in the clear.'

He takes a deep breath. 'It won't help you because the tip came from an anonymous call. But I didn't trick Rosie in any way. I had a duty to follow it up.'

So this is just another dead end.

'Please, Tara, just trust me on this. I'm not ruling Mikey Bradford out as a suspect, but there's no evidence to suggest it was him.'

'Then who? And don't say Rosie. Just don't tell me that's what you think.'

He takes my hand and I'm surprised by how warm it is, even though it's cool out here tonight. 'Whoever did it, I will find them. You have my word on that. And then we will deal with the consequences together. Okay?'

And then he leans forward, pressing his lips against mine. Although it feels good, and I savour every second, one thought crowds my mind.

Can I trust this man? Can I trust anyone?

CHAPTER TWENTY-EIGHT

I wake up early, shattered from a fitful night's sleep, but I force myself up anyway. There is too much to do today, so I can't waste time attempting to sleep.

The house is quiet when I go downstairs, and I'm surprised Spencer isn't up yet, stretching out his day to make the school holidays last longer. I can understand Lisa needing a lie-in, she is mentally and physically exhausted after Harvey's attack, and doesn't seem to be making much progress with her healing. I vow not to burden her with my troubles when she is going through enough of her own.

I have a half-formed plan, and I grab some toast and wash it down with tea, just to fuel me for what lies ahead. And then I make my way across the road, fully prepared to have the door slammed in my face.

But Serena doesn't close the door on me, even though it looks as if I've woken her up. She's wearing a vest top and shorts, because already it is muggy, and her hair is tied back in a messy ponytail.

I speak before she has a chance to tell me to leave.

'Serena, please can we talk? I didn't kill Lee, you have to know that. You must know the police have cleared me.'

'Sometimes they get things wrong.' She spits her words at me.

'Not this time. I know you hate me, and rightly so, but. . . it's really important. Can I come in? Just for a minute.'

She stares at me for too long without speaking, and I begin to feel uncomfortable. But I need to go inside, and once again I'm prepared to put up a fight if I have to.

'Well, you've got guts,' she says. 'I'll give you that much.'

She holds open the door, and I step inside before she can change her mind.

'DCI Hunt really believes in you, doesn't he?'

I ask her what she means, although I already know.

'He came round the other day to check on me, as he often does, but this time he was trying to persuade me it wasn't you. But he insisted that he'd find out who did it.'

I am grateful that he's done this, but don't need him to fight my battles. 'Well, it's true, Serena.'

'He's not so convinced about Rosie, though, is he?'

My gratitude turns to anger. What is he playing at? 'Why? What did he say about her?'

'Nothing. I just got that impression. Anyway, I don't have to explain myself to you, Tara, so why don't you tell me what the hell's going on? What do you need to say to me that's so important?'

We are still standing in her hallway, but I don't expect her to invite me to sit down, so I take a deep breath and begin, unsure how exactly I will get her to understand this.

'It's complicated. But please just hear me out before you dismiss me.'

She sighs, an exaggerated gesture to make me realise I am at her mercy. 'Go on then. What is it?'

'I've said this before but I need to repeat it. I have no knowledge of doing anything with Lee, other than waking up in your bed. I would never have intentionally hurt you; you were my friend, Serena, and that meant a lot to me. I came over here because I got your text and you wanted to see me. There was no other reason for me to be here.'

She opens her mouth to speak but I don't give her the chance. I will have my say first.

'Whatever happened next, I have no memory of. I don't know what happened to me. Maybe Lee gave me more than just wine, I don't know, or maybe someone else did, but I swear to you – I can't remember a thing. And that's why I'm here.'

'What are you saying?'

'I know this is asking a lot, but I think maybe, just maybe, seeing your bedroom again might trigger a memory or something.'

She snorts. 'You have got to be joking. You think I'm going to let you go up there after—'

'We both want answers, don't we? That's the only way either of us will ever be able to move on, isn't it?'

She clutches her head in her hands. 'Why are you doing this to me? Why can't you just leave me alone? I just want to put this all behind me, but how can I when you keep turning up here? When you're always there reminding me.'

'Serena, I promise you I will stay away from you for the rest of my life if you just let me do this one thing. Please. For both of us.'

There is no answer. I count the seconds. Five. Ten. Fifteen.

'Okay,' she says finally. 'But go up now before I change my mind.'

Upstairs, I stop outside the bedroom. Now that I'm here I'm not sure I can go through with this. On the other side of that door is the place Lee died. While I slept. But I need answers and it's now or never.

Turning the handle, I step inside, unprepared for the panic that overwhelms me when I take in my surroundings. The room has barely changed, although it has been cleaned of the blood that was here that night. I don't know how Serena can continue sleeping here, but perhaps she doesn't. It is not my place to ask her.

I walk further in, waiting for something – anything – to come back to me, but the only picture in my head, other than that of Lee's lifeless body, is of me fleeing from the room.

Walking around the bed to the window, I remember scrambling around for my clothes, finding them scattered across the floor. Discarded in a fit of passion? Or made to look that way?

But there is nothing else. No other memories return to me, and my heart sinks as I realise this was futile.

I sit on the bed and close my eyes, shutting away the tears I won't let fall. Still there is nothing. And when I open them again, Serena is standing in the doorway, watching me.

'Anything?' she asks, making her way towards me.

Shaking my head, I am aware I am letting her down as well as Rosie. 'Nothing. I really thought. . .'

'It must be strange,' she says, coming to sit beside me on the bed. 'To have no memory of that whole time. I guess before I wasn't looking at it from your point of view. It must be pretty scary.'

Her words seem to suggest forgiveness, but I remain on guard. I have learned that nobody can be trusted.

'It is. But. . . he was your husband. Nothing's worse than that.'

'Well, he made it easier for me. By having an affair, I mean. It's easier to hate him than to love him. So in a way he did me a favour.'

Trying to block out Mikey's description of that night, I wonder how Serena can mean this. How, for her, life can be so black and white. But aren't Noah and I an example of this very thing? I nod to show her that I understand.

'So you really can't remember anything? Being here hasn't helped in any way?' Serena asks, staring around the room as if she's never seen it before.

That's when I realise she no longer comes in here, and probably hasn't since Lee was murdered.

'No.' At least not what I need to. 'But I thought it was a bit of a long shot.'

For a while we sit together, neither of us speaking, and I can almost believe nothing has happened, and we are exactly how we used to be.

Serena is the first to break the silence. 'You're not going to give up on this, are you?'

I turn to her. 'No. Never. I want to clear Rosie's name, but I also want justice for Lee.'

'Well, if it means anything, I don't believe you were responsible. It's not just what DCI Hunt says, it's what I've known about you all these years. You are not a murderer.'

It is a relief to hear Serena say this, but I know she is about to say something I don't like.

'But. . . I told him that I'm no longer sure about Rosie. She sweet-talked me the other night, Tara, we both know how good she is at that, but now I see things more clearly and it had to be her. There is no one else.'

So many things cross my mind as I walk home, tracing my footsteps from that fateful night. But the first thing I need to do is call Holden. Standing in the drive, I ignore the flickering curtains at Guy and Layla's house and call his mobile, but it goes straight to voicemail.

'Call me,' I say. 'As soon as you can. It's urgent.'

I don't know what he's playing at, but somehow he's managed to change Serena's mind about Rosie, which puts into question everything he has said to me, and what happened between us.

Inside the house, I find Spencer watching television, but am surprised Lisa still isn't up.

'Where's Aunty Lisa?' I ask.

He shrugs. 'Not sure. I called to her and knocked on her door but she didn't answer. I guess she's extra tired today. Mum? Where's Rosie? I haven't seen her for ages, and Aunty Lisa said she's not sure where she is.'

Lisa has helped me out here, then, because we never discussed what I would tell Spencer.

'She's just staying with a friend. Just to have a break.'

'Okay.' He shrugs again and turns back to the television.

It is nearly ten a.m. now, and I should let Lisa sleep, but I need her to watch Spencer for me. If Holden won't call me back then I'm going to the station, and right now I don't care what trouble either of us gets in.

Tapping on the spare room door, there is no answer. Lisa has always been a heavy sleeper, much like Rosie, so I open the door and go inside.

But she isn't there, and her bed is made up. The only other place she can be is the bathroom, but when I check it I find it unoccupied.

Puzzled, I head back downstairs and check the kitchen. Again, there is no sign of her, and no used mug or cereal bowl in the sink or dishwasher.

Back in the living room I turn off the television, and ignore Spencer's groan.

'Spence, I can't find her. Are you sure you didn't hear her leaving the house or anything?'

'No. But I didn't even know you weren't here. I thought you must be in your bathroom because I knocked on your door too. I just thought you were both being lazy today.' He grins because he doesn't realise the seriousness of the situation.

'Half an hour more, that's it,' I say, turning the television back on.

Once I'm in the kitchen, I shut the door and try calling Lisa's mobile. It rings for almost thirty seconds before her voicemail kicks in, but finally I can leave a message.

'Lisa, where are you? I'm worried. Call me as soon as you can.'

And then I send her a text, repeating my message, just to make sure she gets at least one of them.

Racing back to the living room, I ask Spencer what Ryan is doing today.

'I don't know. Think his mum's dragging him shopping or something. Why?'

'Do you think she'd mind if you tagged along?'

His face lights up. 'Can I?'

'Go and call him. Quick. Tell him I'll drop you wherever is easiest for them.'

As soon as he's gone, I try Lisa's phone once more, but again it goes to her voicemail.

I have more luck with Holden, though, and he finally answers his phone, his voice almost a whisper.

'Are you okay? I've just had to come out of a meeting but they'll need me back in a sec.'

There are so many things I need to say to him, but Lisa has to take priority now. At least I know where Rosie is, and that she's safe.

'I think my sister's gone missing,' I say. 'She's not in the house and we haven't seen her all morning. I've tried calling her mobile but she's not answering. I'm worried, Holden, this just isn't like her. She didn't even want to leave the house so I can't imagine where she's gone.'

'I'm coming over,' he says.

'No, I need to go to her flat. Can you meet me there in one hour?'

'I'll be there,' he says. 'But don't go in there on your own. Wait for me outside.'

His words are meant to reassure me, but they have the opposite effect. Now the possibility that something has happened to Lisa feels even more real.

So once again I find myself outside my sister's building, only this time everything has changed. I try her mobile again, and her house phone, but, as I've come to expect now, there is no answer.

Holden is late, and twenty more minutes pass before his car pulls into Lisa's road. He parks behind me and hurries out.

'Sorry. Something came up. Still no answer from your sister?'

'No.' I point to her building. 'She lives there. Third floor.'

Together we walk towards the entrance.

'When did you last see her?' he asks.

'Yesterday evening. Before I met up with you. She said she was having an early night.'

'So you left the house about half nine?'

'Yes, it must have been, because we met at about ten, didn't we? Well, she definitely went to bed before I left.'

'So let's say half nine was the last you heard from her, because if you were in the house when she left you would have heard her, right? It's a pretty big house, but not big enough for someone to slip out unnoticed, unless everyone's asleep.'

I agree with him.

'So that means she left when I was out with you, or early this morning.'

He frowns. 'But you would have heard her this morning.'

Now is not the time to confront him about Serena.

'I had to pop out for a bit. But Spencer was up early and he didn't see or hear her. And when he knocked on her door she wasn't there. Or at least he got no response.'

'So the most likely scenario is that she left some time in the night.'

He pauses as we reach the front door, and I press the buzzer. I hold my breath as we wait but seconds pass and there is no answer.

I pull out Lisa's key, and Holden clasps my hand in his.

'She could still be there. Sleeping maybe. Or just needing a break from. . . the world.'

'She would have told me. Holden, she wouldn't let me worry like this.'

'Come on,' he says, pushing through the door as soon as I've unlocked it. 'Let's find out what we can.'

We reach Lisa's flat door, and dread envelops me. If Harvey could batter her like he did, then what else is he capable of? Noah's words ring in my ears. *Don't jump to conclusions.* But it is difficult not to when I know my sister wouldn't just disappear without telling me where she was going.

'Lisa?' I shout, the second we are through the door. 'Lisa? Are you here?'

There is no answer, and I turn to Holden.

He holds up his hand. 'Wait here.'

But there is no way I'm not following him. 'No, I'm coming with you.'

'Seriously, Tara, just wait here.'

But of course I don't. I am right behind him as he checks each room, with no sign of Lisa. And then we get to her bedroom, and I'm about to tell him she's not here when we both hear a whimper.

I burst through the door, shouting her name, pulling free of Holden's grip as he tries to stop me. It is dark and I can't see her. The curtains are closed, and with her blackout blind down it might as well be the middle of the night.

The whimper again, louder this time, coming from the other side of the room. We both must see her at the same time: Lisa's arm flailing up from the floor on the other side of the bed. Holden pushes past me to get to her, and when I've caught up he is already kneeling beside her.

She is dressed only in her underwear, dried blood splattered over her face, and every inch of her body is covered in bruises. I rush to her and wrap my arms around her.

'Be careful,' Holden says. 'Lisa? Can you hear me?'

She gives a barely perceptible nod.

'Good. Now don't move, but I'm calling the ambulance now, okay?' He turns to me. 'Stay with her, and don't let her move.'

This time I cannot stop the tears from falling and they drip onto her battered skin. 'I'm sorry,' I whisper.

She squeezes my hand in reply.

'Harvey?' I ask.

She nods.

'Do you know where he is?'

The shake of her head causes her to wail in pain.

'Okay, no more questions, let's just get you to the hospital and you can tell us what happened when you're up to it.'

'He's. . .' she says, her voice frail and unrecognisable. 'He's. . .'

And then she lapses into unconsciousness.

CHAPTER TWENTY-NINE

I pace the hospital waiting room, desperate for news, counting the minutes since the doctor said Holden could speak to Lisa. At least she is doing okay, her passing out due to shock and lack of food more than her injuries. She is a tough woman, and I know she will be okay. What I don't know is what she was trying to tell me about Harvey.

Finally, he appears, the expression on his face one I've never seen before, and can't identify.

'What did she say? What happened? Where is he?'

'Tara, slow down a second. I did get a chance to talk to her, but I'm not in charge of this, even though we found her. It's the local police who will investigate, and they've just been in with her. I now need to go and talk to them, and they'll also want to speak to you. But she wants to talk to you and tell you everything herself.'

I am already heading towards the door.

'Tara? I'll be here when you've finished.'

She looks a bit better now that she's had medical attention, but there is barely a patch of her normal skin colour visible in between the bruising.

Sitting beside her bed, I take her hand. 'How are you doing?'

'Exactly how I look,' she says. 'But, Tara—'

'I should never have left you alone in the house. Tell me what happened.'

'It's all my fault. I went back home last night, to get something. Grandma's wedding ring. Harvey's still got a key and I just couldn't bear the thought of him going there and taking it. It's not even the money it's worth, it's what it means. I couldn't lose her ring, Tara.'

Lisa was always especially close to our grandmother, so I can understand this.

'But you should have asked me to go. Even in the middle of the night. You know I would have got it for you.'

'You've got enough going on so there was no way I wanted to disturb the only peace you get. It was about two in the morning. I got a cab.'

'Why didn't you at least leave a note? I was going out of my mind. And with good reason.' But looking at her in this state, I decide to drop it. 'Anyway, none of that matters now. So carry on, what happened then?'

'I'd only been there a couple of minutes when I realised I wasn't alone. He was in the flat, Tara. He must have been hiding out here, right in plain sight, and I stupidly didn't even consider that he could be there.' She fights back tears. 'He came straight from the bedroom and dragged me in there. . . then he did this.' Now her tears come hard and fast and she is powerless to stop them. 'There was nothing I could do. I couldn't fight back, he's too strong. I must have lost consciousness because the next thing I remember is you and your detective coming in.'

I lean down and wrap her in a hug, careful not to hold her too tight. 'It's not your fault. None of this is.'

Her body tenses. 'But it is, Tara. That's what I need to tell you. It is my fault. All of it. Everything is my fault.'

'Stop saying that.'

'Please, Tara, you're not listening. Before he left, Harvey told me. . .' She breaks off as her crying becomes uncontrollable. 'He said that. . . he. . . killed Lee.'

For a second I think I must have misheard, but then she re-peats what she's said and there is no mistaking it. Lisa is telling me that Harvey killed Lee. But it's impossible. They didn't even know each other: there is no link between them. I wonder if the medication she's been given, or even the attack, has confused her somehow.

'Lisa, that can't be right, what exactly did he say?'

'He told me that he killed Lee, and he meant it, Tara. I can still picture the grin on his face. And then he said that either you or Rosie will go down for it, and that I'd have to live with that for the rest of my life.'

This doesn't make sense. 'He's lying, Lisa, he must be, he's just trying to freak you out, to scare you.'

'Stop!' she shouts. 'Please, just listen to me!'

'Okay, okay, just try to stay calm. I don't want you doing yourself any more damage.'

She attempts to pull herself upright, but can't quite manage it until I help her.

'I need to tell you this, Tara, and it won't be easy to hear. But you have to know that I love you. All of you. Noah too. You're my family and, with Mum and Dad, you're all I've got.'

I know she means this but I am waiting for what's to come. She is clearly struggling with something, and I sense that our whole lives are about to change.

'I've always enjoyed my freedom, Tara. Being able to do what I want, whenever I feel like it. Travel the world without being tied down to anything or anyone.'

'I know. It's what I love about you. And envy sometimes, be-cause my life couldn't be more different.'

'But that's just it. Eventually it wears thin, and. . . it's just nice to settle down. To feel like you belong somewhere.'

'Lisa, what exactly are you trying to tell me? I feel like you're stalling. Whatever it is you know you can just say it.'

But nothing prepares me for what she says next.

'I met someone before Harvey, and I really fell for him in a big way.' She stares at me, as if she's willing me to finish her sentence.

And with a sickening dread in my stomach, I know exactly what she's about to say. This is about Lee, as everything always ends up being about him.

I cannot speak, but I sit and stare at my battered sister, wondering how this can be possible. 'You and Lee were together,' I say. It is not a question, and I don't need confirmation, I just need to know how that happened.

'I know it's a huge shock,' she says, 'and you don't have to say anything, but please just listen and then I'll answer any question you have.' She doesn't wait for my agreement. 'We met a couple of years ago when I came round to see you. You weren't there but Lee was in his front garden and we got chatting. Do you remember my friend Yvonne? Well, she was looking for someone to landscape her garden so he gave me his mobile number. It started from there.' She exhales a loud, laboured breath. 'It was just texts to start with. We had a lot in common, and I think he needed an escape. Well, you know what he was going through with Serena.'

Still I cannot speak.

'I won't go into detail – I can't, it hurts too much, but it was pretty intense very quickly. We. . . loved each other.' She looks at me, studying my face. 'That's how I know nothing happened between the two of you. Your colleague is lying. Lee just wouldn't have done that – he was a decent man, Tara, despite falling for me.'

'He was married.' Finally I find my voice. 'Lisa, how could you do that?'

She begs me to reserve my judgement and let her continue, so I do. But I cannot look at her while she speaks. Instead I stare at the bare, sterile walls, at the labels on pieces of equipment.

'It went on for over a year and a half, and I'm ashamed to say this, but even when I met Harvey I was still seeing him. But then

I broke it off, and I really tried to make it work with Harvey.' She shakes her head. 'What a mistake that was.'

So now there is a link between Harvey and Lee, and it's stronger than I would have thought possible. I am still having trouble comprehending how this all happened, and how oblivious I have been to what was right under my nose.

A nurse comes in to check on Lisa, and it buys me some time to sort out what I will say to her. I am angry with her: for lying, for doing this to Serena.

Once we're alone again she continues. 'I had no idea Harvey knew until last night. But. . . I don't know how he could have found out. Lee and I were always so careful. We never met anywhere close to either of us.'

But the truth always comes out in the end, that's one thing I have learned from all this. Lies and secrets are only ticking time bombs, waiting for the moment they can wreak the most havoc.

'So you broke it off with Lee? When? How did he take it?'

'A few months ago. He was upset and kept trying to meet up, but I didn't give in, Tara, as much as I wanted to. I did the right thing in the end.'

But this is only a tiny consolation. 'I suppose.'

'But do you see now? That it's all my fault Lee is dead? If I hadn't got involved with him then Harvey would never have. . . I just can't believe he was such a psycho. How did I not see it? He moved in with me, and the whole time he knew what he'd done. It makes me feel sick.'

That is exactly how I feel at this moment. 'I have to go, Lisa.'

'What? No, please don't leave me yet.'

'I need time to take this all in. You're my sister and I love you; that will never change. But I just need some time. I'll be back when I can, I promise.'

And I walk away, consumed with guilt that I am leaving her in that state, but desperate to get away, because I have had all I can take of lies and deceit.

In the car, I sit without starting the engine, drumming my fingers on the steering wheel. I'm so consumed with my thoughts that when my mobile rings it startles me. It is Holden, and I scoop up my phone and press it to my ear.

'Didn't you see me waiting for you at the entrance? You walked right past me. Are you okay?'

'I can't believe it,' I say. 'It was Harvey. This whole time we had no idea. And all along. . .'

'Yes, I know. I'm sorry, Tara. But at least it proves you right about Rosie.'

I can't help but notice him saying you instead of us. He has never believed in her.

'So what happens now?'

'This is the situation: we don't know where he is. We're using every resource at our disposal to find him, though, so I don't want you to worry.'

But as always happens when he says something like this, I can do nothing else.

'You mean he might come back for Lisa? And please stop giving me the police-speak.'

He sighs. 'Yes, that's exactly what I mean. He's already murdered once, so. . . well, I don't need to spell it out for you. I've arranged for police to be stationed outside your sister's room, but once the doctors say she can go then there's not much else we can do, other than regularly checking in with her. We just can't spare the manpower on the off-chance Harvey will come back.'

In that moment, I know what I have to do. I might barely be able to look Lisa in the eye, but I can't let her go back to her flat alone. 'She can stay with us,' I say. 'I'll keep her safe.'

'We'll find him, Tara. But I have to be honest with you, it's not going to be easy. The fact that he confessed to Lisa tells me he had a plan in place to evade us. Otherwise he would never have had the confidence to do it. He may be getting help from people. I asked your sister if he had access to large amounts of money, and she didn't think so, but couldn't be sure.'

That's because she didn't know him at all.

'But, like I said, we're already doing everything we can.'

Hearing this means very little now, though, because I have lost faith in this man. He promised me he would find Lee's murderer, but the reality is that Harvey confessed because he wanted to hurt Lisa. There was no detective work involved, no cleverly piecing together evidence, or working on instinct. It fell into Holden's lap. So how can he expect me to believe in him?

'I need to go now,' I say. 'I'll talk to you later.'

And once I've disconnected the call, the only person I want to speak to is Noah. He was due to come home today, leaving Rosie in Manchester, and I only hope he hasn't left yet. I need to speak to her, to tell her that she can come home, that everything will be okay now.

'I can't believe it,' Noah says, once I've filled him in on every detail. 'What a sick and twisted world this is. And Lisa seeing Lee? I'm just. . . speechless.'

'The main thing is Rosie can come home now.'

'Hang on, is that a good idea? Harvey's still out there, and if Lisa's staying at the house then it puts you all at risk.'

'I need her home with me, Noah. I need my family.'

'Then I'll bring her, Tara. But I'm moving back too.'

* * *

Rosie runs into my arms, tears flooding down her cheeks, while Noah stands at the door, carrying their bags.

'I knew it wasn't you,' I whisper into her hair. 'I always knew.'

This makes her cry even harder, but I know her tears are from gratitude.

'Dad told me everything,' she says. 'Poor Aunty Lisa. But. . . I can't believe she was. . . seeing Lee.'

'Neither can I. But we have to move on from that and be here for her.' Even as I say this, and mean it, I know it will be hard for me to look at Lisa and not think of it. 'She'll be out of hospital in a couple of days, and is coming back here to stay with us for a while longer.'

'Until they find Harvey?' Rosie asks. 'But what if he comes here?'

'I'm here now too, so you don't have to worry about that,' Noah says, placing their bags on the floor. 'Now, why don't you go and get unpacked and let your mum and me talk for a bit. Okay?'

I can tell she is about to protest, but thinks better of it. 'Okay. I'll be upstairs if you need me.' She gathers her bags and gives us both a kiss on the cheek.

Watching her head up, I am overwhelmed with relief. And fear.

'Where's Spencer?' Noah asks.

'I called Ryan's mum and asked if he could stay there the night, if we have Ryan on another night before school starts again. She was more than happy with that.'

'Good, at least we know he's safe.'

'Harvey's not after us, Noah, I'm sure of that.'

He picks up his bag and gestures for me to follow him upstairs. 'How can you know? He clearly wants to get to Lisa, and we're her family so. . .'

'Hasn't he already done the worst thing to her by. . . killing the man she loved?' The words feel strange in my mouth; I will never get used to the idea of Lisa and Lee together. 'And anyway, he left me alive, didn't he? Why would he do that if he was intending to get to Lisa by harming one of us?' I've thought about this a lot since Lisa's revelation. Harvey could just as easily have murdered me, but he chose not to.

We reach the bedroom and shut the door behind us. Glancing at the en-suite, I think of Holden and the day the two of us were in there together.

'He's a psycho, Tara,' Noah says, as he starts to unpack. 'Who knows what more he's capable of?'

But I am still convinced it is only Lisa he wants to harm. And no matter what she has done, I will do whatever I can to make sure he can't hurt her again.

CHAPTER THIRTY

For four days we wait for Lisa to be discharged from the hospital. Worried about her slow recovery and the damage to her internal organs, the doctors have prolonged her stay. But this is a relief to me; she is safer there than anywhere else.

Noah takes the week off work and the four of us stay cocooned in the house, barely out of each other's company, the shadow of Harvey looming over us. The police are still hunting for him, and Holden updates me regularly, but I've told him we cannot see each other for now. I'd like to think he understands that my family has to come first. But either way, I am grateful for him keeping me in the loop.

In these dire circumstances, Spencer, Rosie, Noah and I have been brought closer together, bonded by our mutual fear and concern for Lisa, and on Thursday morning we sit at the garden table playing Scrabble. It is something to occupy us while we wait to hear if we can bring Lisa home today.

But none of us have our minds on the game, and we throw down words half-heartedly, no one bothering to keep score.

Someone knocks on the door and Noah gets up to answer, while Rosie, Spencer and I collectively hold our breath because we are on edge, ready for anything.

'It's just the postman,' Noah says, placing a pile of letters on the table as he sits back down.

Rosie peers at them. 'Is there anything for me?'

I flick through the envelopes, but they are all for Noah, except one, which is addressed to me. I am about to put it back in the pile to open later when I notice the company name across the top. It is the gallery I submitted my painting to, all those weeks ago. I scoop it up again and clutch it to my chest.

'What's going on, Mum?' Rosie asks. 'Who's that letter for?'

Noah and Spencer both look up from the game to watch me. 'It's for me. But I'll open it later.'

This piques Noah's curiosity. 'Why later? Who's it from?'

I show him the envelope. 'It's the gallery.'

Spencer leans forward to get a look. 'Open it now, Mum, you have to!'

But I tell him not to get excited, that I'm sure they write to everyone, even those who don't win, just to thank them for their entries.

'Isn't it better to know, though?' Noah says. 'Either way.'

He is right, and besides, it will give me something else to focus on, other than worrying about Lisa and whether the police will ever find Harvey. A rejection from the art gallery I wanted so desperately to be represented by may just spur me on to keep trying.

Quickly I rip open the envelope, taking in every word then reading it again just to make sure I'm not mistaken.

'I've won,' I say, to all of them, and to myself at the same time. 'I can't believe it; I've won.'

I hand the letter to Noah, just for confirmation, and his huge smile tells me I haven't misunderstood.

There is a blend of congratulations and compliments, but I can't take it all in. This news, which at any other time would have me walking on air, just cannot be celebrated right now. Not with Lisa in the state she's in. I tell them we'll talk about it later, once everything's been sorted out, and we all agree before focusing once more on our game.

* * *

'Are you and Dad back together now?' Spencer asks, while we all wait for Noah, who is agonisingly slow at taking his turn.

Noah and I both look at each other, and I'm sure he's as unsure what to say as I am. We have been sharing our bed again to sleep in, but with no physical contact.

'We'll see what happens,' Noah says, finally placing some tiles on the board. 'Let's just worry about your aunt for now.'

'She's so brave,' Rosie says. 'It makes me so nervous when I think of what she went through.'

I squeeze Rosie's hand, and admire how well she is taking all this. After all, she had deep feelings for Lee, so to discover her own aunt was involved with him must take some accepting. Not to mention the fact that she was falsely accused of murder.

The television in the kitchen is on, and we can all hear the news bulletin stating that the police are looking for someone else in connection to Lee's death. But the neighbours still avoid us, are still afraid of us. No doubt we will for ever be tainted by what happened. But there is something comforting about the fact that Guy and Layla will not speak to, or even look at, us. I prefer it this way.

My phone rings as I'm trying to choose a word, and Mikey's name appears on the screen. I ignore it and mute the volume; he no longer has anything to hold over me, because everything he said was a lie. Once Lisa's home, I will draft a letter to the school, telling them exactly what Mikey has done. I have no more pity for him and he doesn't deserve to keep his job. I don't even want to know why he did it. I can only assume it was to hurt me.

Noah looks at me but doesn't ask who it is; instead, waiting for me to offer the information.

'Mikey,' I mouth, because I don't want the kids asking about him.

He nods and goes back to staring at his Scrabble tiles.

Thankfully, the next call I get is a welcome one: Dad telling us he's just spoken to the doctor.

'Good news, love. They say Lisa can leave this afternoon. They're happy with her progress but said she needs to take it easy. You'll see to that, though, won't you? You know she's more than welcome to stay here, though.'

But I won't let my parents be put at risk. It is better if Lisa is here with us. I assure him we'll look after her and tell him I'll pick her up.

'I'm glad Noah's back home,' he says, and hearing his words, I realise that I feel the same way.

'Is this weird for you?' Lisa asks, as I help her into the house. 'Because I could stay with Mum and Dad. I really hate what I've done, Tara, so I understand if you can't be around me right now.'

I explain that it is hard, but I'm not going to turn my back on her, and she tries to hug me but winces at the pain it causes.

'I know,' I tell her. 'You don't have to thank me or say anything about it. Let's just get through each day.'

Thankfully, Spencer appears, eager to help by taking Lisa's things upstairs.

'Do you want to watch a DVD with me?' he asks. 'I don't mind you choosing which one. We can watch on Dad's iPad.'

Lisa manages a smile. 'Of course I will. But it might take me a while to get upstairs so you go and set it up.'

'I'll bring you up some snacks,' I say.

And as I head to the kitchen, I acknowledge how good it feels to be doing something so normal. So unrelated to anything.

But still I can't help feeling on edge, because surely it is just a matter of time before we set eyes on Harvey again.

* * *

'It's strange, isn't it?' Noah says, as he climbs into bed. He turns off the lamp, but the glow from his mobile phone illuminates his face.

'What is?'

'Everything that's happened. If you really stop to think about it, it's actually hard to believe. It's the kind of stuff that happens to someone else, isn't it?' He pauses and mulls this over. 'Actually, I'm wrong. It's worse. It's what you can't even imagine would be possible.'

I know what he means, but for me it has been only too real since the moment I woke up in Lee's bed.

'I keep thinking about when we went over there for dinner,' he continues. 'How nice he was. He really had me fooled.'

'Well, just imagine how Lisa feels. She shared a bed with him.'

I roll onto my side, so that we are facing each other.

'It's made me realise a lot of things. How glad I am that I didn't get mixed up with Amelie again.' Under the sheet, he takes my hand in his, and I let him. 'Which reminds me, I need to show you something.' He leans across to his bedside table and grabs his phone, tapping on it before passing it to me. 'Read those messages from Amelie. We had an interesting text conversation yesterday, and I want you to read it.'

I take the phone and scroll through the exchange. And by the time I've finished, I am convinced Noah has been telling the truth about her. I hand it back to him.

'I told you she was lying,' he says. 'She blatantly admits it in those messages.'

'I know. Sometimes it's just hard to see the truth when it's hidden in so many lies.'

He grabs my hand once more. 'It's always been you, Tara. Even after everything that's happened. I trust you. I know you.'

I think of Holden, and our unfinished business, and feel a wave of guilt. Am I cheating on him by sharing my bed with Noah? By letting him hold my hand? By the fact that it feels good? Solid and familiar. But all Holden and I shared was a kiss, and maybe the promise of something to come.

'But too much has happened,' I say, keeping my hand in his. 'Far too much. How can we ever trust each other again?'

'It's not like either of us really cheated, Tara. Surely anything else can be overcome?'

He wants an answer but now is not the time I can give him one.

'Can we wait and see? There's just too much hanging over us at the moment, and until they find Harvey I can't think about anything else.' This is the best I can offer him.

'Okay, whatever you need,' he says, still clutching my hand. 'But I'm not giving up on us, Tara.'

Lisa seems a little better in the morning when she joins us for breakfast. She is still unsteady on her feet, and is barely recognisable underneath her bruising.

'I could have brought you something up,' I say, standing up to help her into a chair.

'No. I'm sick of lying around all day, I need to be up and about. It's good for me.' She attempts to smile, but winces in pain. 'Are we okay?' she says, lowering her voice, even though Noah is concentrating on a phone call and the kids are still asleep.

I nod. 'Don't worry about anything, Lisa.'

Again she tries to smile. 'No, just the crazy murderer who did this to me.'

'He's not getting into this house,' Noah says, finishing his phone call. 'Trust me, Lisa, you'll be safe here.' The determination in his voice shows me Harvey will not easily get the better of us. But that doesn't mean he won't try.

'Thanks, Noah,' Lisa says, biting into a slice of toast. It takes her a while to swallow a small piece, and she quickly gives up and puts the toast back on her plate. She turns to me. 'Tara, is that Mikey still bothering you? He must have heard it on the news by now. I told you he was lying.'

I came to this conclusion as soon as I heard it was Harvey, but it's strange that Mikey still tries to call. I'm beginning to think he will never give up.

'He can't hurt Rosie now,' I say.

Lisa nods, but looks away, and I wonder if she is remembering that she had doubts about Rosie's innocence. 'What have you both got planned for today?' she asks.

'Nothing,' Noah says. 'We're staying right here with you.'

'I'd love to say you really don't have to do that, but the thought of being alone terrifies me. I'll get over it, I know I will, but right now it's just all so. . . raw.'

'No need to explain,' Noah says. 'We're not leaving you alone.'

It should be me saying all this to Lisa, not my estranged husband, but I still can't bring myself to accept what she's done. She turns to me but I look away. And then I think of something that might just help me forgive her.

Serena doesn't take much convincing; she is more than ready to confront Lisa, and now the two women sit on my sofas, neither one of them saying anything.

'I thought I'd know what to say to the woman he was seeing when I found her,' Serena says eventually. 'But now you're right here in front of me I actually have nothing to say to you. I'm done with Lee. He's dead because he fell for you, and in a way that's all the closure I need.'

Since Lee's murder I have seen a different side to Serena, but these words are the most callous I have heard her utter.

Lisa leans forward, wincing as she does so. But her pain has no effect on Serena.

'I made a horrible, horrible mistake, and I'm sorry. I know that means nothing, but I'll have to live with this for the rest of my life.'

We all do, I think. *Every one of us.*

Serena stands up, even though she's only been here for a few minutes. 'Well, if you're expecting forgiveness you can forget it. And you looking like that doesn't make me pity you. It's justice.'

She turns to me. 'I'm selling the house, Tara, so, hopefully, I won't have to be here much longer. I can't wait to get away from. . . well, everything. But do you know what makes me the saddest? The fact that I've lost our friendship.'

She doesn't give me a chance to respond, but turns and walks out of the living room, out of the house, and out of my life.

'I'm so sorry,' Lisa says. 'I really tried.'

I know she did, and I also know how stubborn Serena can be, even though this time it is fully justified.

'Well, what did you expect? And to be honest, she at least came here.' Even though I suspect that was to get a good look at the woman who was sleeping with her husband.

'You're right. I have no right to complain about anything. Even this.' She gestures to her body.

'What you did was bad, Lisa, but you didn't deserve that, so never believe that, okay?'

She nods, but I can tell she's not convinced.

'I'm curious about something,' I say. 'Seeing Serena today made me think of it. Was Lee going to leave her?'

It takes her a moment to answer. 'Yes, but I wouldn't let him. It was too much of a mess. And it brought it all home to me how bad it was that I was involved with him, and breaking up his marriage. I didn't want to be the person who did that.'

'Does that mean he didn't actually want to have a baby with her? They went through all that fertility treatment, so was he just stringing her along?'

Lisa looks away, and I'm glad that she feels ashamed.

'He wanted one to start with, but it got too much. The pressure was really getting to him.'

This is familiar. It's what Lee told me that night.

Someone knocks on the door, too loudly, and Lisa jumps. In the hall I hear Noah answer it, and thank someone for something.

'It's just a delivery,' I say, 'nothing to worry about.'

'This time,' Lisa says, her arms shaking. 'I'd better get used to it, because eventually it will be Harvey, won't it?'

CHAPTER THIRTY-ONE

After a few more days we are all restless, desperate to get out and see something other than the walls of our house.

'Why don't we go out for dinner?' Noah suggests. 'All of us. We don't have to go far, but it would be good to have a break.'

But there is no break for Lisa. Wherever she goes, she still has to live every second in fear of Harvey.

'You take the kids,' I suggest. 'I just don't feel up to it.'

Noah shoots me a look, but won't say what he's thinking in front of the kids: *I'm not leaving you alone when that maniac is somewhere out there.* 'No, we should all go,' he says, 'or we can all just stay here. Together.'

'Oh, please, Dad,' Rosie says. 'We need to get out, and it will do Aunty Lisa good. Please can we go?'

Even when Lisa agrees, and says it sounds like a great idea, I can tell Noah wants to fight this decision, so I need to assure him I will be fine.

'I need to start a new painting,' I say. 'Now that I've got representation at the gallery, they'll need to know I can produce more than just one good painting. So a couple of hours on my own will be great.' I keep hidden that there is no chance of getting into the zone to paint, but I do need some time alone. I need to gather my thoughts and then try to sort things out with Holden.

'Come on, Dad,' Spencer says. 'Please!'

It takes a few minutes but, eventually, Noah gives in.

'Okay, let's go then.' He turns to me. 'But we're only going to the high street.'

That look again.

'I'll be fine. Go and try to enjoy yourselves. We've not had enough of that lately, have we?'

But we both know this will be difficult.

Once I'm alone I double lock the door, leaving my keys in there, just to be sure. Then I check the back doors and every window. It is still warm tonight, but I close them all anyway. I would rather it be oppressively hot than take any chances.

Only moments ago having this time to myself to sort things out with Holden seemed like a good idea, but the reality is something else. The house is quiet as I'd expected, but it's almost too quiet.

Dismissing this fear as irrational, I pull my mobile from my pocket and call Holden. I press the phone to my ear to let the dial tone drown out the oppressive silence of the house, but it is a while before he answers.

'Hi,' he says, sounding wary. 'Are you okay?'

Grateful to hear his voice, because the regret I feel at staying here alone is quickly building, I tell him I'm fine and ask how it's going with the hunt for Harvey.

'Not good,' he says. 'We think he carefully planned to disappear because he's thoroughly covered all his tracks. His passport is missing, but it doesn't look like he's gone abroad. It's as if he's disappeared off the face of the earth.' He snorts. 'But he can't stay hidden for ever.'

Some people do, though, and that's a fact. But I don't burst his bubble. It might help him to be positive, to really believe he will finally find Lee's killer, because just knowing who it is won't be enough.

'I know. But what happens in the meantime is worrying too. I feel like I'm constantly looking over my shoulder, waiting for him to appear.'

'I'm sorry,' he says.

But what is he sorry for? None of this is his fault.

'How's your sister doing? I was checking up on her in the hospital and she seems like a nice girl; she just made a mistake,' he adds.

I wonder if he's thinking of his ex-wife as he says this.

There is an ache inside me for what will never be, for what we will never have.

'Thanks for doing that, Holden, you didn't have to. And thanks for everything you've done.'

'I wanted to.' He coughs and there is a long pause before he speaks again. 'I heard Noah's moved back in.'

I tell him this is true. 'He just wants to make sure his children are safe.'

I look at the clock on the wall as I say this, once again conscious of being alone, but it will be at least a couple of hours before they are home.

'And you, I'm sure,' Holden continues. 'Anyway, I think it's a good idea that he's moved back.'

'Do you?'

'Yes, Tara. Look, I want what's best for you, and if that's for you to be back with your husband then I like to think I'm a big enough man to understand and accept that, despite my personal feelings. I've got a job to do, for now at least, and that has to take priority.'

'Noah and I aren't back together,' I say. 'But. . .'

'It's okay, you don't have to say any more. I get it.'

I explain that there's just too much going on for us to have a chance at working. And it's better to end it now before it even got off the ground.

'It already was off the ground,' he says. 'But, anyway, I'm sure we'll talk soon. Just take care of yourself, and Lisa.'

'I will. Thank you. For everything.'

As soon as we end the call I sense something isn't right. It's not that I can hear anything, but I feel the heavy weight of unwanted eyes on me. And then, before I've had time to process exactly what's wrong, he speaks.

'Tara.'

Frozen, my body withdrawing into itself, I know there is nothing I can do. I am cornered in the kitchen, and he must be standing by the patio doors. Doors I'm sure I checked were locked only moments ago.

Slowly I turn around to confirm what I already know: Mikey is standing in my kitchen.

'What the hell are you doing in here?' I try to keep my voice measured, but even though I'm relieved it isn't Harvey, I'm still afraid. 'Get out. Now. Or I'll call the police.'

He holds up his hands, but inches further towards me. 'I just need you to listen to me. That's all. And then I'll go.'

'Why should I listen to a word you've said when all you've done is lie? Just get out, Mikey.' I hold up my phone, which I'm still clutching, but this only makes him take another step in my direction.

'I don't think calling the police is a good idea, Tara. And weren't you just on the phone to that detective? Sounds like things aren't really working out there.'

I should have known Mikey would know about Holden. 'I don't know what you're talking about,' I say.

'So who's lying now?' He sighs. 'Look, I haven't come here to. . . do you any harm, but there's something you need to know. I've been trying to call you and you never return my calls, so I had no choice but to come here.'

'There's a reason for that,' I say, hoping he won't notice me backing away, inching towards the door so I can make my escape. 'You have no hold over me now, Mikey. Haven't you been watching the news? The police know who killed Lee now, and Rosie has nothing to do with it.'

'That's exactly why I'm here,' he says. 'Because they've got it wrong.'

'You never give up, do you? What are you hoping to achieve here by continuing to protest that it was my daughter?'

He reaches me now, grabbing my arm so that my phone slips to the floor. 'Tara, you need to listen to me. I was not lying, and nothing I've ever said to you has been a lie. The only thing I'm guilty of is hiding my feelings for you, but that doesn't matter now. I know we will never be together, and I've actually applied to do supply teaching so I'm not going back to the school in September. I will be out of your life.'

I wrestle free of his grip. 'So leave now.'

'Not until you listen to me. I'm trying to tell you that the police have got the wrong person. I saw your daughter that night, just like I said I did. It was her, Tara, not this Harvey.'

I shake my head. 'You're unbelievable,' I scream. 'Just leave my family alone! Get out of my house now!'

I grab hold of him and shove him backwards, forcing him to fall against the edge of the worktop.

'Violence obviously runs in your family, doesn't it?' he says, recovering from the blow he has taken to his side.

And then I lunge for him again, even though he is far bigger than me and could probably stop me with one finger.

'Okay, I'm going. You won't listen—'

That's when I let out the loudest scream it's possible to produce. It pierces the air, and there is no way the neighbours won't have heard it.

I start shoving him towards the patio doors, jabbing into his wounded side, but he stops suddenly when we pass the table.

'What's that?' he says, pointing to the seat of one of the chairs.

Despite my anger, curiosity gets the better of me and I peer over the table to see what he's talking about. But it is just a hair clip.

Mikey rushes forward and picks it up, waving it in front of my face.

'See this? This is what she was wearing that night! I remember now because it sparkled in the dark. Look, it's got crystals.'

And with his words, the ground falls away beneath me, everything crashing down around me. Just like I always knew it would.

CHAPTER THIRTY-TWO

I sit in the kitchen, waiting for them to come home; hoping, desperately, I've got this wrong, but knowing the truth. Perhaps I should be scared, but I'm not, because I know she won't hurt me. But then how can I be sure of anything any more? I have been so wrong about everything up until now, my instinct letting me down in a huge way.

But by the end of this night I will know everything. And then I will deal with the aftermath.

They get home around ten p.m., their laughter and chatter echoing through the house, fuelling my pain and anger. How can she act as if everything is normal? As if she hasn't committed such a heinous crime?

Lisa walks in first, unsteady on her feet. 'Hey, Tara, how was your evening? Did you make a start on your painting?'

Rosie follows her in, and starts rooting around in the fridge, pulling out a carton of orange juice.

'Yes, I made good progress,' I say, my stomach churning.

'Don't bother asking to see it,' Noah says, joining us. 'She keeps them top secret until she's finished.'

'She has to, Dad, that's her artist's prerogative. Creative people always have their funny ways, don't they, Mum?'

It is a struggle to answer her, and my body turns hot, bile rising to my throat. 'Yes, we're a funny bunch of people,' I manage to say. 'Where's Spencer?' My question is directed to anyone, and the sooner I get an answer the better.

Noah sits at the table. 'I told him to go upstairs and get ready for bed. It's getting late.'

'Rosie, can you come with me for a minute? I need to show you something.'

She shrugs but does as I ask, and I'm grateful she hasn't made a fuss, grateful that Noah and Lisa are busy discussing something so that they hardly notice us leave.

Back in the kitchen, Noah frowns at me. 'What was that all about?'

'I just needed to talk to Rosie. Nothing too important.' The lie tumbles from my mouth, but this time I am justified.

Noah's frown remains on his face. 'Well, as long as she's not in any trouble. Hey, this might actually be the first time in her life she's really not in any trouble. Isn't that something? Anyway, if you'll both excuse me I just have to send some work emails.'

As soon as he's left the room, Lisa begins telling me about their evening.

'It was so nice to get out, and I actually forgot about everything for a couple of hours. You know, it's a shame you and Noah can't work things out. He's really pulled through for us all, hasn't he?' She doesn't wait for an answer but looks at the patio doors. 'Are they locked?'

'Probably. But it doesn't really matter, does it?'

She turns back to me. 'What? What do you mean?'

'Why don't you tell me?'

Her eyes widen. 'Tara, you're scaring me. What's going on? What are you talking about?'

I stand up, knowing that in her state she won't be able to do the same. 'You know, for once, I want the truth from you, Lisa. Time's running out so you need to speak quickly.'

She stares at me, her mind ticking away. She must know, but she continues her charade. 'Tara, please, just tell me what's going on. Is this about Harvey? Or Lee? Because you know I'm sorry, so there's not much more—'

'Just stop!' Although I want to shout at her, I can't let the kids overhear us. Or Noah, for now.

I walk towards her and lean down. 'Do you recognise this?' I thrust the hair clip in her face, keeping a tight hold of it.

Despite her bruises, the colour drains from her face. 'Yes, that's mine,' she says, reaching for it, her voice not as confident. 'I've been looking for that today. Where did you find it?'

I pull my hand back. 'I'm surprised you didn't get rid of it. It's evidence, after all, isn't it?'

She stares at it. 'Evidence of what? Tara, what are you talking about? What's going on?'

'I'm talking about you murdering Lee.'

Cold silence. It is what I expected.

'So you're not going to say anything? Defend yourself?'

'Tara, I. . . I still have no idea what you're talking about. But it's late and I'm tired. Can we just talk tomorrow?'

She stands up, but I push her back down, ignoring her shriek. I am now immune to her physical state.

'What I don't understand is Harvey's involvement. Did you plan it together? It's all over for you, Lisa, so you may as well tell me what happened.'

She tries to run then, but doesn't get very far before I grab hold of her, whispering into her ear.

'If you at least show some remorse they might go easier on you. Why don't you think about that?'

And then she sinks to the floor, burying her head in her hands. When she looks up her eyes are cold and hard. 'Have you called the police?'

'They'll be here any minute.'

'How. . . how did you know?'

I shouldn't bother telling her. I should let her spend the rest of her life wondering. But it is not in me to be that cruel, and I want the satisfaction of watching her face as she realises how easily it has all fallen apart for her.

'Mikey came here tonight. He insisted the police had the wrong person, and that it was Rosie he saw with blood on her. He wouldn't let it go. And then, and you'll love this part, just by chance he saw your hair clip while I was trying to make him leave.'

'But. . . I. . .'

In my mind, I have already worked out where she went wrong, but I need her confirmation.

'You probably got rid of the patterned shorts you were wearing, didn't you? But you forgot about the shiny hair clip you must have tied your hair up with.'

I hold it up and twist it around in my hand. 'And I bet there's all sorts of DNA on here.'

She gasps then, and part of me wishes she would contradict me, and convince me this is all a mistake, but the fear in her eyes is unmistakable.

'It was Rosie. She must have been wearing it.'

I ignore her. 'What I don't get is how Harvey fits into this. Why did he beat you so badly?'

She shakes her head. 'I'm not saying another word. Let the police come for me, I just don't care any more, Tara.'

As I watch her, unable to comprehend what she has done or why, she no longer looks like my sister. No longer feels like my sister. No longer is my sister. In this moment, our whole lives growing up together have been tarnished, blackened and made worthless.

'And I've only just thought about the ring. You must have planted it in Rosie's room, because Harvey's never been here, has he? You tried to frame your own niece for murder. The two of you are the most despicable people. You're evil to the core.' My blood boils, and I try hard to resist the urge to drag her to her feet, just so I can watch her fall to the ground. 'And it was one of you who made an anonymous call to the police, wasn't it? Because that wasn't Mikey.'

She says nothing, but stares at me with an expressionless face.

'Mum and Dad,' I say. 'What the hell is this going to do to them?'

'I don't care. I'm sick of trying to live up to you, to be as good as you. I'm sick of their disappointment that I haven't settled down and had children yet. Well, none of that matters now.'

Hearing her words sickens me. I will not let her use our parents as an excuse for what she's done.

'They have never played favourites, Lisa, so how dare you say that? And even if they did, it's got nothing to do with Lee.' I join her on the floor. 'I thought you loved him? Why would you do that to him?'

'You're dying to know, aren't you? It just eats you up inside that you have no control over this, and no control over what you did that night.'

'What?'

'I don't need to spell it out for you, do I? You heard a blow-by-blow account of it from your stalker. I'll just let you think about that.'

Noah bursts in before I can reply. 'What the hell's going on? The police are here looking for Lisa.'

He takes in the scene before him: me sitting on the floor next to the crumpled mess of my sister.

And then I hear Holden's voice, and someone else's, and the kitchen fills up with bodies. There is no chance for me to take in who is here, or what they are saying. My eyes fill with tears and all I can do is watch as several arms lift Lisa up and lead her away.

Someone tells Noah to make sure I'm all right, and I think it is Holden, but how can I be sure of anything any longer when the one person I trusted the most, the person I would have bet my life would never harm me, has ripped me apart inside?

PART THREE

CHAPTER THIRTY-THREE
SIX WEEKS LATER

It is almost six weeks before Lisa agrees to see me. In that time, I have had no answers, and can only make assumptions as to why she killed Lee. She won't talk to the police, won't talk to anyone. But finally one of my letters has got through to her, and she is ready to supply me with answers. Harvey is still missing, and I'm convinced she knows where he is, and was helping him evade the police.

They have moved her to a psychiatric unit, fearful that she will try to end her life, or cause harm to someone else while she awaits a trial date, but I'm not convinced of this. I think it is all an act to get off as lightly as possible. I would put nothing past her.

A guard leads me to her room, where she is kept in isolation, and I gasp at how sparse and lifeless it is. I have only ever seen cells of this kind on television, but they never seem to look this cold.

She sits huddled in the corner of her bed, skinnier than I've ever seen her, her knees pulled up to her chin, and her feet bare. I almost want to hug her, and cradle her in my arms, but then I remember why I'm here, and why she's here.

There is a wooden chair by her bed, and I drag it back towards the door, safely out of her reach.

'I've come for answers, Lisa,' I say, looking behind me to make sure there is still someone outside the door, just in case.

'I know.'

At first I think that's all she's going to utter, but then she continues. 'You want things all neatly wrapped up, don't you? So that you can move on with your life? That's why you're here, isn't it?'

'Yes,' I say. I will not tell her that I've also been desperate to see her, just because she is still my sister.

'I'll do that for you,' she says. 'Because I love you, Tara.'

'Don't say that to me. Just tell me what happened.'

She begins talking, and with every word she says I want to flee from this stifling room.

'I loved Lee. And he loved me. But it was starting to get difficult because he just wouldn't leave Serena. He said he couldn't do that when she was going through so much with her fertility problems.' She takes a deep breath. 'But I could have lived with all that, because I knew he loved me, and that I'd always come after Serena. He chose me. Until he suddenly ended it.'

Now it all becomes clear. What Lisa couldn't deal with was Lee having a new woman. And when she came to his house that night, she saw me with him. I don't know how much of it she witnessed, but it was enough to trigger insane jealousy. I ask her for confirmation of this, and all she does is nod.

'But why can't I remember anything?'

'Because you were so drunk, Tara, you barely even noticed when I came in. Lee had given me his spare key once when Serena was away, and forgot to ask for it back.'

'So I wasn't drugged? But then surely I'd remember you being there? And you. . . killing him.'

She looks away from me. 'I made sure you had more alcohol. A lot more, and then I left you downstairs and went up with Lee to have it out with him. He was pretty drunk too, falling all over the place. I could have pushed him over with one finger, he was that paralytic. I don't think either of you knew what you were doing.'

I am okay hearing this now. I have had time to come to terms with my mistake. Nothing like that will ever happen again.

'That's the worst part of it all,' Lisa continues. 'The fact that it meant nothing to either of you. I could almost have accepted it if you'd had feelings for each other but seeing you both like that. . . it was just too much. I snapped.'

I almost don't need to hear the rest, but she tells me anyway. Perhaps it is doing her some good to finally speak about it, because for weeks she's not said a word to anyone, not even the doctors who see her every day.

When she's finished speaking, it is as I suspected. The two of them argued, and in Lee's drunken state, he was powerless to defend himself when she came at him with one of his own kitchen knives, fuelled with a rage she couldn't control. And she also had no trouble dragging me upstairs and dumping me in his bed.

'You wanted me to take the blame,' I say, anger mixed with sadness swelling inside me.

She shakes her head. 'No. . . yes, maybe, I don't know.'

Hearing this, I remember something. 'But what about the wine glasses Lee and I drank from? The police made no mention of them when they questioned me, so what happened to them?'

'I had to wash them because I'd touched yours when I forced you to drink. I couldn't risk my DNA being on either of them. I was on autopilot, Tara, as if I wasn't in control of my own movements. Then panic set in and I just ran. That's when Mikey must have seen me and mistaken me for Rosie.'

And all the time he was telling me he saw Rosie running away from Lee's house, I never thought to question whether he'd got the right person. Rosie is as tall as Lisa and they have the same hair colour and build, but it would never have occurred to me that Lisa was involved in any of this.

'So when you realised I wasn't coming forward, you decided Rosie was a suitable scapegoat?'

Other than murder, this is the worst of what my sister has done: making a seventeen-year-old child appear guilty of murder. There are no words to describe my anger.

She admits that she put the ring in Rosie's room. 'When I found out she had a crush on him it just seemed that everything was falling into place.'

If I hadn't known she has lost her mind before, this confirms it for me. I don't want to hear any more about what she did to my daughter.

'And Harvey? Where does he fit into all this?'

She stares at me. 'Everything about Harvey was true, except he didn't kill Lee. But he still battered me, Tara.'

The police have yet to find him, and I still believe she knows where he is.

'I don't know, and I don't care,' she says, when I ask her. 'But can you do me a favour now? I need you to tell Mum and Dad how sorry I am, and that I love them.'

I stand up and bang on the door to be let out. I don't need to hear another word.

Outside the building, I stop and suck in a lungful of air, grateful to be out of that place. I sit down on the steps and bury my head in my knees. I thought I had it in me to forgive Lisa, or to at least try to see some good in her, but I have nothing left for her.

A voice calls my name and I look up to see Holden Hunt walking towards me. I haven't seen him since the day Lisa was taken away.

'Are you okay?' he says, joining me on the step. 'Just coming or are you leaving?'

'I've been in,' I say. 'I've seen her. For the first time.'

He nods. 'Did she say anything?'

'Yes, she did. But not much I didn't already assume.' I fill him in on everything Lisa told me just now, avoiding eye contact when I mention what Lee and I did. I wasn't convinced it was the truth before, but now there is no doubt. And it is the reason Lisa lost control. I am the reason.

Holden takes it all in and then places his hand on my shoulder. 'It's not your fault, Tara. None of this is. I hope you know that.'

'But she still claims she doesn't know where Harvey is,' I say. 'Do you believe that?'

Holden looks into the distance. 'Actually, that's why I'm here. A body was found late last night. In the river near your sister's house. It was in such a bad state that it took us a while to make a formal identification. But Harvey's ex-wife did that this morning.'

I have become so immune to death and murder that the biggest shock in his statement is that Harvey had an ex-wife. Just one more thing Lisa lied about.

'Someone else dead. I can't believe it. Even after what he did to her, he didn't deserve this.'

'That's the thing, Tara,' Holden says. 'I don't believe he did anything to your sister. And I'm working to prove what happened.'

'What do you mean?'

'My theory is that Harvey found out what your sister had done to Lee. Maybe her claim about him knowing about the affair is true, maybe not, but I don't think that's important. I'm working on the belief that he turned up at her flat that night and found her clearing up the evidence of Lee's murder. She might have panicked and felt that she had no choice but to get rid of Harvey, but whether it was planned or not, she still killed him in cold blood.'

He pauses to check my reaction, but there is nothing I can say. It does all fit together.

'I don't think Harvey attacked her, either time, so I'm guessing she did it to herself.'

I gasp. 'But that's not possible, is it?'

'There are all sorts of people out there, Tara. People who will do anything for a bit of cash. And if she was desperate enough to ensure she was never suspected of anything then she would have accepted the temporary pain.'

This just keeps getting worse, and I'm tempted to get up and run. I don't know if I want to hear any more. 'There's no proof, though?'

'Not yet. But I'll get it. We've got her computer and as we speak it's being analysed. If she went on any dodgy websites, even if she tried to cover her tracks, we'll find out. We're also checking her mobile phone. It's just a matter of time before we close in on her for Harvey's murder too.'

Because things always do catch up with us in the end. Even if it's in an unexpected way.

'I'm sorry,' he says, when I don't speak. 'Sorry for everything you've been through. And sorry you've lost a sister.'

I'm about to ask him how he knows what's in my heart, but his phone rings.

He listens to the person on the other end for a minute then says, 'Got it,' and disconnects the call. 'I have to go. But I wish you all the best with everything.'

'You too. Are you still leaving the force?'

'Yes. Handed my notice in a couple of weeks ago.' The smile on his face tells me he couldn't be happier about this decision. 'See you, Tara.'

He stands up, and I watch him head into the building to arrest my sister for another murder.

And then I slowly get up myself and head back home. To Rosie, Spencer, and Noah. We have packing to do and a new house to move into, and a new start waiting for us.

AUTHOR LETTER FROM KATHRYN CROFT

Thank you so much for choosing to read my fifth book, *While You Were Sleeping*. I really hope you have enjoyed reading it as much as I've loved writing it.

I'm extremely grateful for your support, and if you did enjoy the book then I would very much appreciate it if you could take a moment to post a quick review to let others know your thoughts. I'd also greatly appreciate any recommendations to friends and family!

I'm always thrilled to hear from readers so please feel free to contact me via Twitter, my Facebook page or directly through my website.

If you'd like to be kept informed of all my forthcoming releases you can sign up to my mailing list at my website – the details are below.

Thank you again for all your support!

Kathryn x

www.bookouture.com/kathryn-croft

www.kathryncroft.com

@katcroft

authorkathryncroft

ACKNOWLEDGEMENTS:

A huge thank you to Keshini Naidoo, my amazing editor, for her consistently fantastic insight. I wouldn't be where I am without my fabulous publishers, Bookouture, so thank you also to Olly Rhodes and the whole team.

My whole writing journey began with an email from my wonderful agent, Madeleine Milburn, so I continue to be grateful beyond words for her belief and support! And thank you to Thérèse Coen and Hayley Steed at the Madeleine Milburn Literary, TV & Film Agency for being such a pleasure to work with!

Thank you to amazing publicist Kim Nash, and Rich for all your help with this book.

As always, the support of my friends and family is never taken for granted, thank you to each and every one of you.

Once again, I am overwhelmed by the messages and responses I get from my readers, so a huge thank you to all of you, old and new, for all your support.

59935634R00180

Made in the USA
Lexington, KY
20 January 2017